THE WIZARD PRIEST

Dragonspeaker Chronicles Book 2

PATTY JANSEN

GET FREE EBOOKS

CHAPTER 1

I F THIS WERE a legend, She Who Rides Dragons would be an armour-clad heroine sitting on top of her fire-breathing steed, striking fear into the hearts of villains and bringing justice to all the citizens of the city.

But it was not a legend and the only fear was in Nellie's own heart, and in particular, a practical fear she might fall off. In fact, she'd barely managed to clamber onto the dragon's back when it had leapt from the back steps of the palace into the darkness of the night.

When it unfolded huge wings under her, she'd managed to grab onto the part where they joined the body and all she could do was hang on for her life, while the shouts of the people in the back yard of the palace kitchen receded.

Her kitchen apron was definitely an inferior type of armour. It didn't even protect her against the biting cold wind.

She had no weapons either, not that she could have used them if she did.

So here she was hanging onto the dragon's back, seeing the few meagre street lamps lights of the city of Saardam underneath her. She had no idea which part of town this was, only that it was a long way down there, and she did not want to fall.

None of this was heroic.

To make matters worse, the little kitten had come along for the ride, and it was now terrified, hanging onto her side, while digging its claws into her skin. She very much wanted to pull it off her dress and stick it in her pocket, but that meant letting go of one of the dragon's wings, and that option was even less attractive.

Where was the dragon going?

What if it dumped her in a forest where she had no idea how to get home? And if she managed not to fall off and made it safely to the ground, what if bandits who roamed the fields outside the city captured her? What if they stole her clothes and let her roam naked in the forest in the snow, as had happened to some poor farmers not long ago?

But none of that happened.

The dragon, after having gained height, merely circled over the city.

Nellie sat in between the shoulder blades and hung onto a comblike thing on its back.

It was peaceful up here if you didn't think about falling. The houses were so small and if people on the ground were shouting, she couldn't hear it.

She patted the dragon's neck.

"Can you please put me down?"

The dragon had never displayed signs of understanding her and didn't react.

It continued to circle.

Nellie said again, "Please, put me down. I'm cold." Her face was almost too numb to speak.

How did one talk to a dragon? Nellie had no magic. The dragon's box was in the bag she held on her back, but it held no instructions on how to talk to the dragon, or how to get it back in the box.

Her notion that the dragon had come back because she wanted it to seemed ridiculous. One did not tell a magical creature what to do unless one was also a magician.

But she needed to get off. She might get too cold to hold on. Already, her hands hurt.

Suddenly, the dragon made a sharp turn—Nellie gasped —and glided down. It snorted and blew sparks from its nostrils.

What was it doing?

But then Nellie spotted another glow over the city. From a distance, it looked like a bonfire, but it *moved*.

"What is that thing?"

The dragon only replied with another snort of sparks. She wished it wouldn't do that. It might set her dress on fire.

"Are you afraid of it?"

Obviously, because it was flying lower and lower, over a part of the city where streetlights were sparse.

Now she feared that it would crash into something— how could it see anything in this darkness?—or it would land on a roof and fall through, or leave her stranded there, unable to get down. She would freeze to death.

That would be a terrible thing.

She patted the dragon's neck again.

"Please, land somewhere in the street, so I can walk back."

Walk back where?

She couldn't go back to the palace after all those guards had seen her take off with the dragon. By now, her name would be on the most-wanted list.

Magician, killer.

The dragon flew lower and lower, skirting so low over the roofs that Nellie thought she could touch them.

Oh no, those houses were getting far too close. The dragon ducked into the street between them. Its wingtips raked the walls on both sides. Glass shattered.

Then the dragon's feet touched the ground and with a great jolt it ran along. Nellie's hands were so cold that she couldn't hang on any longer. She slid off and fell in the street.

Ouch.

The ground was cold and wet but it was solid and familiar.

She stumbled up, numb from that terrifying ride. She was safe; she hadn't fallen and hadn't been left on a roof. She had survived.

The cobblestones glistened in the light of a single street lamp further down. The houses on both sides of the street were dark, although one or two windows radiated a faint glow. She *thought* she was somewhere in the artisan quarter.

If this were a legend, there would be an army waiting to rescue her from the terrible dragon, chomping at the bit to slay the beast.

If it were a nightmare, citizens would come out of their houses with pitchforks to slay the witch who rode the dragon.

But the only sound was the mewling of that silly little kitten. It had lost its grip on her dress when she fell and now came trotting towards her. She picked it up.

The dragon had come to a halt all the way past the street lamp. It nosed one of its front paws, and then made a little jump, jerking its wings at the same time.

She had expected it to take off again, once it was rid of that annoying thing riding on its back, but it didn't.

It did that funny jump thing again, and again, scratching its nose with its paw. It was *sneezing*, blowing out smoke each time it did. It shook its head vigorously, then rubbed its head on the lamppost. And scratched its nose again.

Another jump.

It tossed its head, uttering a low growl.

There was something stuck in one of its nostrils.

"Come here," Nellie said, reaching out her hand and taking a step closer.

The dragon raised its head and looked at her as if it had forgotten she was there.

"Come. It'll get it out for you."

The kitten wriggled from her grip and trotted up to the dragon.

The dragon lowered its head and sniffed the tiny kitten. But the sniffing made it sneeze again. The kitten jumped and scurried back to Nellie, its tail all fluffed up like a brush.

Nellie was so close that she could feel the warm air of the dragon's breath.

Warmth could mean the difference between life and death in winter. She could survive until the morning without food or water, but if she couldn't keep herself warm, she'd be dead by morning.

The dragon might well be her only chance of survival.

"Come," she said again.

She touched the dragon's snout, ready to pull her hand away. My, its breath was really warm.

It didn't jerk back or try to snap at her hand, so she let it glide over the warm skin, coming closer to the nostril. Its ear twitched.

Her fingers probed into the nostril opening and met the irritating object. Nellie pushed her index finger and middle finger together to grab hold of it and pull it out. It was a splinter of wood.

The dragon shook its head so vigorously that its ears flapped against its neck. It blew out a cloud of warm air, then pushed its head into her hand, as if it were a kitten. She patted the warm snout.

The kitten jumped onto the dragon's head and the dragon lifted it up.

Nellie found it hard to believe that such a creature was evil. Whatever Lord Verdonck and Madame Sabine had tried to do to it must have been bad.

"Those people must have terrified you." She slid her hand over the smooth skin. "I don't know what I'm going to do with you. People will want to kill you. You better go back into your box."

But when she pulled out the box, the dragon shied back. It blew out a gust of hot breath.

"All right, calm down." She put the box back into her bag.

A young voice said, "Whoa, look at that!"

A group of three children peeked out of an alley. They stood in the corner in the faint glow of the street lamp. They were street urchins in worn clothes.

"Is that really a dragon?"

"Don't come closer," Nellie called out to them.

"Is it dangerous? You better watch out, miss. It might eat you."

She still had no idea what dragons ate. Especially this one, which had been locked inside a box for the best part of twenty years. It was a magical dragon, but it felt real and solid. It had to eat something to sustain itself.

"Oh, look at that," another child said. "There's a cute kitten on its head."

The dragon lowered its head, blowing smoke over the street. The children laughed and squealed.

It seemed like the dragon was enjoying itself.

"Did you just fly here on the back of that dragon?" a girl said to Nellie, as if it were the most normal thing in the world. She remembered how both Princess Celine and

Prince Bruno, as toddlers, had no trouble believing their mother's stories about ghosts. Just like these kids had no issue with the fact that a dragon was in the street. They knew what dragons looked like. There were plenty of pictures of eastern dragons, and this was clearly one.

"That's means you're a dragon tamer!" the girl shouted, her voice excited.

The boy gave Nellie a suspicious look. "She doesn't look like a dragon tamer. I don't know any girl dragon tamers. Dragon tamers wear armour, not aprons."

"Girls can be dragon tamers if they want."

"They cannot."

"Can so."

"Children, please." These kids would bring everyone into the street with their shouting. "The dragon needs a place to hide. Do you know one around here?"

The boy's eyes widened. "I can ask my mum if the dragon can sleep in our shed."

"Well . . ." Nellie wasn't sure if the boy's *mother* should become involved.

"Tell it to wait here," the boy said. He ran off into the side alley.

Nellie didn't like waiting here in the street. Even if the dragon wanted to stay with her, she didn't want to be found with it; and besides, she was getting very cold. She walked into the alley where the boy had disappeared, and the other children followed her.

"My brother is stupid," the girl said to Nellie. "Girls can *so* be dragon tamers." She glanced at the dragon. "Can I touch it?"

"It's a wild dragon. It may be dangerous."

"That kitten doesn't think so."

"It's a magical dragon."

"I'm not scared of magic."

"What's your name?"

"Anneke."

"Anneke, is your full name Johanna, after the queen?"

She pulled a face. "I don't like that name. Nobody uses full names. Only nasty nobles."

A couple of people were coming down the alley. It was very dark, and one was carrying a lamp.

A woman said, "Nellie?"

Nellie recognised the voice. "Mina! I was worried about what happened to you."

She fell into her friend's arms.

"You're not the girl's mother, aren't you?" She was pretty sure Mina's children were grown.

"Not me. But Bas was talking about a dragon, and I thought I'd better check this out."

"I feared you were in the poorhouse after you got evicted from the church."

"No, Never that place. It's full of leery men and drunkards. I wouldn't want to subject any children to that. But what about you? Little Bas tells me you have a dragon."

"I wouldn't call it mine. It's following me around and creating a lot of trouble for me, but I don't know that it will listen to me."

Nellie stepped aside so that Mina's light reached the dragon which had followed into the alley. The passage was so narrow that the dragon's sides brushed the walls. Its head was fully in the pool of light from the lamp. The scales and comblike protuberance on its head gleamed in the low light. The orange eyes blinked.

Mina gasped. "My, you really do have a dragon."

"You never believe us," Anneke said.

"You are very good at telling fibs, young lady." And then she turned to Nellie. "The dragon chose to be with you? Where did you get it?"

"It's a long story."

"Lucky we have a nice dry barn. It's a bit cold, but it's better than being on the street. Come with me."

Mina took her down the alley, and the children followed. Nellie looked over her shoulder. The dragon was coming, too.

On the way, Mina told her that after Shepherd Wilfridus evicted the group from the church, Mina had asked a friend for help.

"Zelda is a wayfarer, and she knows all the good places to stay. She has saved all our lives and our dignity besides. Our only other option was the poorhouse."

Mina led Nellie to a tall building on the right.

A plank of wood had once been a door, but it was rotten and the door had fallen off its hinges. Mina and the children pushed it aside.

The warehouse hall beyond was more than two floors high, lit by the flames from a lusty fire that burned in a fire pit in the middle of the floor.

It looked like this had been a stable for coaches and horses. There was even a hayloft above.

The people had put what meagre possessions they had salvaged from the church in the dark space underneath the hayloft. Planks of wood had been removed—and probably burned in the fire—to turn it from a stable into an area where people could sleep in the straw. In an adjacent pen stood a scruffy donkey.

Several people sat around the fire, most of them women.

"Nellie!" one of them called out. Next thing, Jantien came running towards her.

Nellie took her friend into her arms. "Oh, I'm so glad to see you. Are you and the children all here?"

"Yes, all of them. I'm trying to get money to follow my husband to Florisheim. Zelda has jobs for us to do."

Nellie glanced over her shoulder at the other

women. She recognised some who had also been in the church. She didn't know their names, but they were, like Jantien, ordinary citizens who had fallen on hard times.

The children looked at the dragon from the door.

It didn't fit through the door opening and had stayed behind in the courtyard.

Some of the children were very small. A boy had taken a stick, which he swung at the dragon.

"Behave yourself!" Mina called. "Here is Nellie who was so nice to help us when we lived in the church. She does not want any of you to touch her dragon. It's a dangerous magical creature."

The children disappeared into the darkness anyway.

Most of the adults had also gone to the door. The women were not happy to see a dragon standing out there. One woman fell to her knees in prayer. Another went to the corner of the warehouse, got a broom, ready to defend herself.

"That beast has to go," she announced. She was a sturdy type, not afraid to defend herself.

"I don't *think* it's dangerous," Nellie said. Of course, the dragon could definitely be dangerous. "It seems to like the kitten, and it seems to like me, and I think it also likes children."

The woman snorted. "To eat, certainly?"

"If it was hungry, it had many opportunities to do me harm, or to eat these children, or eat the kitten."

A couple of women gathered up the children, who were all watching the dragon, much less scared than the adults. They ushered the little ones back inside. A little girl carried the kitten.

The dragon leapt across the courtyard like a giant cat and tried to squeeze into the door.

The sturdy woman hit its snout with a broom. Another

slammed the piece of wood that served as a door in its face.

"Quick, put some heavy things behind the wood. It wants to come in."

Two women barred the door with a broom and a stick. They were about to drag a bag full of firewood in front of the door when a bright glow oozed underneath the door. The very real dragon had turned back into a fire dragon. The women retreated.

"Evil magic!" one shouted.

The fire dragon flitted through the hall, frolicked up to the ceiling and landed in the hayloft. A shower of magic sparks blew up.

The dragon returned to its former size.

The sturdy woman climbed halfway up the ladder and yelled at the creature from her safe position. She still held the broom.

"Take it back outside!" she yelled at Nellie. "It's gone to sleep. My children sleep up there and I'm not having them in the same place as that creature."

"Mam, it's a warm creature," Anneke said. "I'm not afraid of it."

The girl's mother glared first at her daughter and then at Nellie. She was a coarse, heavyset woman with a strong brow and a severe bun at the back of her head with hair that had gone grey.

Nellie's cheeks glowed.

"If that creature is going is to follow you around, you can't stay with us."

Mina said, "I think that's unfair. Nellie has brought us food all the time. She says the dragon is just following her around. It's not her fault it's here."

"But she still can't stay. It will bring us into danger, that's why."

"It brought Nellie into danger to bring us food. She

risked herself by taking things from the kitchen without the knowledge of the Regent. Are you going to be so ungrateful as to send her away?"

The woman glared at Mina.

"Nellie helped us when our life was hard. So now we will help her, dragon or no, and that is the final word I will hear about it."

She looked around the group. The expressions in the faces of several women were not terribly friendly, but none of them said anything.

"So the kitten is the dragon's real friend?" Anneke asked.

"I think so." Nellie spoke softly, aware that all the women listened.

"Then I will bring the kitten upstairs."

Anneke picked up the kitten.

"You will do no such thing," her mother said. "Stay right here."

"But Mam, she's a dragon tamer," Anneke said. "She came here on the back of the dragon."

The woman said, "Is that so?" She gave Nellie a suspicious look.

And Mina said, "This is Agatha, the mother of Anneke and Bas."

Nellie held out her hand. "Pleased to meet you. I'm Nellie."

The woman gave another snort. She shook Nellie's hand, reluctantly. "I don't do all that magic stuff."

"Me neither."

"Good. Because I want none of that near my children."

"She really is a dragon tamer, Mam," Anneke said again.

"I don't want to hear any more about it."

"Can I take the kitten up to the loft?"

"What did I just tell you?"

"But Mam! Ewout is going up."

One of Jantien's boys was climbing the ladder, peeking up to the loft to spy on the dragon.

"I don't care what Ewout does. Maybe his mother doesn't mind him being struck dumb with magic. But I do. You and Bas will stay here."

The girl started crying and Mina took Nellie to introduce her to the others.

"I'm sorry for creating trouble for you," Nellie said.

"Don't worry about it. Agatha is a little terse sometimes," Mina said.

"I really don't control that beast," Nellie said.

"You'll be fine. She'll warm up to you. Let me introduce you to the others."

Apart from Jantien, Nellie knew a few other people in the group.

Emmie and Lise were a mother and daughter who both used to work in the household of a well-off merchant family. Lise was twenty, and Emmie mentioned that her greatest worry was that, because they were poor, her daughter would never marry.

Gertie, Hilde and Josie had all lost husbands.

"He took off with a trollop from the harbourside," Gertie said. "A whore, that's what she is. Her boobs are bigger than mine, but I bet she can't even boil an egg. Men are disgusting. Be glad you're not married." The latter to Lise.

Hilde's husband had died of consumption. Like Mina's, her children were older, but they had all left town.

Josie's husband had gone missing at sea several years ago. She had lost her first and only child through illness.

Misfortune through hardship or illness was the glue that held these women together.

Koby hung out with them a lot. She was twelve, the

eldest child in the group, but her face had already lost all her childish softness.

"Both her parents are dead," Mina said in a quiet voice. "She has an uncle, but he doesn't want to care for her. It's very sad. I try to help her where I can, but she's very closed to outsiders."

Most of the children were Jantien's. Ewout, the oldest, still stood on the ladder gawking at the dragon, and the dragon gawked back at him. He had gone a few steps higher, and his younger sister was right below him, while Anneke and her brother glared at them from where they sat.

Ewout said, "Yes, he likes the kitten."

"He?" Mina said.

"It's a boy dragon, hadn't you noticed? He's got . . ." He made a swinging motion in front of his lower body.

The children laughed and a few declared that they wanted to see it.

They all crowded at the bottom of the ladder. Jantien told them to take a peek, but not go to the top of the ladder.

Anneke crossed her arms over her chest and kept glaring at her mother, and Agatha pretended not to notice.

"And this is Zelda," Mina said to Nellie.

The final woman in the group to meet Nellie was of tiny stature. She wore several layers of clothing of a foreign style, with big colourful patterns. A faded yellow scarf sat around her hair. The wisps that poked out from underneath were black. Her eyes were dark brown, like those of a cow, even if she had pale and freckled skin. Her face was sharp, with a rather big nose. And were those really golden earrings that poked out from underneath her scarf?

She looked Nellie up and down.

"Hmph, can you work?" She spoke with a curious accent.

"I've worked all my life. Depends what kind of work."

"Do you know anything about donkeys?"

"Not really. I worked in households."

"Ha! Washerwoman. That's all people do around here. Wash, wash, wash. No wonder the water is so foul. Do you know about plants?"

"Herbs? A bit."

"Good. You can come with me."

"What? Now?"

What sort of strange woman was this?

"Ha! No. Tomorrow. We sell herbs. You come with me. It's a good job. We have money to eat."

Nellie glanced at Mina, but Mina smiled and nodded. "It's all right."

"Ha, all right. Of course it's all right. I'm Zelda. I make the people better. Local woman say the herbs are good, so the rich woman believe the herbs are good. Woman feels better, gives more money. Ha."

"What about the dragon, Zelda?" Mina asked.

"Dragon make us rich."

"I meant how can we hide it?"

"Dragon makes poop. We can do much things with dragon poop. We can dry it, we can make it into a salve, we can make pills. Rich men will pay a lot because dragon poop makes them like a dragon, you know, in the bed. When the dragon does a poop, bring it to me, children."

Anneke and Bas laughed. The other children came down the ladder to see what was so funny.

"What do we get when we bring you poop?" Ewout asked.

"Ha! You're getting smart already. You get poop, we get money. We can buy sweets, no?"

The children's eyes shone.

Mina still insisted, "But how can we make sure no one sees the dragon?"

"No one will see. Dragons are lazy. They sleep and sleep and sleep. They make much poop."

Her straightforward attitude was refreshing, and because Zelda didn't seem to be concerned about the dragon, Agatha let her children join the others in the hayloft. Because, apparently, the prospect of "poop" and money overcame all.

Nellie went to check on the dragon. He lay in the hay, with his tail curled around his body. The children all leaned against his flanks, their cheeks rosy from the animal's warmth. The kitten snuggled next to Anneke.

With that settled, the women set about making beds in the stable. Nellie was given a blanket to share with Gertie. It wasn't warm enough, but when they covered themselves with straw, it was quite snug. Oil for the lamp was scarce, and it was too dark for Nellie to read from the Book of Verses, but she kept her satchel close to her head. She missed her room in the palace and she feared for the coming winter, but for now she was dry and didn't freeze.

CHAPTER 2

NELLIE LEARNED the next morning what Zelda's business entailed.

She rose before dawn, and when the women woke up, she distributed tasks among them. For example, it was Mina's task to cook while Lise and Emmie went to get water at the well. When they came back, they distributed the water into two pots. One was for cooking; they placed the other in the corner of the warehouse for mysterious purposes.

After a brief breakfast of watery porridge, Zelda handed out further tasks.

Gertie, Hilde and Josie were to go to a place referred to as "the shop" and had to work there. Before they left, Zelda handed them a wooden box that looked like a drawer from a herb cabinet. Inside lay a soft brown-orange object that resembled a large egg, but was not as evenly shaped.

This morning, Anneke had brought this thing down the ladder, the first delivery of dragon poop.

"Spread it out over the bench to dry," Zelda said to

Gertie. "Then put the powder in a jar. We'll use it in salves. You might want to visit the butcher for sheep's fat."

Zelda said she would look after Nellie herself. She told Nellie to get changed into something warm but not too shabby. She then took the donkey out of the pen.

Young Koby was coming, too, but the others were all staying in the warehouse.

The morning was freezing. An icy mist hung in the streets, turning all the buildings varying shades of grey.

"Do you know where we're going?" Nellie asked Koby as the two of them followed Zelda and the donkey. Zelda was not one of the most forthcoming people about her plans. When Nellie had asked her the same question, she had only said, "You'll see."

"We'll be seeing Zelda's patients. She visits sick people at home and gives them remedies."

First, they went to a small workshop that lay behind an empty shop front in the main street of the artisan quarter. The building that faced the street had been empty for some time. All the windows were boarded over and the wooden door showed signs of rot.

Many of the surrounding shops were abandoned, too.

Inside the workshop, it was cosy and dry. The space was small—it had probably been a storage space for the shop—and the fire easily kept it warm.

A big metal pot hung over the fire, bubbling steam.

Gertie, Hilde and Josie were already at work at the benches. Gertie was scooping big blobs of paste from a pan into glass jars. Hilde was grinding dried leaves into powder and Josie was cleaning jars in a tub of steaming water.

A tray on the bench held orange-brown bits of dragon poop. It was quite rough and contained little bits of what looked like chewed sticks. What did dragons eat?

Zelda pushed a tray into Nellie's hands, pulled many

jars and bags off the shelves that filled one end of the workshop and loaded them onto the tray. When it was full, she sent Nellie to the cart that stood in the small courtyard outside the workshop.

The poor donkey stood waiting, its ears drooping and head close to the ground. It didn't even look up as Nellie deposited the heavy tray into the cart.

Koby brought another tray.

There were three boxes, and when the cart was ready Zelda came out, dressed in a woollen cape. She led the donkey by the reins out of the courtyard.

They went into the main street and turned left toward the merchant quarter of the city.

It was still misty—the type of air that made droplets of moisture on everything and seeped into clothes until it penetrated the warm cocoon inside and went to the bone. Nellie looked with envy at the smoke rising from the chimneys of the houses they passed. Once she had been warm and comfortable like that. She remembered standing inside and looking at the poor milkman, the poor baker's son and the man with the grocery cart who were out in the weather every day.

When she stopped the cart, Zelda explained about the first person they would visit.

"This woman always complain about bad airs. She complain, complain, even if it make no sense what she complain about."

"So you can't do anything for her?"

"I still give her herbs."

"But if there's nothing wrong with her—"

"Her wrong is all in the head." Zelda tapped the side of her head. "My medicine make her happy."

Goodness, what was in those jars? The only ingredients Nellie had seen were the collection of herbs.

"Do you want me to carry the basket?" Koby said.

She had prepared a pretty basket with a cloth lining and all manner of jars.

"Yes, carry it to the door. Then you wait, look after donkey." Zelda pointed at Nellie. "You come with me."

"But I know nothing about herbs," Nellie said. "I just know some of the minor remedies. I don't know anything about salves and potions."

"Don't worry about that," Zelda said. "Your part will be easy. Let me do talking. When I ask you question, you answer question."

They went up the steps, where Koby was already halfway with the basket, to the door which was painted in rust brown. When Zelda knocked, a fresh-faced young maid opened it.

The girl smiled at Zelda. "Come in. The mistress is waiting for you in the parlour."

They entered the house. It was strange. At one point Nellie would have been that maid.

She didn't know the people who lived in this house, but she knew the type. They were merchants who had recently come into some money and wanted to show it off. The house was every bit as elaborate as Mistress Johanna's had been, but all the furniture was new and had not yet been passed through the generations.

The maid opened a door to the left and led them into the parlour. It was a splendid room, with glass-fronted cabinets containing porcelain statues, beautiful matching chairs and a couch with green and white striped fabric with tiny pink embroidered roses, and huge paintings on all the walls, depicting idyllic forest scenes and a castle by a river.

The lady of the house sat on the couch next to the fire. She was rubbing her hands as Zelda and Nellie came in.

"Oh, Zelda. I am so glad to see you. You have a new helper."

"Yes madame. Did you remember that I was talking about well-known local herb woman? You told me that you would rather use local remedies, so I found someone for you. She has even worked in the palace. Well, this is her."

The merchant's wife regarded Nellie with renewed interest.

Nellie's cheeks glowed.

She definitely did *not* agree with this. What was this about doing the talking?

She opened her mouth to protest, but one sharp look from Zelda stopped her.

Zelda settled the row of jars she had taken from the shelves that morning and explained what each of the concoctions was for. Every now and then, she would ask Nellie a question to which only yes or no would be inappropriate answer, like is that right? Or didn't you tell me so this morning?

The woman looked Nellie, but never once questioned Zelda's implausible stories.

And there were many.

Nellie had seen what Gertie, Hilde and Josie were doing in the workshop, and hadn't seen any of the ingredients that Zelda claimed to have put in.

Not only that, but Nellie knew for certain that chamomile extract did none of the things that Zelda told the woman it did.

But the woman listened to all of it.

Zelda's so called secret ingredient was a tea, which supposedly cured everything.

It consisted of several herbs. When Nellie took it to the kitchen to have the servants prepare the extract, Nellie recognised bits of chamomile and dandelion and some other local herbs which grew plentiful in the surrounding meadows and road verges.

There was no secret ingredient in any of it.

When she carried the teapot back into the parlour, she almost felt like throwing it into the hearth.

This was the reason so many people distrusted wayfarers like Zelda. Because this was not proper herb medicine. It was a swindle.

But the merchant's wife drank the tea, and she said she already felt much better.

Then the time came to leave, and Zelda flapped her hand at Nellie to pack all the jars and go into the hallway to wait there. Nellie did so, anger growing inside her. She wanted no part in this quackery and didn't want to be the "local woman" face to Zelda's business. She wondered if Zelda had tried the same trick with the other women.

As Nellie waited in the hallway, the maid came past and opened the door to the room. Zelda crouched on the carpet at the merchant wife's feet, while the woman counted out coins. Nellie spotted at least two silver florins. Quite a lot of money.

Nellie didn't see what Zelda did with the coins, but presumed she put them in her coat pocket before coming to the door, bowing profusely and stating that she would come back next week.

Then it was on to the next patient, only a few houses down the street. Here they met another woman complaining about sore feet. Her feet did indeed look terrible, red and blue and swollen, but Nellie had a suspicion this had more to do with the expensive shoes she bought which turned out to be a bit too small.

Instead of suggesting she wear more comfortable shoes, Zelda sold her a jar of salve, and also some of her secret tea, which in this case would soothe pains of sore joints and feet.

In the next house, an elderly woman complained about constipation. Zelda again gave her herb tea. She encouraged the woman to share it with her entire family, because the grandkids were making a racket in the kitchen, and the woman complained that her daughter would never shut them up. If they ran out, Zelda would bring more because, while food might get scarce in the city, herb tea was in plentiful supply.

Each conversation developed along a pattern.

Zelda told the merchants' wives that the tea did everything they wanted it to do and then got paid lots of money for it.

At the end of her round through the merchant quarter, Zelda knocked on a few doors where she went up herself and instructed Nellie and Koby to stay with the cart and the donkey.

Each time a bewildered servant opened the door, Zelda did her sales pitch. She appeared successful most of the time. The servant would talk to her, and sometimes they took the free sample she offered. A few people made arrangements to see Zelda later.

One man shouted at her. "Get out of my sight, you filthy thieves!"

Zelda sped back to the cart. She snorted as she climbed back onto the driver's seat. "A very rude man that," she said. "I come to help him, and he yells at me? Very rude man."

But Nellie wondered what she herself would have done when faced with a peddler wanting to sell remedies for ailments. She probably would have told the person to go away, too, especially if she was peddling a chamomile tea for exorbitant prices.

When they got back to the shed, they unpacked the cart and put it away.

Gertie, Hilde and Josie had left, but all the items for the next day of trade lay ready on the bench: the bags of samples, the large jar of dried leaves, and the jar with dragon poop which she had no doubt would be sold for ridiculous prices.

Two silver florins for some chamomile tea!

Zelda's pocket was jingling with coins, and when they walked back through the main street in the artisan quarter, Zelda gave Koby some coins to buy sweets for the children.

She also bought a bag of flour for porridge, but the rest of the coins still jingled in her pocket.

Nellie wondered what she did with it, and why she didn't give it to Koby.

"You can be my local woman now," Zelda said. "We make good team."

Nellie didn't want to do any such thing. "Where do you get that special tea?" she asked.

Zelda smiled. Her teeth were brown. "Is very special indeed. I buy it from a man in town who gets it from up the river. Herbs grow where the water is clean and free of filth from dirty cities."

"Who is this man who sells such valuable things?"

"Mr Oliver, but he rarely has tea. You have to ask for it, and then it may be out of stock. Only very special times of the year you can get it."

That was not the answer Nellie had suspected, and she wondered how much of it was true. Judging by all the rest of Zelda's stories, probably not that much. But Mr Oliver was a well-known merchant of all kinds of foodstuffs. From his warehouse in the harbour quarter, he sold fine sausages and jams and other confectionery. He would sell tea, too, if there was any tea to be had. Now that the ships had stopped coming from across the ocean, the normal teas and exotic spices had become rare.

Nellie felt tempted to ask Zelda about what she did with the money in her pocket, and whether this was just a good day, but she guessed the feeble relationship could probably not withstand those questions. Besides, the women might not have much chance to make a living otherwise, even if Zelda held back earnings from them.

Back in the warehouse, the other women were cooking the midday meal. The flour Zelda had brought received much appreciation. Nellie felt sick because she knew two silver florins could have bought so much better food.

She spoke to Mina when they were both collecting new wood from the pile outside the door.

"It's all quackery," Nellie said. "Everything she tells those women is a lie. She is deceiving nice people and saying I am a well-known local herb woman."

Mina shook her head. "Don't worry, she has done that to all of us. If any of the merchants worked out that we are just poor women, she would use someone else as the next new local herb woman."

"But it's unsavoury."

"It's not the most honest of ways to make money, but it keeps us fed."

"Were you already doing this when you lived in the church?" Nellie was getting a queasy feeling about this. She remembered the time she had come into the church when Jantien was out, "doing a job". Was this what she had been doing? Selling quackery to unsuspecting honest citizens?

Would Zelda have used the innocent children as well?

"It doesn't make much money," Mina said.

"Have you been with her inside the merchant houses?"

"I can't go with her. Everyone in town knows I am just a poorhouse woman. She takes Jantien's children to help her and mind the donkey. She says children make people nicer to her."

"It's no wonder she prefers to take children. She is deceiving all of us. I saw how much money she was making. She gives you the bag of porridge, but she keeps most of the money for herself."

Mina shrugged. "Isn't that the case for all people who make lots of money? They let us do all the work and they get the harvest."

"Aren't you angry about that?"

"We have no other way to survive. Tell me how else we can get food."

And that was the ultimate problem. Nellie felt sick. She did not want to rely on this thievery to make her living.

She might have another solution so that the women didn't have to do this. It might be dangerous to her, but she could sneak into the kitchens and Dora could give her food. If she waited at the gate until Henrik was on duty, he would let her through. Then she just needed some way of carrying all the food out here.

She didn't like begging either, but would rather that than rely on thievery to make ends meet.

The plank that formed the door to the warehouse slid aside, and Agatha came into the courtyard.

"I'm going to the warehouse to make potions," she said. And she disappeared into the alley.

Mina said in a low voice, "Whatever you do, be careful around Agatha. She is a very angry woman, and she is a strong friend of Zelda's. She believes that all rich people are evil and should be scammed out of as much money as possible."

"Is there anyone in this group who isn't angry?"

"It's very hard not to get angry when you're always worried about where your next meal is coming from and whether you will have a place to sleep."

That was true, and Nellie felt ashamed of having asked the question. "I'll be your friend, Mina, whatever happens."

CHAPTER 3

FOR THE NEXT few days, Nellie didn't leave the warehouse much.

Zelda went out on her rounds, but she took only Koby and Ewout, Jantien's oldest son. He was ten, and quite a handsome young lad with his thick mop of blond hair. Nellie hated to think how many hearts he melted with those big blue eyes, and how many purses opened at the thought of him living on the street.

Zelda either didn't need someone to pose as a local herb woman, or she noticed Nellie's reluctance to play that role. Even when she was at the warehouse, she always looked for ways to make money. She sent the kids to trade ointment for eggs. She told Agatha to go to a house in New Harbour to pick up a parcel. It contained two bottles of syrupy liquid, which she took to the workshop where Hilde and Gertie mixed it with water until it filled twenty bottles of "apple wine", according to the label.

The dragon poo was dry enough to be ground and turned into an ointment. The main ingredient was wool fat, which came in a barrel and smelled terrible. It was full of sticks and grass so needed to be heated and strained before it could be mixed with the poo powder. The resulting paste was drab brown, so Zelda told them to mix it with black soot.

"If it's black, people think it's very powerful," Zelda said.

Nellie wondered how impressed the merchant wives would be with getting soot all through their clothes.

Fortunately, the work kept Nellie warm, and Gertie, Hilde and Josie were good company. Josie, especially, had an infectious laugh.

Nellie asked them what they thought of the fact that Zelda sold simple dried leaves as a wonder remedy with no proof that it worked.

"Isn't that the case with all these concoctions?" Josie said.

"Some of them do work," Nellie said. "But nothing like what she tells these women."

Hilde shrugged. "I have never known the herb sellers to be any different. They will talk up their potions as if they're the best thing. It would surprise me if these noble women didn't understand that. One thing about rich people: they didn't become rich by being dumb."

"Then why are they buying this tea?"

"Because the lady from next door, whose family has even more money, bought it and swears by it? Rich people do things for all kinds of strange reasons we will never understand."

But there was always a reason. Nellie had worked for these families although the Brouwer family had never taken part in displaying wealth. You knew they had it when you walked into their house, in the same way you knew these merchants were trying to appear more important than they were.

It disappointed Nellie that none of the women were worried about Zelda's sales swindle, but maybe that was what happened when you were desperate: you didn't care so much about right and wrong.

Nellie hoped that this would never happen to her, but could see it might, and it frightened her.

Doing the right thing had already caused her a lot of trouble. She had only wanted to return the dragon box to the church, and now she was homeless. She was still waiting for the fallout from her escape from the palace.

Nellie expected hordes of guards to come looking for her by now, but if they did, they were looking in the wrong parts of town. In fact, the silence after her escape worried her a lot. She couldn't believe the guards really wouldn't have a clue of where to look for her, which meant that those guards were occupied with other things. If they weren't worried about a dragon loose in their town, what problem occupied them?

But no matter how well Nellie listened to the shards of gossip brought in by the women from the streets or the market place, she didn't get any indication of what it would be.

Since her escape, the palace had gone eerily quiet. Of course she was no longer living there, but she had the feeling that people would hear from the Regent on a regular basis, especially if there were soothing words to be told about the presence of a dragon in the town.

The Regent was pompous enough to speak to the citizens from the steps of the palace, as he had done on several occasions. He would say everything was under control, that his men would find the beast and kill it, and the people would cheer and the Regent would boast about how he was the best and how he deserved to be king. He loved opportunities like that.

But the steps of the palace remained conspicuously empty.

And as much as Nellie thought the Regent was a

ridiculous windbag, she was starting to wonder about the lack of reaction from the palace.

People had seen a *dragon* in the city. If that wasn't a good enough reason to bring the Regent to the palace steps, then what was?

It was not as if no one knew about the dragon. Not that anyone had seen him, but after a few days the women who went to the markets reported that a lot of people knew about the dragon in the palace and had an opinion on it—whether it was real, whether it was good or evil, and where it might have come from.

Nellie told the women most of her story: about her father's book and how it described that the church had been buying dark artefacts and that the dragon box was part of it, that it had been stolen from the church, but that the church didn't want it back. That the dragon appeared to like her, or at least hadn't scratched her. She left out that she had the key to the crypt and that she had more or less stolen the box from Lord Verdonck's chest. She did say the Regent tried to accuse the dragon of killing Lord Verdonck, but if the women didn't care about Zelda selling quackery to merchant women, they cared even less about the Regent.

Nellie cared, because some of the suspicion fell on her.

The dragon barely showed himself. He slept in the hayloft, surrounded by the children and an increasing number of cats.

Every day, the children collected the orange poop and traded it with Zelda for sweets and sausages.

When and what the dragon ate, no one knew. Nellie suspected that during the day he would assume his magical form to hunt, but cats and children didn't appear to be on the menu.

For her part, Nellie kept her head down, trying to figure out what she would do when it became necessary for her to leave the group. She no longer had a home to go to. The palace had been her home for the past twenty years. Her parents were dead, the house had never been theirs, her father's brother was dead, too, and because the two brothers hadn't liked each other, Nellie had never been close with her cousins on that side. Her mother's family lived in a village outside the city where they owned a mill. She could go there and would be welcome, but it was a good distance to travel, and the coaches didn't go when there was snow on the ground. And it would be hard to turn up as an uninvited guest with a dragon in tow.

She helped the women. She helped Jantien look after the children. She helped gather firewood, which the women took from the two neighbouring abandoned warehouses. The group had found an axe which was extremely blunt but good for wedging loose wooden planks and shelving that could be used as firewood. Chopping it to manageable lengths was hard work with the blunt axe, but it kept her warm.

Food was not terribly scarce, because of Zelda, but Nellie grew increasingly uneasy with the woman's activities.

She happened to be in the workshop when an angry man demanded his money back because the "Dragon magic extract" he bought had caused him a terrible rash.

Zelda did repay him—but Nellie thought only because she and Josie were watching—the two whole florins he had paid for the jar. What an outrageous price. She wondered how many people suffered in silence.

And not much later, while going to buy wax for sealing bottles, she watched Zelda in the street with Ewout and one of his younger twin sisters, both dressed in rags. She instructed the children to approach people, especially, it seemed, well-dressed women.

As she watched, one of the women instructed a maid to give Ewout some coins.

Nellie's cheeks glowed. Zelda was teaching the children to beg.

"Did you know that?" she raged at Hilde and Josie in the workshop. "It's disgusting. We're proud women. We can work. We can sell things. We don't beg."

Hilde snorted. "Can't say I'd want any of my relatives to see me ask for money."

"Exactly. We can do better than that." Nellie was glad they finally agreed with her. "We can look after ourselves in an honest way."

"I can make jams," Hilde said.

"I can sew," Josie said.

But there was no fruit in winter, and a list of clients who would pay for mending clothes would take a long to time to collect. And quite a few of the merchants' businesses weren't doing well. Those wives probably did their own sewing now.

The problem would be how to get through winter.

"You can keep getting leftovers from the palace," Hilde said.

Nellie had thought about it. She didn't want to go back to the palace, because someone would want to arrest her there, but could not see another option. It was go back to the palace or continue to live off Zelda's activities.

"I also heard that the Regent will start handing out food from the city stores soon," Josie said.

"Oh? I haven't heard that," Gertie said.

"That's because it's a rumour. I spoke to my brother-in-law, and he heard it from people who work at the stores. I think the Regent is afraid that if he doesn't hand out food, people will steal it. Some is already being stolen."

"I think it's because the Regent wants to buy our support to be declared king," Nellie said. "It's only the start of winter. Supplies are not that low yet. He'd be stupid to hand it out now."

"That's what I heard," Josie said.

But if it happened, a group of women and children would amongst them have enough rations to build up a supply. Then she would only need to get leftovers from the palace every week. That sounded much more acceptable.

Nellie decided to try it. After all, Henrik and Dora would help her.

Early morning was the best time. The bakers would have left, most of the nobles wouldn't be up yet, the guards would be at the end of their shift and would expect people to come to the kitchens to deliver things, so they might not pay that much attention to visitors.

What was more, she was curious to know what had been going on in the palace, and she wanted to let Dora know she had found a safe place.

So she got up early while the others were still asleep, stoked the fire and put a pot of water to boil so there would be water for porridge and tea.

Then she wound a scarf around her head in the way Zelda did hers. She should get one of those colourful ones to make the disguise better, but this would have to do. Then she went into the pale blue predawn light.

After the cold and wet weather, the temperature had again fallen below freezing, and a blanket of snow covered the city. That was what winter in Saardam was like: wet and cold, with the occasional few days of snow.

Dawn was a quiet time at the marketplace. Most of the market stallholders had not yet arrived for the day's business, especially in the cold weather.

Normally, the visiting merchants would linger in the glow of the street lamps, discussing business with colleagues, but it was cold and snowing, so they were all still in the taverns, leaving the snow to settle on the ground, disturbed only by a prowling cat which, by the twitching of its tail, seemed most displeased about the weather.

Oh, for a nice warm bed.

Several times in the past few nights, Nellie had almost picked up her blanket and gone upstairs where the dragon slept in the hayloft. The children always said his body was warm and that he would let them sleep against his warm flanks. It seemed so much more comfortable than sleeping downstairs.

Nellie crossed the marketplace between the empty snow-covered stalls, up to the gates of the palace.

The palace guards stood in their guard boxes. She hoped that one of them would be Henrik because he would let her through without asking too many uncomfortable questions. Or so she hoped.

But neither of the guards was Henrik. It had been silly of her to hope.

Nellie debated waiting until she could see him, but that would only make the men suspicious.

So she pulled the shawl closer over her head and went up to the guard box.

"I have spices to deliver to the kitchen."

She showed them the basket she had brought to carry the leftovers. No one would know the pots in the basket were empty.

These two men she only knew vaguely. Fortunately, they let her through, and Nellie crossed the snow-covered forecourt.

It looked like all the guests from the banquet for the birthday of the Regent's son had gone home. The stables were empty. There were no more coaches standing outside and no more horse boys gathering around a fire laughing and talking.

The guards at the palace entrance looked bored,

standing by the closed doors by the light of a few lamps. One of them was stamping his feet, the other clapping his hands around himself, making his sword rattle in the scabbard and the metal in his belt jingle as he did so. Neither of them were Henrik either.

Nellie sped past the bottom of the steps, through the familiar lane that ran past the side of the palace and into the back door that let her into the kitchen.

The moment she entered, Dora turned around.

"Didn't I tell you to shut that—Nellie!"

She had been stirring a pot at the stove, but flung her ladle on the table and ran to the door.

She enveloped Nellie with a warm, strong hug. "You're still alive. I was so worried."

"No, I'm fine. Life could be better, but I'm fine."

Then another kitchen worker came in.

"I thought I heard your voice." Corrie ran up to Nellie and hugged her.

"How is your foot?" Nellie asked. In another time, that seemed lifetimes ago, Corrie had fallen down the stairs and could barely hobble around the kitchen.

"All good again. You're coming back? What happened? Sit down. Tell us all about it."

"I'll have some tea, but I can't stay long."

"What? You're not staying? Your room is still empty."

"I know. I would like to stay, but I can't."

Dora asked, "You want the leftovers?"

"Yes. I'm looking after a group of the children and their mothers who were evicted from the church. We have little food."

Dora said, "Let me make you a nice bag, then."

She went into the pantry.

Nellie sat at the table, surprised at how quickly this place felt strange to her. It was so comfortable and not so long ago that she was working here herself.

Corrie said, "We heard rumours a dragon took you from the palace. Is that true?"

"Yes, it is. It was not like I had any choice."

Corrie gasped. "How big was it? It could eat you."

"He's quite big, but he wasn't interested in eating me."

"Where is that dragon now? We keep hearing rumours about it, that it flies over the city at night and eats people's cats and dogs."

Nellie spread her hands. "I don't know. He flew off." Although she would love to put the record straight on cats and dogs. *Her* dragon did not eat cats and dogs. He got on much better with animals than with people.

Dora said, "Last we heard, the shepherd said the dragon killed Lord Verdonck."

Nellie snorted "The *shepherd* said that? Why?" The shepherd had been nowhere near Lord Verdonck or the dragon.

"He said the deacons were preparing his body—"

"Wait. The Regent let *deacons* prepare the body?"

Corrie frowned. "Yes? Is that unusual? It needs to be done before the burial."

"Lord Verdonck hated the church. Did his son allow the deacons to prepare the body?"

"Now you say it, people commented that the stuck-up son had some strong words to say about it. But anyway, what I wanted to say was that when the deacons went to wash him, they found scratches on his leg so large that only a dragon could have made them, and that was how they figured it was the dragon that did it."

That would almost have made sense, if not for the fact that Madame Sabine had scratches, too, and she was still very much alive. But that was a secret known only to Nellie.

She remembered seeing the body being carried out of

the palace into a waiting coach. Someone would have had to prepare the body for burial.

Dora said from the pantry, "Lord Verdonck's son was real angry and has threatened to take the Regent before the Burovian court for neglecting to ensure the safety of all guests in the palace. That's a big thing with the nobles, apparently. And I've heard it from good sources that many people were at the banquet who shouldn't have been, and all of them had invitations, too."

"If they were invited, then the Regent had himself to blame," Nellie said.

"Yes, we all know he's not the brightest spark," Dora said. "I don't know how much of this is true, but it's said Madame Sabine wanted to do the invitations, but her husband said no, and he passed the task off to the church, because they would have to approve the list anyway."

Nellie had heard that, too, and from a more reliable source than just rumours: from Madame Sabine herself. Thinking back to that strange visit to the consort's room, it occurred to her that Madame Sabine had a much better handle on the situation than Nellie had thought.

"Whatever you all think, Lord Verdonck had the scratches," Corrie said. "The deacon told us. He saw them."

Dora said, "You don't die from scratches."

"If they go bad, you may. I imagine a dragon's scratches can easily go bad."

Nellie said, "You served at the tables in the days before the banquet. Lord Verdonck was there. If he was about to die from bad scratches, he would have limped, or seemed unhealthy. Did you see anything unhealthy about him?"

"An unhealthy obsession with Madame Sabine's bosom, maybe," Dora said, and they all laughed.

She came back to the table and poured herself some tea.

Corrie said, "So do you don't think Lord Verdonck's son will be happy that the Regent holds a dragon responsible for his father's death?"

Nellie shook her head. "I doubt it. Adalbert Verdonck is many things, but stupid is not one. He hates the Regent with a passion. He demands not just to know whose hand put poison in his father's food, but who ordered it. He is an angry and powerful young man."

Corrie asked, "What is the son going to do? If he demands his money back, what will the Regent do?"

Nellie shrugged. "Ask the church to loan it to him?"

Dora said, "The shepherd will tell him that he can have the money, but in return, he has to give up his wish to become king."

True. "He could raise taxes."

Corrie snorted. "If he does that, there will be a lot of unhappy people in Saardam."

"There sure will," Dora said. "You mess with people's money at your own peril."

Corrie said, "If the Regent declares himself king, then he can do whatever he wants."

Dora nodded, clutching her cup. "That's the long and short of it. And it may well be the start of another winter of discontent."

Nellie remembered the last of those winters. She had been with the group of former refugees who had returned to Saardam after fleeing the city when the Fire Wizard and his magicians occupied the city. They had eventually driven him out, but not without a fight and loss of life.

"You know who has been asking about you? That guard, Henrik is his name, isn't it?"

Nellie's heart jumped. "What did he want to know?"

"He was concerned and wanted to know where he could find you. He was sitting right where you are now. I had to tell him I had no idea where you were."

"Tell him I'm safe."

"But where are you sleeping? Not in the poorhouse, I hope?"

"No. There are a lot of empty shops and warehouses in the artisan quarter."

"Whoa, that's a creepy place."

"It is, but it's dry and the people who abandoned those buildings didn't always take all their things with them."

"So can I tell him that? You're in the artisan quarter?"

"Oh. I don't know . . ." It felt embarrassing, and she didn't want Henrik to see her living like a pauper.

"Why not? There is clearly something going on between you and him."

"No, there is not," Nellie said. "And anyway, I don't work here anymore, I live with outcasts and homeless people. I'm a pauper. Why would he be interested in me?"

"Because he is. Why won't you talk about it?"

"Because I have better things to do. Like making sure we don't starve to death."

"But he could vouch for you so you could have your position back. I don't understand."

Because they didn't know about the dragon box. It was tempting to come back here, but Nellie knew it would never last. Once it became known she had stolen the box, maybe she would be blamed for Lord Verdonck's death. After all, she had visited his room and had given him herbs. If Madame Sabine wanted, she could easily blame Nellie.

She put her empty cup down. "I better go before it gets light and too many people get up."

Dora nodded at the hessian bag that now sat at the end of the table, bulging with wrapped leftovers from the pantry. "Take that. Come back every day if you want. I don't understand you, but we'll help anyway."

"Thank you." Nellie hope that one day she could

explain everything, and they would all sit around the table and have a good laugh about it. For now, though, that time seemed further away than ever.

She picked up the bag and went back outside into cold. The wind came straight from the snow-covered forests of the east and bit into her skin. It was going to be a cold winter. The Regent should *not* squander food from the stores for the sake of buying his way to the throne. They would need that food later in the year.

By the first of dawn light, Nellie walked through the dark alley around the side of the palace and back into the forecourt.

The guards at the gate said nothing and let her pass unhindered.

Nellie crossed the marketplace where a few stall-holders had arrived. They were talking to each other in the glow of a street lamp and appeared to be watching something.

Two men stood at the door to the main church, one with a light while the second nailed a sheet of paper to the church door.

Nellie stopped next to the merchants.

"What are they doing?" she asked.

"You tell me, missy," a man said, while rubbing his gloved hands.

The man with the hammer had finished his job. The other man lifted the lantern to look at the paper. And then, satisfied with their job, the two came down the church steps.

Nellie thought she recognised one of them: he was one of the city guards who worked for the mayor.

They greeted the group of merchants watching and turned into the street.

A couple of the merchants climbed the steps and

Nellie followed. By now, it was light enough to read the text on the paper, written in plain script.

It said:

Declaration.

Henceforth the following shall be forbidden:

All activities that involve magic.

The possession of objects that involve magic.

The plying of craft that uses magic.

Persons found to be in breach of these conditions shall be arrested.

Regent Bernard.

CHAPTER 4

NELLIE WALKED BACK through the streets of the city to the artisan quarter. When she came past the shops, people were still unaware of that horrible piece of paper on the church door. That piece of paper that would make their activities illegal.

Most of the shop owners and many of the carpenters, tailors, bakers and anyone who plied a handicraft had limited amounts of magic. At least the ones who were good at it.

She wasn't sure why the Regent's aimed to get rid of all the craftspeople in the city. If no one was left to bake the bread, how would people eat? If all the musicians left, then who would play at his banquets? Who would cook? Who would build houses? Who would make beautiful furniture? Who would sail ships? Anyone could get a team of sea cows and let them drag a barge up the river, but to sail across the sea, navigate the treacherous sand bars without running aground, that required wind magic.

Maybe the Regent had a plan that non-magical people he approved of would replace them, but he didn't appreciate the amount of craft required to be a baker or a carpenter, and that to do well in those trades, a magical affinity with the subject was almost required. Regent Bernard came from Burovia. Wasn't magic much more accepted there? It made no sense.

The people opening their shops for the day's trade knew nothing of the Regent's declaration. Here and there, guards stood in groups. They were not palace guards in royal livery but city guards in blue, young men who assisted the city council in maintaining safety in return for the city council assisting their families. Not as well-trained, and not as well-equipped either.

Some spoke to each other. A lot of them were young. One of them was asking a superior questions, and the patrol leader replied in a curt voice: "We wait for that to happen, all right? I told you before, I don't know."

No, they weren't happy with this latest development. They might have their orders but were probably waiting for the citizens to be given the chance to read the Regent's declaration and make their own decision to leave. The guards would prefer that, because it meant less work for them and, besides, the prisons were already full.

Nellie ran into a crowd of onlookers gathered in a square.

The town crier stood on a stone pedestal ringing his bell. His voice echoed between the surrounding houses.

"By decree of the Regent, all magic shall henceforth be forbidden in the city. Anyone who has any magical ability, or is in possession of any magical objects, shall now be required to notify the guards and to hand in the offending objects. Their choice is to leave the city or be arrested."

The message was short and, when he finished and rang his bell, he was besieged with questions.

Nellie couldn't hear what the citizens asked him, but he shouted out, "I am only a town crier. I didn't make the decision. I'm repeating to you what the palace has told me to say. I don't know why the Regent made this decision. If you want to know, I suggest you go up to the palace and ask. I don't know."

Several citizens called him an idiot and a sell-out.

"The Queen would never have allowed this!" a man called out.

"I agree. Long live the queen."

Except the queen was dead.

The poor town crier looked increasingly uncomfortable. He glanced over the heads of the people to the guards at the edge of the square. They had not moved, so far.

In the tumult, he raised the paper and started again, because more people were coming out of their houses.

It was only a matter of time before someone would throw rotten eggs.

Nellie continued down the street.

The distressed face of the poor town crier made her think about Henrik again.

If one got a coveted spot in the prestigious palace guards, for how long should you keep the position if you were ordered to do things you found cruel? For how long did you trust that the institution you served had the best interests of the country and its citizens in mind?

Her father had been in the same position with the church. As their accountant, he saw how the church spent its money. He didn't agree, but did that mean he should stop being an accountant for the church? Did it even mean he *could* do that if he wanted? Because he had a family to feed.

It was all easy saying self-righteous things if you were just a bystander.

She'd said nothing about the Regent's banquets either, because she needed to work, just like her father had.

For now, she had to warn the other women. Zelda clearly had some magic, and probably so did some of the others. And then there was that issue of having a whopping great big dragon in the warehouse and the dragon box that was in Nellie's bag. They needed to hide all those things, although how she would hide a dragon that refused to go back into its box, Nellie wasn't sure.

Nellie turned into the alley that led to the courtyard surrounded on three sides by warehouses. Since she was carrying the bag of bread and other supplies, Nellie was welcomed with cheers.

A lusty fire burned in the fire pit. Steam rose from the tin that served as kettle and that hung over the fire. The women had set up a temporary table made of two kegs and a couple of planks of wood and had set out bowls in which Mina was ladling porridge for the children.

Seeing them all lined up and attacking their food as soon as Mina set the steaming bowl before them almost made Nellie cry. These children with their pale faces and bright eyes deserved better than this. They deserved better than to learn how to beg.

The children finished in no time and scrambled up the ladder to the hayloft.

Nellie watched them go, still feeling uncomfortable that she had no idea what the dragon ate.

Mina handed her a bowl of porridge. It was watery in substance, since they didn't have milk; and they didn't have sugar, but it was warm and filling.

No one said much while they ate.

Nellie had dumped her bag onto the table and Koby, having eaten with the children, piled up the contents on the table.

Dora had slipped in two loaves of fresh bread and a chunk of ham. And cheese. It was a good haul.

Jantien brought the tin they used as a teapot and the

collection of dirty and chipped cups. She poured steaming tea into the cups and the remaining water into the porridge pan where the porridge she could not scrape out had already congealed on the sides.

NELLIE WRAPPED her hands around the warm cup, knowing she would have to upset these women again to tell them about the Regent's decree. She started in a soft voice. "On the way back from the palace, I saw two men putting a decree from the Regent on the church door."

Emmie and Zelda gave her sharp looks. Emmie looked worried, but Zelda's expression was foul. In the past days, she had gone from wanting to use Nellie as a fake herb woman to keeping her out of her workshop.

"What did this paper say?" Mina asked.

"It said that everyone who uses magic and who has artefacts of magic will be arrested."

Zelda snorted. "No matter what King or Queen or Regent in the palace, they always put up these silly pieces of paper. It is like this: they need us, they don't want us in their city. They're afraid. They say we steal. They're afraid that we teach the citizens superstition. Church doesn't like superstition."

Nellie assumed that by us she meant magicians. Magic was strong in the wayfarers and this might even be why they weren't welcome in so many towns. They weren't welcome in Saardam either, but their numbers were too great for the guards to expel them without a fuss.

"I don't know what their reason for putting it up is either, but there are many guards around," Nellie said. "I saw them waiting on street corners ready to search houses and question people."

Zelda snorted again. "They do that every couple of years. They make a fuss. They go blah-blah-blah evil magic blah-blah-blah hand in your stuff. Nothing ever comes of it."

Nellie didn't believe that. For one, when King Roald had been in the palace, he had never issued a decree for all people with magic to hand themselves in.

But she didn't want to argue. "Whatever you believe, we can't afford any more trouble. First, the Regent thinks you have stolen things, and they take all your possessions. Next they come in and drive you out of the safety of the church. And now they want to scare us away."

"I'm not scared," Zelda said She crossed her arms over her chest. "We look after ourselves. We always have. We don't need Regent to say yes or no, we can do this or can't do that. Regent know nothing about us."

"I only want to warn you that there are guards around and they might come in here. Is that a bad thing?"

"Not a bad thing," Agatha said. "But something like that happens a lot around here. Did you see the town crier?"

"I did."

"He's out there every morning blathering about stuff the Regent says. People bring their rotten eggs just because he says the same thing every day. It's all just rubbish from the Regent. Did you hear about the one where he was going to declare himself king?"

Several of the women laughed.

This was not the type of reaction Nellie had expected. Why wouldn't they understand that this was serious? Maybe when your life was constantly in peril, you grew numb from threats like these.

She tried again. "I still think we need to hide the things we don't want them to find. If they find magical items, we'll be put in jail. If they find we have magic, they'll arrest us."

Agatha huffed. "We got no magic."

Right. One didn't go there with her.

Agatha continued, "Why are you telling us this anyway?"

"I want to warn you," Nellie said. "Just so that we know who to be most careful about."

Agatha snorted again. "You come in here, and because you've helped us out in the past, you think we should be so grateful that we drop to our knees to worship the ground you walk on?"

"I don't think that at all!" What was wrong with these women?

Agatha said, "Yes, you do. That's typical for these people from the palace. You think you can boss us around while you bring danger to our children—"

Jantien interrupted, "Please, stop, Agatha. She's not bringing danger—"

"Yes, she is. Remember where she comes from: the palace. She has friends there. She is a danger to all of us, with her . . ." She glared up to the hayloft where children's voices drifted down, mingled with the soft snoring of the dragon. "If there is anyone who's a danger to us, she is. She has no right to warn us or boss us around."

She tightened her arms over her chest.

Nellie's cheeks grew hot. Agatha was right about the dragon. "I'll have to try again to get him back in his box."

"Good luck with that."

Nellie finished her tea in silence. For now, Agatha had won the discussion and Agatha seemed very much into winning things.

What had she expected when she joined this group of women to whom she had been bringing leftovers from the palace? Eternal gratitude? No, but more friendliness than this.

Even the suggestion that she would tell anyone at the palace rankled her. As if the palace would care about this group of ragtag women, some of whom might have a bit of magic. As if she were that type of person. She might not be perfect—nobody was—but to suggest that she would betray the group was an affront to her personality.

She was only trying to help.

In the straw, by the makeshift mattresses and the scratchy horse blankets in the former stable, she found the satchel that she had taken from the palace, with her father's book and the dragon box inside.

She brushed the dust off, and took it up into the hayloft.

The children had collected all the loose hay into a giant heap and had dragged blankets onto it, to the dismay of Jantien, who complained that the children looked like farm boys covered in straw.

But Nellie suspected it was quite warm, especially so because the dragon lay in the middle of the heap, with his legs bent at the knees, and tail and neck curled around his body. He opened an eye when Nellie came to the loft, but then closed it again.

The children sat on the wooden floor, playing a game with pebbles that involved rolling them across the floorboards. Anneke and her brother Bas were there as well as Koby and Ewout and all the other children.

"Come and play with us, Nellie," Bas said. He shuffled aside to make room for her.

"No, I'm sad to say I can't. I would like your friend to help me. He needs to hide."

"Boots?"

Nellie laughed. "Is that what you call the dragon?"

Anneke said, "Yes, it's like he's wearing boots, because his feet are darker than the rest of him."

"Well then, I'm going to have to ask *Boots* to go back into his box."

"No! He keeps us warm."

"It may not be necessary for a long time, but there are guards looking for magical things. I want him to hide."

Watched by the children with wide eyes, she produced the box from the satchel.

The dragon jerked his head up. His eyes were suddenly bright and round, the irises vicious orange.

"I don't think he likes it," Bas said.

No, the dragon didn't like it at all. To be honest, she wouldn't like it either, having been locked up inside the box for the best part of twenty years.

"You have to help us," Nellie said to the dragon. "I'm sorry, I need you to go back inside so we can all be safe."

She opened the box.

The dragon's head shot up further. A puff of smoke blew out of its nostrils.

"There are guards looking for you. They will kill you and kill us if they find you here. You don't want to go back into the church crypt, do you?"

She had no idea whether the dragon understood what she said. So she took a step forward.

Now the dragon jumped to his feet. His tail waved around, narrowly missing the heads of some of the children.

"Whoa, be careful, children. You best go down while I do this."

"You're scaring him with that box," a little girl, Jette, said. She was only seven, still with soft blond curls dancing around her head.

The dragon turned to her. He let out a brief growl.

Jette walked to the top of the ladder. "You be good, Boots. You behave yourself. If Nellie says you should go in the box, you better go in the box."

Several of the other children were packing away their game.

"Come on, children, go down. It's only for a little while. You can come back and play soon."

"But we'll forget where we were," Bas said. He was marking the floorboards with a piece of chalk to indicate where each of the pebbles were.

Nellie told him, "There is no need to do that. Just hurry."

While she was talking, the dragon reached out with a forepaw and hit the box out of Nellie's hands. It bounced over the floorboards. The kitten scooted out from under the straw and inspected the inside of the box.

"Whoa! Be careful."

Anneke said, "I don't understand why he needs to go into that box. If someone comes, Boots can just fly away."

Agatha called from downstairs, "Children, if Nellie says go downstairs, you go downstairs. Now come down that ladder or I'll spank your bottom."

Wide-eyed, Anneke and Bas scrambled down, leaving Nellie alone with the now agitated dragon. His ears were twitching, his tail was twitching and his head was waving from side to side. He glanced to the box and then to Nellie.

Smoke trailed from its nostrils.

The box lay on the hay-covered floor between them. When Nellie took a step towards it, the dragon shied back, pushing his rear end into the wall.

"You really don't want to go back into that box, don't you?"

She spoke in a soft voice.

The dragon didn't react. Smoke drifted from its nostrils and its ears continued to twitch.

"I helped you, didn't I?" Nellie said. "Now I need you to help me."

Again, no reaction.

"You're causing a lot of trouble," she continued. "Do

you think it's going to be worth it? Do you think Prince Bruno is still alive and waiting for you?"

The dragon turned his head to her.

Did he recognise Prince Bruno's name?

In her memory, Nellie saw the chubby little prince as she had last seen him: a toddler with a soft face and big brown eyes. His hair was dark and very straight, and in summer, his skin would have a lovely bronzed tint.

She used to read stories to him, and he would listen, sucking his thumb. He always chose stories about animals, unless his sister made Nellie read stories about fairy princesses and witch queens.

The dragon made a soft whining sound.

Nellie felt sorry for the poor creature. "You miss him, right?"

A dragon without a master should roam free in the forests or mountains or whatever the dragon's eastern home looked like. He should be able to soar through the sky, not be tied to a silly little box.

Why was the dragon still tied to the box?

Nellie held out her hand, palm up.

The dragon bent its neck forward, brushing her finger-tips with its snout.

She took a step forward. The dragon leaned its head into her hand. She patted the warm scaly skin and scratched behind the ears and under the bearded chin. The dragon half-closed its eyes.

"You like that, huh?"

If she reached out with her right foot, she could just push the box back into her reach. But as soon as she bent to pick it up, the dragon's head shot up and its eyes widened again. He let out a low growl.

"Whoa, calm down."

She went back to scratching the dragon's head.

"All right then, stay up here, but don't move and don't

make a noise. If you want to see your master again, you'll have to help us and keep very quiet."

The dragon let out a low rumble. Smoke curled from his nostrils.

Nellie climbed down the ladder, taking the empty box with her.

Mina looked at her, hopeful, but Nellie shook her head. "He won't go into the box. I told him to stay quiet."

"How is it going to stay quiet? You said it doesn't listen to you," Agatha said.

"No, he doesn't!" Nellie whirled at her. "It's not like I asked him to come or to bring me here. And I don't know why you think I can solve all your problems because I can't. I'm doing my best, right? I have no magic and don't know how to tell a dragon what to do. You go up there and try!"

Agatha stepped back. "You don't have to get so angry."

"Yes, I do. All you can do is snipe at me. I'm doing my best." Nellie's eyes pricked. She could do nothing right for these women.

Agatha snorted. "It's all useless quackery anyway, with this box and all that."

Anneke said from behind her mother, "Don't be angry at Nellie. I *like* Nellie. I *like* Boots. And she did try to get him into the box. I saw it."

"Don't talk your nonsense," Agatha said.

"I saw it," Anneke said.

"You were down here. Now keep quiet."

Agatha was right, Anneke had been down here. There was only one way she could have seen what had happened in the hayloft: if she had wood magic and had been touching the ladder, because it protruded above the floor level of the hayloft.

CHAPTER 5

NELLIE THEN TOLD the dragon to stay up in the hayloft and told the children to cover him with anything they could find.

But she was very unhappy about it, and so were the other women. If the dragon had gone back into the box, she could easily have hidden it. Now she had to hide a full-size dragon *and* the incriminating box that had been stolen from the church.

Nellie wondered whether, if Prince Bruno were here and he was still alive, *he* could control this creature. How did one tell a dragon what to do in absence of its master?

Some of the women, led by Jantien, were hiding all their meagre possessions in the straw and various other places in the warehouse.

There must have been some earlier disagreement because Jantien kept looking sideways at Zelda. "I don't care what she says, I don't want to lose everything I have once again. I had some bronze candleholders that belonged to my husband's family I was going to sell so I could afford to travel to see him. Those supposed guards stole them, and I don't know whether I'll ever see him again."

Her eyes glittered.

Nellie said, "That's all right. I'll help you." She had lost all her possessions several times, and she knew how important those little mementoes became when you had nothing else to remind you of the good life.

Jantien did not have much left in the way of possessions, except some spare clothes for the children, and a little box with hairpins.

"It used to belong to my mother. I would die before I sell it." She wiped a tear from her cheek.

Gertie and Hilde had lifted a couple of cobbles and dug a hole underneath. The women put all their valuables in there.

Nellie felt so miserable she thought she could cry. She thought of the little table in her room in the palace that she had been unable to take and that would probably now go into the dusty storage room from which she had rescued it in the first place. Maybe the Regent would even sell it, and she would have no money to buy it.

Koby brought her own treasure: a little brooch with three tiny gemstones. "It's my grandma's. I don't want to lose it."

Poor Koby.

Zelda was watching all these activities with an expression of scorn on her face. She had made it clear that she had wanted the women to make ointment.

She stomped around the warehouse. "I need to do work. I will lose customers."

But when Jantien suggested that she help hide the valuable items, she snorted and left.

"What is up with Zelda?" Nellie asked Jantien when the two of them went to collect wood in the adjacent warehouse.

"I don't know. But many people don't trust her."

"Why is she with the group, then?"

"Because Agatha was friendly with her, and she said Zelda wanted some women and children to come work for her."

"Have you been to see her 'customers', too?"

"I have. We visited a family with a sick old grandma. She was thin as a skeleton and had all these horrible lumps all over her skin, some of them burst open. Zelda insisted that the family put ointment on them even if it hurt the poor old dear so much that she was crying. But it was all right because she couldn't speak anymore, anyway. The poor dear died a week later. I said to Zelda I wouldn't come anymore, with what she charges for those ointments and tea that's nothing more than chamomile and other herbs from the meadows."

Nellie said, "She says she gets it from Mr Oliver."

"Maybe she does, but there is nothing special about the tea. To be honest, she could just pick the leaves herself. She wouldn't need to buy them from Mr Oliver's expensive store."

Yeah, that part might be a lie. Nellie couldn't see why Zelda would buy leaves from Mr Oliver either.

"I would like to go somewhere else," Nellie said. "I don't like selling quackery to people who believe they're buying a medicine that works."

"No, me neither, but Zelda has money and gives us food."

"We can get our own."

"I'm so ashamed of all this," Jantien said, and her eyes welled with tears. "I'm ashamed that the children see me do this work for this woman I wouldn't even say hello to in the street. Ewout and Jette are old enough to understand. I hope when they get older, they'll understand that I had no choice. I hope that my husband will understand when he comes back."

Nellie put her hand on Jantien's shoulder. "It's all right. Look after the children. That's the most important thing."

Jantien nodded, but her eyes glittered with tears.

"I don't even know if I'll ever see my husband again. I have no idea where he is."

"Didn't you say he went to Florisheim?"

"That's what he said, but if he arrived safely, surely he would have let us know?" The tears again welled in her eyes.

Nellie wished she could make everything better, but this time she had no king and queen hidden in her group as they did in the hard but glorious time when they defeated the Fire Wizard. They were a bunch of poor women and a dragon who wouldn't listen to them.

The wood was chopped, and Jantien and Nellie carried it into the other warehouse where some others were already preparing the midday meal.

Zelda had brought a bowl of dried beans, and they needed to be soaked and boiled for a long time before they were ready to eat. The leftover ham and potatoes Nellie had brought were not enough to feed all of them, but with the beans, it would make a nice soup. The smell was wonderful.

Suddenly, Koby came rushing into the warehouse. She had gone out to collect clear snow to melt for water, but her buckets were still empty.

"Guards are coming into the street!" she shouted, panting.

"Be calm, child," Agatha said.

"There are so many of them, and they've gone into Yolande's shop and are throwing everything into the street. They've also gone into the house next door, you know, where the two brothers live, and are taking out things like clocks and other devices made of metal."

Zelda started, "That's what you get when you—"

But Mina cut her off. "Children, go up into the hayloft, and be very quiet. I'm going to have a look."

"No need to panic," Zelda said. "They're always looking for stolen things in those shops."

Mina rounded on her. "And we have no stolen things? We don't know what they're looking for. I'm not going to take any risks."

Nellie followed her out of the warehouse.

Indeed, a couple of men were standing outside the shop on the corner. Like the ones who evicted the people from the church, these did not wear uniforms. They were not men who Nellie recognised, either. At least, they were not regular palace guards being sent out to do this work. Yes, she was still thinking about Henrik. The fact he continued to ask about her made her more uncomfortable. If he would not renounce the deeds of the guards, then she didn't know if she could trust him and didn't want his attention.

Yolande's shop on the corner sold homemade sweets and spices. It was a quaint little business, no bigger than a few steps wide in each direction, and crammed with many shelves with little boxes, glass containers and jars and other quaint items. It was a relic from the days that the artisan quarter was filled with shops like these and that the well-off citizens would come here for the novelty, the days that people would come to see Mustafa's exotic animals and the jugglers.

Now, the shop window was dusty, the paint peeling and the sign that said *Yolande and Dirk's Sweets* faded. Dirk had been dead for years.

Three guards stood outside the shop next to a pile of

jars, some broken, some tipped over with their content spilling onto the trampled snow.

There were a couple of men inside the shop, and a woman's voice drifted out.

"I have done nothing wrong. Now get out of my shop, you're ruining my business."

Next thing one man came out of the shop, dragging the old woman with him. She had a bent back and walked with a walking stick.

"Keep your hands off me. I have done nothing wrong," she was yelling, and thwacking him with her walking stick, but he paid her no heed.

The two brothers from next door stood in the open door to their house, watching the goings on. Nellie wondered why didn't they do anything to help the poor woman, because they were both healthy men. But there were guards inside their house as well.

Someone came out carrying a box full of metal items, adding it to a collection already in the street. The loot included bronze candleholders, wooden boxes with pearl inlay, ornate frames with pictures, wall clocks such as were owned by rich families.

The two brothers stood unemotional and hard-faced as the guards raided their home.

"Are these their belongings?" Nellie asked. She couldn't imagine people in this part of town owning those pretty objects.

Mina said, "They sell those things. Sometimes at the markets, but usually they sell them to shops. They're pawnbrokers. They buy those things, usually for a low price, from well-off people in financial trouble, and resell them."

Nellie felt so dumb. It was as if she had entered another world where she was like a child and needed to learn everything.

Pawnbrokers. Everyone except her probably knew this already.

The only way she knew pawnbrokers was how her father always spoke disdainfully of them, especially if he was forced to deal with them because the church wanted to buy an item off a pawnbroker.

Her father always said making a profit off another person's misfortune was a tacky way to make your living, but her father was quick to judge others, and despite the fact that he dealt with people from all corners of society, he had never understood the plight of others, or had any sympathy for them.

She said, "So what are these men doing? I thought they were supposed to be looking for magical items."

Mina snorted. "I think they're looking for ways to enrich themselves."

A wagon with a horse stood around the corner from Yolande's shop. A few people sat in the open tray, huddled against the cold. The guards dragged Yolande to the wagon, still shouting, lifted her up and made her sit down.

"What are they going to do with her and the others?" Nellie asked.

Mina shrugged.

"Does she have magic?"

But Mina didn't know that either. "If they say you have magic, you have magic. Doesn't matter if it's true or not."

And that was the horrific truth.

Nellie and Mina retreated into the alley and ran to warn the others that the raiding party would turn up soon.

The women stood around the fire, a circle of worried faces. Mina told them to keep talking, but there was nothing to talk about. They all wanted to be quiet so they would hear the approaching footsteps.

"Keep stirring the pot," Mina told Koby.

The children in the hayloft did their job and were very

quiet. There was no sign of the dragon either. Hopefully, he would sleep through all of it.

No one spoke.

The only sound was the occasional clonking of the spoon against the side of the pot as Koby stirred.

Nellie was hungry. The soup smelled really good.

Sounds came from the street, filtered through the alley: a shout of a man, or the whinnying of a horse. Nellie presumed that more people got put onto the cart.

Then heavy footsteps came down the alley, accompanied by male voices. It sounded like at least three or four men. One of them gave an order. Sounds outside indicated that they tried to open the door to the nearby warehouse, but the state of that building was such that it was dangerous to enter.

One of the men swore, followed by a crash.

Nellie guessed the door had fallen off its hinges or part of the roof had fallen in. At any other time, this might have been funny. The women always told the children not to play in there.

Then someone banged on the door of the warehouse.

"Open up, in the name of the Regent."

The women looked at each other, and slowly, Mina walked to the door. She pushed the plank aside a crack.

"Are you hiding any items of magic?" the man yelled.

Nellie couldn't hear Mina's reply, because the dragon took this moment to lift his head out of the straw.

Oh no.

Mina was saying, "We are just a group of women and children. We are poor and have nothing."

The door crashed open, and a man pushed her aside.

Mina almost fell as the men charged in. They stopped in the middle of the warehouse.

They looked around.

The leader's gaze rested on Koby, still stirring the pot.

"Having a party here?"

Nellie had packed away the bread and the remains of the ham so they could use it later, but the cups and plates were still on the table.

The man walked to the table and put his hand on the teapot. Yes, it was still warm.

He kicked one of the bricks that surrounded the makeshift fire pit.

Koby retreated, giving him a suspicious look.

"Leave her alone," Mina said.

The other men spread out around the warehouse. They picked up and threw aside the bags that the women were using as mattresses, sometimes finding little items of interest; but because the women had hidden all their valuable possessions under the cobbles, they didn't find too much.

One of them found Zelda's collection of herbs.

"What's this?" he asked.

"Chamomile tea," Zelda replied, her face defiant.

"And what do you know about chamomile tea?"

"We use it because we cannot get real tea."

Something in her attitude must have irritated him because he pulled her up by her shawl. "You're a herb woman?"

"I am a woman who uses herbs sometimes. Because they grow in the field and they're free."

"Indeed. You're a herb woman. You use magic to deceive and betray people. Where are you from?"

"From nowhere. I've lived in this town for over ten years."

"But you are not from here, anyone can tell that. You are a foreigner with magic, trying to subvert the people of this town."

"I've done nothing that bothers you."

"Haven't you? Then tell me about these things." He held up his hand. "Stealing. Bothering citizens. Selling stolen goods. Cajoling the bereaved into giving up their possessions. Selling poisonous concoctions to nobles."

He counted on his fingers.

Zelda looked at him, her face hard. "You're looking for people with magic. I did not hear you accuse me of magic."

He snorted. "We'll be watching you."

"You're welcome. I can do exotic dances for a very good price."

"And you're a filthy whore, too. Tell me why I should want to watch your old and wrinkled arse."

One of his mates laughed.

Another man was questioning the other women. They stood in a group, and Agatha's voice drifted through the hall.

"We don't have anything like that."

The man gestured at the mattresses in the space under the hayloft, and his fellows searched through it. One man was walking from one side to the other side of the sleeping area with a metal stick and two handles. With his big and heavy boots, he stomped across the hay-filled mattresses.

Nellie wondered what he was doing. She had seen people use this device when she was in the forests of Burovia where people would divine for magic.

"Ah!" His face lit up.

He pointed down. A colleague dug in the straw at his feet.

A moment later, he came up with Jantien's bag.

She clapped her hand over her mouth.

"Was there anything magical in there?" Nellie asked.

Jantien shook her head.

The man found a tatty singlet with pearl buttons. He waved his metal rod over it, then tossed the box to his colleague.

Jantien called out, "No, you can't have that. It belongs

to my mother."

"This is an item of magic."

"It's just a singlet!"

"It's an item of magic. You are arrested in the name of the Regent."

"You can't do that. I have six children to look after. Let me go. Let me go!" She tried to twist herself out of the man's grip.

"The Regent says no magic, and he means no magic." He jerked at another colleague who grabbed Jantien's free arm. "Take her to the others."

As she was being dragged out, one of her children, in the hayloft cried out. "Mama! No! Mama!"

One of the guards looked up. He nodded to his colleagues.

"Check up there."

Oh no.

Two men climbed the ladder.

Nellie held her breath. The first one reached the top of the hayloft and called down, "Hey, there's a bunch of children up here."

And then he gasped. "What's that? It's a—"

A giant roar interrupted him.

"A dragon!"

The man clambered onto the hayloft, pulling his sword.

The children screamed, and the dragon roared again.

Agatha yelled, "Get down here, kids!"

But two men were climbing the ladder, so that was impossible.

And then a fireball burst through the door of the warehouse with such force that the half-rotten wooden plank exploded.

It slid to a halt on the floor. It unfolded four paws, a snarling head with vicious teeth.

The women screamed and ran.

Nellie hid behind the barrel of water, peeping in between the barrel and the wall.

In the middle of the warehouse stood a fire demon in the shape of a mean guard dog with a strong, square-jawed head and powerful shoulders. Its eyes were red as glowing coals, moving from one side to the other as it took in the women cowering in the corner. The guards gripped their swords, pale-faced, knowing they were about to die.

A big ball of fire erupted from the top of the ladder.

Oh no, the dragon. He stood with his mouth open, hissing a spout of fire. No, he would set fire to the entire building.

The guard halfway up the ladder jumped down and drew his bow, aiming at the hayloft.

The other men in the warehouse shouted. A couple surrounded the fire dog, swords drawn, as if swords could do anything against a magical creature. It let out a low growl and crouched as if getting ready to attack.

The dog wasn't interested in the men at all, but only had eyes for the dragon.

Nellie didn't think. She grabbed the bucket that stood next to the water barrel, dunked it into the ice-cold water and threw the water over the fire dog.

The stream of water hit the burning figure with a hiss of steam. The creature shook itself. Its fire-laced fur issued steam into the cold air. It turned its head to Nellie. The look from its red eyes burned with evil.

Nellie jumped behind the water barrel with a squeak.

That was dumb. Now it would attack her.

Next thing, the dragon sailed from the hayloft, his claws outstretched. He hit the fire dog in the back. It screamed. The two rolled over the floor, scattering burning wood from the fire.

Nellie yelled, "Stop it, stop it!"

But she wasn't sure what she would do if the two creatures stopped fighting. She was just afraid that the dragon would be injured. The dragon had his claws dug into the fire dog's sides and the dog held the dragon's throat in its jaws.

The dragon shook his head, billowing fire. The dog yelped, letting the dragon go. The dragon jumped into the air, ran through the middle of the fire pit, scattering a shower of sparks. The fire dog jumped after him, but missed, because the dragon's wing hit it in the face. It rolled over the ground, setting fire to the random bits of straw.

The dragon took no

notice. He ran across the floor, straight through the fire, and launched himself into the air. The sound of his wingbeats receded in the distance. The fire dog shook itself and vanished in a puff of sparks.

Within moments, a big group of guards came running into the warehouse, shouting, swords at the ready.

"Arrest everyone!" the patrol leader shouted.

There was no time to make a plan. It was everyone for themselves. No time to find the children or take any possessions.

Nellie ran across the floor. A door in the back of the warehouse led to a path that ran along the canal. She didn't think; she ran past the back of warehouse, past people unloading stock from the low barges that could navigate the canals, past the brewery and the city's food stores, until she could no longer hear the shouting.

Then she hid in an alcove, catching her breath.

It was cold. The day was misty and the humidity of the air seeped into her

clothes. She only had the clothes she wore. She was still hungry.

The dragon was nowhere in sight.

CHAPTER 6

IT **WAS COLD** in the misty morning along
the canal.

Nellie stared over the surface of the water,
disturbed only by two ducks paddling across an area near
the opposite side, which was free from ice.

There was nothing to do, except to return to the warehouse and gather what she could salvage after the raid, find
the people who were still there and then . . . start again
and struggle to survive.

The thought of going back to the palace crossed her
mind. Now that the dragon had escaped, the proof that
she had stolen him had become irrelevant. Hopefully, the
dragon was smart and had gone back to wherever dragons
came from. Still, she had the box, and she would forever
be afraid that the dragon would turn up. And there would
be questions, most likely from Madame Sabine. And
lacking a dragon would make it more likely that the
Regent would blame her, and not the dragon, for Lord
Verdonck's death. That threat would always hang over her
head any time she came near the palace.

When Nellie entered the warehouse, she found Mina,

Gertie, Hilde and Lise with Koby and Jantien's children, all standing around crying and hugging each other.

They turned to the door as soon as Nellie came in. Faces lit up.

"Nellie! You're alive."

Koby ran to her and gave her a hug, and Mina followed.

Zelda sat on an upturned bucket in a corner, giving the group an evil look. Agatha sat with her, with Anneke and Bas at her feet, and so the lines in the sand were drawn.

"Where are the others?" Nellie asked. A few faces were missing from the group. Gertie and Hilde were there, but Josie was not. Emmie was also missing.

"They took Jantien," Koby said.

Yes, that was another missing face.

"The children," Mina said.

All six huddled together, the youngest only four. By the Triune, the poor things. How were they going to survive? Nellie crouched next to them.

"When is mama coming back?" Jette asked.

Nellie couldn't bring herself to say what she feared. "We'll look after you. You won't have to be alone, and you won't have to go hungry." It was all she could say.

"Boots was really angry at those guards. He will get mama."

Nellie couldn't bear to tell the children that their dragon was also gone.

From her spot on the upturned bucket, Zelda said, "Go on, be a hero. Just remember why we're in this trouble in the first place."

"It is not her fault!" Mina shouted.

Zelda snorted. "She brought the creature in here. And then dared accuse me of being dishonest."

"We are all in this together. We need each other to

survive. If you don't want to be here, then leave, because—"

Gertie interrupted. "—Stop it, Mina. Bickering won't get us anywhere."

Zelda continued, "We were fine until she came, stuck-up bitch from the palace, thinks she's better than us."

"Stop it!" Gertie and Hilde shouted at the same time.

Zelda crossed her arms over her chest and glared at Nellie.

Nellie's ears glowed. Nobody had ever said things like that about her. She had given so much just to help people. How dare this witch suggest that she . . .

But as usual, when she got angry, she lost the capability of making sensible replies. She just froze up.

Mina said into the tense silence, "What has happened has happened. There is not much point in arguing who was at fault or why this happened—"

"It was because the guards were looking for people with magic," Koby said. "I heard them say so."

"Leave it, child," Mina said. "It's done. We can't change what happened. We need to all help each other and do what we can to find the others. We'll need everyone to respect each other. Please don't fight because it only weakens us. Are you all with us?"

Gertie and Hilde nodded. Nellie nodded, too, and so did Koby, and Emmie's daughter Lise.

Agatha, seated next to Zelda, did not.

"Mama?" Anneke said. "I want to stay."

Mina turned to Zelda, who said nothing, but pulled her arms closer about her chest.

"Agatha?" Mina asked. "Can we count on you?"

Agatha glanced at her daughter, tucking a strand of hair behind her ear. She blew out a breath. "Oh, all right. I have the little ones to take care of."

"Thank you," Mina said.

Anneke clapped her hands. "Yes! I don't want to go anywhere else. Thank you mama."

"Zelda?" Mina asked.

Zelda said nothing, and Mina said nothing either for a while. They glared at each other.

"We appreciate your knowledge and your free spirit, we really do," Mina said.

Finally, Zelda spoke. "Yeah, because that's what this is about: I know where to find things you can use and eat. But, no, thank you. I know when I'm not welcome."

Zelda picked up her bag and walked out of the warehouse. She left behind a tense silence.

"Who will get us the tea and the beans?" Anneke asked.

"Don't even ask," Mina said. "It's bad enough that this had to happen."

"I only tried to help," Nellie said.

"It's not your fault. You did well bringing us the leftovers from the palace."

"I can keep doing that." Nellie cringed. She didn't want to go back to the palace, but she had to, just to help these people.

"Thank you. We appreciate it."

Gertie sighed. "It is a pity though. Together we stand much stronger than divided. She did know a lot of useful things. With winter coming, surviving until it's over will be our main problem. We'll see about all the other stuff, like finding a better place, and maybe going somewhere else in spring."

The women fell silent. Some of them nodded, and Hilde hugged Agatha.

Then Nellie said, "How about we try to free Jantien and the others?"

Mina snorted. "If you know how we, a group of ragtag

widows and children, can do that, I'd be happy to hear about it."

Nellie didn't know. It was always Mistress Johanna who had the brilliant ideas. But it wouldn't hurt to find out where the people had been taken. Then, once she knew that, maybe an idea would come to her—

—An idea that involved a dragon—

—That had probably left the city a long time ago.

She needed to make a plan, but plans were not her strong point.

After making sure that the guards had gone, Nellie ventured into the street. She needed to think, away from the immediate concerns of survival. They still had enough food for a day, two if they stretched it.

The main street through the artisan quarter was a chaos of discarded and broken household items and people trying to recover those items. Groups of men stood in the street, arguing about the raids. The talk was of ruined stock and possessions stolen from houses.

A group of merchants hotly debated who these guards worked for. Nellie stopped to listen.

"They were not in proper uniform," one man said. "They're mercenaries paid by the Regent to search the houses of people they suspect of hatching plots against him."

"Why would he send them in here? All the people who conspire against the Regent are in the palace already. They're all nobles and their hangers-on, all the fat cats who get invited to the banquets. These men were looking for something."

"They said they was looking for magic," said another man. "The Regent put the rules on the church door that there was to be no magic allowed."

"That's what they *say*. You never know what it's really about."

"Yeah, the Regent wants himself crowned king. He'll be wanting to shut up any that don't agree with him."

"In the artisan quarter, man? Who in this crappy part of town would have the money to stick in his craw that much?"

"The Science Guild, that's what."

"The—what?"

"You don't know about them? They're the ones who meet at the back of Jacques de Ruyter's house. They're no friends of the Regent's, or the church for that matter."

The men went into gossip about who did or did not belong to this group that Nellie had never heard about, so she continued walking.

She suspected that this was about finding a dragon. Someone had tipped off the guards she was in this area. It could have been someone who had watched from a darkened window when the dragon had tumbled into the street. It could have been a neighbour. It could have been Zelda, or Agatha.

Further down the street, people gathered around a woman who wailed about the arrest of her daughter.

"She was just fifteen, never done nothing wrong!"

The coldness in Nellie's heart grew. What sort of guards took a young girl away from her family?

How could the Regent order this?

Signs of destruction were everywhere. The men had bashed in doors and destroyed shops when searching for magical items. They had even ransacked the markets. The contents of a herb seller stall lay on the ground. Several of the man's jars were broken, the contents spilling in the snow. A lot of the stallholders had already started to pack up, many of them angry, saying they were leaving, never to return.

A group of people stood on the steps to the church, looking at a second piece of paper on the door.

Nellie joined the group and shuffled forward until she could read the text.

It said:

In our efforts to rid the city of the evil practitioners of magic, we will conduct an open court for people who have been charged with performing or being in possession of items of witchcraft. The session will be held in the marketplace, and people from the church will preside over the proceedings.

The date was only two days from now, and none of the onlookers knew what would happen to people who were judged to be magicians or how those judgements would be made.

Nellie rushed back to the women in the warehouse and told them about the declaration.

"What does it mean—there will be a process?" Hilde asked.

"I think the Regent and mayor and shepherd will hold court in the marketplace to decide whether the prisoners are guilty."

Agatha scoffed. "How can they tell that?"

"These men can tell, that's all I know," Mina said. Her voice sounded ominous. "They use church relics that can pick out witchcraft. I've seen it before. The shepherd has a skull with ruby eyes. He holds it up in front of your face and the eyes glow when they feel witchcraft."

Nellie felt cold. She had seen this dreadful thing.

Agatha said, "I thought they weighed people. Anyone less than four stone is held up by magic and is a witch."

"What happens to the people who are witches?" Koby asked.

"Likely they will be thrown into the dungeons," Mina said.

Agatha said, "They don't want to feed any more mouths down there. I think they'll be hanged or burned at the stake."

Mina hissed, "Shhh, don't say that in front of the—"

The children all watched, eyes wide. Nellie didn't think the little ones understood, but the older ones, Jette and Ewout, certainly did.

Nellie had been through this before. Alexandre, the fire magician, also made a point of making an example of anyone who disagreed with him. She remembered Mistress Johanna's own father being put up on a stake to be burnt and how the intervention of the people had saved him and the other prisoners.

"We have to do something," she said, hugging herself.

The others nodded.

But saying that was easier than figuring out what to do. It was hard enough to figure out how to survive. If she had any say over the dragon, would she give the dragon up to the Regent to save these people? What would the Regent do with him?

The women gathered all their possessions and brought them all in one spot to determine if there was anything they could sell. Many of the items were worthless mementoes of long-dead family members, or lost homes. In Nellie's case, she was determined to hang onto her father's book and the dragon box for as long as possible. She promised to continue to go to the palace for leftovers.

But there was more work to be done and fewer people to do it, and no one knew an easy way to make money like Zelda did.

Once the meagre meal of dry bread and the remainder of the soup had been eaten, Nellie asked the children to bring down their bedding from the hayloft so they were together and kept each other warm. Some of the young ones cried for their "Boots" and Nellie had to explain that the dragon was a free creature.

By the light of the fire, Nellie sat in the hay, surrounded by the children. The kitten had been mewling all day—missing its friend—and it curled up on Nellie's lap.

"Tell us a story," Anneke said.

So Nellie told a story about a girl who was headstrong and wanted to be a businesswoman.

"That's funny, because all girls want to be princesses," Anneke said.

"Well this girl did not want to be a princess. She wanted to take over her father's business because that was what she was good at. But her father was a widower, she was his only daughter, and he needed someone to leave their estate to."

"What is that?" Ewout asked.

"An estate is a house or a piece of land or a business."

Anneke said, "But she already had the business. It was hers, wasn't it? Because it was her father's."

"It was," Nellie said. "But unfortunately, that is not how people see these things. There always has to be a man who owns these things because women cannot own it by themselves."

"What about you? Do you own anything?"

Nellie laughed. "If I did, I would not have been working as a maid for all of my life. Now, do you want to hear the story or not?"

"Of course we do."

"All right. One day the king held a great ball and all the girls in all of Saardam were invited. He wanted them to dance with his son. He needed to marry his son, because he had no other children. But the prince was rude and not good in the head. And during the ball, a great magician invaded the city. He could throw balls of fire with his hands, and he burnt all the houses around the palace. The girl fled, as the king and queen were killed. But the prince also fled, and when the magician's men tried to take him prisoner, he jumped into the harbour. You see, he could swim. And the girl and her friends . . ." Nellie stopped. *She* had been there. She remembered fishing the man out of the water, weighed down by his heavy cloak. She remembered the horror of realising that the man was Prince Roald. She remembered how scared she had been of him, and of his outbursts where he would bang his head against a wall or a tree, and how upset she had been with his rude and lewd remarks. "So the girl and her friends fished him out of the water, and they escaped together. They could see the entire city in flames and knew everyone was dead. They knew the survival of Saardam depended on them. So the girl ended up marrying the prince anyway, but it was her own choice, because she chose to save the country."

"You're talking about Queen Johanna," Anneke said.

"Yes, I am. That is very smart of you. The queen and the few people who were still alive fled up the river because the evil magician still lived in the palace. The girl and her new husband couldn't be king and queen until he was gone. She had to save the country from his evil, and she did that by uniting all the people against the evil magician. And when her own father was going to be burned at the stake, she led a crowd of people into the market square and they all created such a fuss that the guards did not know what to do, and most of them weren't terribly loyal to the fire magician anyway. They only did what he said because they were scared of him. As soon as they saw that the common people might win, they abandoned him and helped the Queen."

After a small silence, Anneke said, "Is the Regent an evil magician?"

Nellie looked at her, frowning. "No, he isn't, why do you ask?"

"Because he sits in the palace, and the church won't make him king. Also, everyone says the prince is still alive, so he should let the prince be king."

"There are rumours about the prince. No one knows for sure if they're true."

"If they're not, then why won't the shepherd make the Regent king?"

"Because . . ." Because the shepherd had selected the Regent for incompetence and didn't want him on the throne. Because . . . well, what if the church knew Prince Bruno was still alive and this was the reason they didn't want Regent Bernard to become king?

Also, in the days with Mistress Johanna and Prince Roald, the church had been on their side, and most nobles had been against the Fire Magician already. This time, a lot of nobles liked the Regent, at least for as long as they could come to his banquets. Most of the merchants didn't mind that the Regent was holding banquets as long as they could trade. And the Church . . . she shivered. She was sure that most of the deacons, and shepherd Adrianus and the other shepherds of the smaller churches were with the people, but they had to obey Shepherd Wilfridus, and Nellie wasn't sure of the good intentions of Shepherd Wilfridus at all.

Anneke said, "What about making a fuss with all the people? Isn't that the thing we should do?"

"When we get a chance, yes. But first we have to have a plan." A plan that involved making most of the city angry enough to do something.

"You have a plan?"

"Not yet, but we will think about it, the adults and I."

By that time, most of the children were already asleep, and Nellie returned to the fire with the other women.

The mood was grim.

Mina finally voiced the one concern that had bothered Nellie for most of the day. "If it was clear to the guards that Zelda was a herb woman, then why did she not get taken?"

"I reckon it's because she's friends with the ones doing the arresting," Hilde said. "She sells concoctions to the nobles and tells them about the things she hears on the streets. Why would those men have come down our dingy alley? There are so many other old buildings and warehouses. They only went to places where they knew people had magic."

That was a disturbing thought.

"If that's true, we can't stay here," Nellie said. "We need to find a better hiding place."

Preferably one in a place where the guards would not come looking. And a place away from the artisan quarter and its colourful characters, away from the gaze of Zelda.

"Do you know a place that's better than this?" Mina asked.

"I might."

It was so easy to pretend that this little group of women and children could make any difference. Last time, the enemy had been just one person, who happened to be a foreigner who happened to have invaded the city, a fact that most citizens remembered all too well. As she had said in the story, most of the citizens had been afraid of this man, who burned their houses whenever they said something he did not like.

This time, everything was different. Not only was the Regent not hated, and had not himself performed any evil acts, but he also had the support of the church.

Nellie didn't want to fight the church because most people related to the church were good people. The problem was that this time, there were no clear lines in the sand. This time, the people who could make a real difference—the people with money—weren't angry. This time, there was no one man up there shouting *I am your enemy*. It wasn't clear who, or what, they were fighting, only that

Saardam was slowly dying as citizens left, were accused of having magic or became too poor to survive.

The winter would be long.

It was cold in the warehouse that night, and the fact that they were all sleeping together in the hay made little difference.

And as she lay awake staring into the darkness, Nellie had another worrying thought: she had given the dragon the choice of freedom. He had chosen to hang around. She could think of only two reasons he would do that. The first was food, although he didn't seem to need people to feed him whatever dragons ate.

The second was that his master was still alive somewhere in the city.

CHAPTER 7

I T WAS NO LONGER SAFE to stay in the warehouse. It was probably no longer safe to stay anywhere in the artisan quarter because the guards would just keep looking for whatever they were looking for, besides magical things, and would pick up more people. They would use any excuse to arrest people, including waving around a metal rod. They were looking for people to scare and intimidate. And they were doing it in the artisan quarter because many of the citizens of Saardam cared little about those who lived there and because they had always been "strange" people and wayfarers. So they couldn't stay here anymore. Nellie had an idea where they might go, but she needed time to check it out. But first she had to go back to the palace for more leftovers the next morning. Now that Zelda was gone, it would be even harder to feed everyone.

She got up early so she could be back in the warehouse while it was still dark. The less she showed her face, the better.

The snow-covered streets were nearly deserted. Here and there city guards patrolled the streets, but the raids from yesterday had left no traces except a lot of footsteps in the snow and the occasional bits of broken glass. All the items the guards had tossed into the street had either been carted away or collected by scavengers.

The windows in the palace were still dark, especially those on the first floor that faced the courtyard. This was where the Regent, Madame Sabine and their sons and courtiers had their residence. Nellie used to live up there when Johanna was alive. Every morning she had risen early to get the children out of bed. Celine was always fast asleep and was cranky at being woken up, but Bruno was full of beans. He would run out of the room the moment the door was open, and liked screaming in the foyer because of the way his voice echoed in there. He would not sit still and, no matter how many times Nellie or the Queen told him, he would not say thank you or wait his turn. He was a truly boisterous toddler whose hero was his father, who visited from his office in town regularly.

Those memories seemed impossibly long ago.

The guards in the guard boxes looked tired and ready to be relieved at the crack of dawn. They were stamping their feet and swinging their arms until Nellie came up to the entrance when they asked where she was going. She again used the excuse that she was delivering spices to the kitchens and had no trouble getting in.

The kitchen seemed like the only place that was warm and where people were awake in the entire building.

When Nellie came in, Dora was preparing a couple of ducks for roasting, Corrie sat at the table scraping carrots, and Els and Maartje were both getting breakfast ready to be taken upstairs.

"Nellie!" Corrie abandoned her carrots and came to the door to give Nellie a hug. "We heard about so much trouble in town. We were afraid you weren't going to come."

"I have to be careful, but it takes a bit more than that to keep me away." Nellie undid her shawl. It was quite warm in here.

"You want some tea?"

"I wouldn't say no to that."

Nellie sat down at the table and received a steaming cup of tea. Her hands were cold, so she wrapped them around the warm porcelain.

"Roasting ducks again, aren't you?" she asked Dora.

"You know how much the Regent loves his ducks."

Dora sat at the table opposite her. She studied Nellie with an intense look. It was rather uncomfortable. Nellie felt as if she was being scrutinised. Had anything happened here in the last day?

"You don't look good," Dora finally said to her.

No, Nellie knew. This morning, she had attempted to straighten her hair, but her comb had been lost somewhere and her hair was too knotty to fashion into a nice bun. She had no mirror either, not even a window where she could look at her own reflection.

Over the past few days, she had been so cold that now that she came into the warmth, her cheeks were glowing. She guessed the skin looked red and chapped and as blotchy as that of the poor children who came to work in the scullery.

"We were searched yesterday," Nellie said, while looking into her tea. "A lot of people were arrested."

"I heard something about that," Dora said. "What was that about?"

"The Regent put a declaration on the church doors that all people with magic and magical objects would be punished. They raided a lot of shops and took a number of people prisoner. We're trying to find out what happened to them. A few of our group got taken. One of them is the mother of six children in our group. Her husband is no longer in town, so we are looking after the children, but we need to find a safe place for them."

"You can always take the children to the orphanage."

"I could." But Nellie didn't want to do that. Just like the poorhouse was no place for women, the orphanage was no place for children whose mother had been arrested. "I prefer to look after them until their mother comes back."

If she came back.

"If you come with me to the linen cupboard, we can give you some sheets and some old blankets."

"That would be very nice, thank you. But first we have to find a safe place to stay and we have no money."

"Can the children work?"

"I'm sure they can, but the oldest is only ten. He can do little jobs, but there are not many of those around."

"Consider a job where he needs to be small. The sawmill might want to employ him to clean out the machines. I think you should come back here, too, if you can."

Yes, maybe, when all this calmed down. Although so much had changed that Nellie wasn't sure she would ever go back to the palace to cook meals for rich noble guests.

"I don't know that I can or that they will ever accept me."

"It's about the dragon, isn't it? You still have it, don't you?"

"It's not mine. It's a wild creature. It flew off, and no one knows where it is."

"We heard stories about a dragon flying over the city. The guards were all in a panic and wondering how to catch it."

"They can't," Nellie said.

"The Regent seemed pretty determined. He called all the guards in the audience room and gave them a real talking to. Apparently, he said there will be no method or expense spared. Adalbert Verdonck demands answers."

"Is Lord Verdonck's son still at the palace? I thought he left."

"He did. He left for his father's funeral, but came back. I saw him coming into the gates yesterday. People were saying that he requested a formal audience with the Regent, and then spent the next hour tearing into the Regent and the court, and the Regent didn't get a single word in. Apparently he demands a full investigation into his father's death. I'm sure the Regent is trying very hard to present the audience with a dragon."

Which might also explain the obsession with finding magical people.

"Can't the Regent just deny the investigation?" Nellie didn't want the investigation either. She was sure that in cases like this, involved servants were called to give evidence.

"He can, but it won't look good for him and he doesn't have the final say. He's not king."

"I bet he's not happy."

"Not at all. And now that all the guests are gone, it's just him and Adalbert Verdonck. They say the most horrible things to each other."

"What's he going to ask in this investigation?"

"I presume he's going to bother the Regent until the Regent finds someone who can be forced to take the blame for Lord Verdonck's death. Remember what happened after the death of the royal family?"

Nellie shuddered. She remembered all too well. The hearing had gone on for days, as the shepherd who presided over it asked every noble who survived to recount the events in the palace that day.

Even if the king and queen were both dead, none of the nobles wanted to talk about magic. At first they blamed the deaths of the people in the music room on bad wine, but the stories about Princess Celine's exploding magic were just too strong.

A few sensible people had argued that, if only the palace had magicians qualified to train her, it would not have happened, but those voices had soon been drowned by hysteria and extra church services where people would throw all their "magical" possessions onto a bonfire before coming into the church to be "cleansed".

It was awful because everyone was afraid the neighbours would tattle on them for having magical heirlooms, which forced families to give up the only items of value they had.

A chill still crept over Nellie's back when she thought of the service Shepherd Wilfridus had given at the end of the hearing, when he spoke—no, yelled—red-faced and wide-eyed, of the evil that had pervaded the city that must be expunged and that henceforth all forms of magic must be banned.

She said, "These hearings are no good for anyone except the men in power. When two men in power go head to head, it can't be good for anyone."

"You said it. If Adalbert Verdonck knew what was good for him, he would shut up and leave town."

"There must be a significant amount of money involved."

"Or someone else is behind it all. It's said Adalbert Verdonck is friendly with King Leopold of Burovia and may be paid by him to spy on the Regent."

That was one thing Nellie didn't miss about being close to the rulers of the city: the constant scheming. She *desperately* did not want to get anywhere near this hearing, and yet she was sure she *would* be called in.

In Nellie's case, there had been no one in Lord Verdonck's room except the lord, Madame Sabine and the son.

One was dead and the other two could hardly be called unbiased witnesses.

Enough people knew she had the dragon. The jump from there to being able to communicate with him was not big. Then, if the hearing was swayed by the Regent into believing the dragon had killed him, Nellie was a suspect. Even if the hearing decided Lord Verdonck wasn't killed by the dragon, Nellie would still be a suspect. Because she'd been there, because she had brought herbs, and because she was only a maid and no one would defend her.

By the Triune, she should stop coming here.

When she opened the dragon box, when she went into the crypt to check on her father's words about the things that were down there, when she asked Shepherd Adrianus questions, when she took off her bonnet, when she fled the palace, something had changed in her.

Gone was the Nellie who kept her head down. If only she could stop grovelling to these people for their leftovers, she would do it. Let the Regent drown in leftover duck sauce.

She rose and picked up the hessian bag. "Well, I better go, because they'll be wondering where I am."

"Oh, Nellie, we're always here to help you," Dora said. "Just between you and me, make sure you have your name registered as a citizen of Saardam."

"I already have that. Why?"

"You didn't hear this from me: the Regent is about to open the city stores and hand out emergency food to residents."

Nellie had also heard that from Josie. "That seems a silly thing to do this early in winter. What is he going to do when winter hits hard? It seems he's trying too hard to be popular. That's going to backfire."

"Being popular is no doubt part of it. He wants to be

crowned king and he can't do that without support from a good portion of the citizens. But I've also heard this from the guards: they're doing it also because they want the citizens to empty the stores before the less than savoury people in the city have raided the entire stock."

Yes, Josie had also spoken about theft. "Is it that bad?"

"They tell me that increasing the guard level doesn't stop the thievery, and they're not sure how the thieves get in. They're smart robbers, not the average street urchin. If I were you, I would register your names for the hand-outs, and with a bit of luck, you'll get enough to last the winter."

"Thank you for telling me."

Nellie hugged Dora.

Whatever happened, she would love Dora as a sister. One day, life would be better, and Nellie would invite all her friends to the little house she would buy at the edge of town and they would all laugh about it while sitting around the fire in the kitchen.

Nellie left the kitchen and walked down the narrow passage between the side of the palace and the garden wall.

It was still dark here, and very cold. Nellie needed to keep her eye on the ground to avoid frozen puddles or sections of slippery snow.

She didn't see the person at the end of the passage until the silhouette detached itself from the palace wall. She didn't know who it was until she smelled the perfume and felt the softness of fleshy arms and the ample bosom against her back, and the hand that grabbed her shawl and pulled her so she could barely move.

A soft voice said, "I believe you have something that belongs to me."

Madame Sabine.

Her voice sounded sweet, but Nellie did not miss the threatening undertone.

"Whatever are you talking about?" Nellie said. She struggled against the consort's grip, much stronger than she would have expected for such a pampered woman.

"Don't be stupid. You removed something from Lord Verdonck's room. Didn't your parents tell you that stealing can get you into a lot of trouble? You saw a pretty box and thought 'Let's take that?'"

"I don't steal. The dragon was stolen several times. I have documents that prove that he belongs to the church. He was never yours anyway."

"He?"

"You hadn't even noticed that it was a little boy?"

Nellie was trembling so much her lips felt stiff. She wished Madame Sabine would let go of her shawl so she could stand straight.

"You have no business holding onto this thing."

"You're right. Come get him back if you want. I recall last time that didn't end so happily."

Madame Sabine pulled the shawl tighter. Nellie could feel the long nails right through the fabric.

"Don't be smart with me."

"Or you will sack me from the palace?"

Madame Sabine let a long, angry silence lapse. Her breath steamed in the cold air.

Nellie would love to know what went on in Madame Sabine's head. She would have loved to know what had happened that had given Madame Sabine and her lover Lord Verdonck those scars.

Finally, Madame Sabine said, "Fine. You win for the time being. But don't think that we are finished. I do believe we are on the same side, although I would love to set my husband's guards on you to stop your impertinent behaviour."

"That would be a very bad idea."

"What business do you have to threaten me? You're just a kitchen maid."

And Nellie was so sick of hearing this that something inside her flipped. In a deep place inside her soul something said *enough* to being treated as if she were unimportant.

She spoke in a low voice. "I am a confidante of our beloved queen who was a woman who always considered the citizens of Saardam before herself. I helped our queen drive out the Fire Wizard. I have no magic except my faith in the goodness of people. I have no power except that of the truth of my word. *You* are the wife of a ruler imposed on us. Your husband eats himself stupid while the citizens go hungry. Your husband persecutes people for stupid reasons just so he can pretend he's serious about finding a criminal. You can't even be faithful to your own husband, let alone this country. You stole the dragon box, which belongs to the queen's youngest child. You have the scars on your back to prove it. I can tell your husband about those scars. I can tell him about your affair and how you were planning to leave the city. I can tell him how you and your lover planned to use the dragon, except that you never figured out how to do it. I can tell the church you stole their dragon. And they would all believe me because it's the truth. I may be a maid, but I'm not stupid."

Madame Sabine let a small, tense silence lapse before she finally let go of Nellie's shawl.

"No, I see. You're not."

Nellie tucked her shawl back in its rightful place.

Madame Sabine continued, "But if you're going into threats, I have a much better one: I can tell that upstart of an Adalbert Verdonck that you poisoned his father."

"And he would know it's untrue, because he was there both times I visited Lord Verdonck's room and he will know if you change the story, and he'll tell everyone you did it. Because I haven't decided if you and I are on the same side, but you and he are definitely not."

It was all bluff, but Madame Sabine said nothing. Her position in the palace was tenuous since neither her husband's men nor the citizens liked her very much. Nellie didn't quite understand what game she was playing, but it was a dangerous one.

Nellie walked into the palace forecourt as quickly as she could, her legs trembling.

CHAPTER 8

I T WAS STILL DARK when Nellie came back to the warehouse to deliver her haul. There were now not as many of them, and breakfast was a sad affair. The children wanted to find "their" dragon, but Mina told them to stay inside the warehouse.

"We don't want to lose all of you, too," she said.

"But Nellie is going out," Anneke protested.

Nellie said, "I am going to look for a safe place for us all to stay, so that the guards don't come back again."

"Then can we have Boots back?"

"He is a wild creature. I don't know where he is or what he's doing, and I can't make him come back."

"But he can come back if he wants?"

"Of course he can."

"You're not angry with him?"

"No, I'm not."

"Mama is angry with him."

Nellie looked around the warehouse, but Agatha had gone out to get more firewood. It wasn't that strange that the women was angry with the dragon and wanted him to go away. If the dragon had kept quiet—but, then, he had reacted to Jantien's screams. Another thought: would the dragon have known Jantien was the mother of most of the children? The dragon had listened to her when she spoke of Prince Bruno, and he had seemed to be looking for affection. From her, from children and animals.

She wished the dragon would just have gone back into the box. It would have saved everyone so much trouble.

Nellie went out again after breakfast, and walked through the snow-covered streets that were rendered in hues of white and grey, reflecting her mood.

At the marketplace, she ran into a big group of people congregated around the church steps. They were merchants and ordinary citizens listening to an announcement by the town crier. He had just finished and was rolling up his piece of paper.

People were throwing him angry comments.

"I'm sick of this," a man said. "If someone broke into the stores and stole food, then they should find the thief, not blame us for it."

"It doesn't surprise me one bit," another man said. "I haven't noticed the Regent cutting down on his banquets. They eat pheasant and duck and exotic spices and dried fruit. People in the city are hungry. It's no wonder that some of them take what they need."

"Yes, that's right. Blame the poor because they can't fight back."

The town crier came down the church steps, clutching his roll of paper, not looking at any of his former audience.

Someone in the crowd yelled, "Oy, do we get a say about what we think of this Regent? He's got less sense than my ten-year-old son."

Someone else said, "Yeah, Queen Johanna would never have feasts in the winter. She knew life is hard for us when the boats can't come. She would share from the stores, not put guards in front of the door to stop us getting the food that we paid our taxes for."

Several people cheered.

Nellie wrestled through the crowd. She was keen to get out because the situation might get nasty. The atmosphere hummed with anger. "Hand us the thief or the whole city suffers," was hardly the best way to deal with theft from the stores. These types of thieves were not dumb. Food thieves were the lowest form of thieves, and if people knew who they were, they would have told the guards long ago.

The streets away from the market place were a lot quieter, especially at the harbour. The winter weather had stopped most of the activities here. Only a few ships still came in from the ocean at the best of times, and the quay-side where they normally moored lay empty. Of course right now most of the harbour was taken up by ice.

Nellie walked along the snow-covered quay. The closer she came to the end of the wharf, the less disturbed the snow. At the end, the only footsteps that disturbed the pristine white were the prints of ducks.

Beyond the end of the pier that sheltered the harbour with the white-painted lighthouse at the end, the broad delta of the Saar River was grey with mist. In summer, you could see the apple orchards on the other side, but today the shore was barely visible through the mist. The water was calm, with little patches of ice floating downstream.

This place had been the beginning and end of a lot of her adventures.

Only a few weeks ago, she had come to the office on the other side of the harbour to receive the box and her father's book that had been the beginning of this new episode in her life.

If she thought about all the adventures she'd had, she

might be forgiven to think it was her destiny to help great people change things for the better.

Even in the way the dragon trusted her, he acted like he knew she might lead him to someone who could make a difference. Mistress Julianna had even said so, no matter how much Nellie didn't believe in superstition and fortune telling.

Except she was all out of ideas now. All the people she loved had been killed or could not help her. She didn't even understand what she felt towards Henrik any more. She hated to think he would support the actions of the guards in the last few days, dragging all these poor people to the prisons. What in all the heaven's name had Jantien done that justified taking her away from her children? The poor little mites.

What was the Regent trying to do, kill this town with his ridiculous rules about magic?

She stopped abruptly. She felt like she was being watched.

In the middle of the harbour was a small area of open water. Something disturbed the surface, a dark glistening creature that made the water ripple. It was too large to be a fish.

The head of a sea creature came up from the water, its whiskers glittering with drops. It had a blunt snout and small, beady eyes. A sea cow.

She didn't believe the sea cow was what she'd felt watching her, but she was glad to see it. Some wild herds lived amongst the muddy seabeds of the Saar river delta, lazily grazing on the weeds that grew in the shallows. You could sometimes see the herds swim across the river as they raised their heads or flippers above the surface.

The river traders, like the Brouwer Company, used to keep flocks of them to pull their ships up the river. Some boats still went up and down the rivers, and some traders still kept small teams of sea cows to pull the vessels, but the large companies had gone, and most of their animals had been set free.

The Brouwer Company, owned by Mistress Johanna's father, had a shed and sea cow barn at the end of the wharf. In the company's heyday, their two riverboats, the *Lady Sara* and *Lady Davida,* were often moored there. The *Lady Davida* had been sunk during the struggles when the Fire Wizard invaded the city, but the *Lady Sara* had taken many trips up and down the river even when Johanna was Queen and after her father had sadly passed away. After the Queen's death, leaving the Brouwer Company without an heir, the ship had lain idle in the harbour for a few months, before being sold to a river trader in Aroden. The barn itself had been abandoned, and this was where Nellie was headed.

Most of this part of the wharf was now in disrepair, with the warehouses alongside falling to pieces. Repeated fires either from magic or accidentally lit by sailors had not helped matters.

Something moved in the corner of her eye, but when she turned her head she saw nothing.

By the Triune, who was spying on her? The quay behind her lay deserted. The quayside was too high for most of the river ships.

Across the harbour lay the beautiful river ship of the Guentherite order. The curtains of the cabin windows were closed and the sea cow harness neatly stowed on the deck.

She remembered that somewhere along this part of the wharf, she and Mistress Johanna had fished Prince Roald out of the water after the palace had burnt. At that time, Mistress Johanna's father had still occupied the warehouse, and Nellie, Mistress Johanna, Mistress Johanna's mad friend, and the Prince had sailed upriver to find help.

They had needed to go quite a distance before they found anyone alive, and it had been a desperate time.

The memories chilled her. And she couldn't shake the feeling that someone was watching her.

When she went into the main door of the old Brouwer Company sea cow barn, she could see out the roof in a few places where the roof tiles had been blown off. Light streamed through these holes into the dusty space.

A workbench along the wall would once have held tools but, over the years, various people had removed those and presumably sold them. The leather straps for the team harnesses still hung on hooks above the bench, all covered in a thick layer of dust.

The wooden harness itself had only partially survived people scavenging for firewood. Only the rear beam—the heaviest of all—was still intact. She mentally looped the leather straps through the eyelets and could almost feel the weight of the thing when lowering it into the water.

Looking after the sea cows had been one of the things she learned when travelling upriver with Mistress Johanna on that frightening flight from Saardam.

The basin in the middle of the barn was still the home of a couple of sea cows. The creatures stuck out their heads when she walked along the edge. Maybe they hoped she would toss some cabbage leaves into the water. They would stick their broad, bristly snouts above the surface, and would slurp and slobber while they ate.

But Nellie hadn't come here to reminisce. There was work to be done.

She judged the roof good enough to keep out most of the rain.

The workbench would make a nice table and the barrels could be chairs, and the storeroom—

But what was that?

The dust on the paving bore scuffmarks that looked

recent. A couple of carrots lay on the ground. Fresh carrots, because if they'd been here even overnight, they would have been frozen to mush.

This barn was already someone's hideout.

"Is anyone here?" Nellie asked.

The sound of her voice died in the silence.

She looked around for other signs that people lived here: bedding, a tin of water, a bag with possessions. Other than the carrots, she saw nothing.

It was strange and eerie, as if she was entering someone else's house, someone who was very careful about not leaving anything behind when he went out.

Except carrots.

Maybe in the storeroom.

It lay off the side of the barn separated by a rickety wooden door that creaked terribly. Faint light filtered through the tiny window in the top corner. The floor was covered in sawdust that gave out a musty scent.

In the past, this room had been used to store items related to ships and their maintenance. There had been barrels of oil, coils of rope and spare parts like leather straps and eyelets for harnesses and other such things. Some barrels remained on the shelves. Probably they would need to be recaulked before being useful again.

There was also some rope, but it would probably break as soon as someone tried to use it.

In the corner stood a couple of newer items: a bag with carrots, a basket with smaller bags of beans and flour, a cooking pot, and a collection of mismatched cups and bowls, all clean. There was also a stack of horse blankets, neatly folded.

The sawdust on the floor bore no signs of recent disturbance.

As if these things were put here just for her and her group. It was eerie.

But the place was dry, and it was away from the searching patrols in the artisan quarter.

Nellie measured out the space by taking big steps across the room. The group had nine children and six adults. It would be a tight squeeze to all fit in the room when they needed to hide or when it got cold, but it was better than the warehouse in the artisan quarter where everyone knew where they were—or it would be, if it weren't for those abandoned supplies and the feeling that someone was already using this space.

Nellie went back into the main warehouse. As she did so, a number of sea cows plopped their heads under the water.

Two of the sea cows were crunching carrots. Did they have the carrots before? She couldn't remember.

Could sea cows climb out of the water? She had never seen them do so.

Two cats hid under the benches, crouching down. In the old times, there used to be a lot of cats here, because the captains often caught fish on the way down the river. But that was a long time ago. There hadn't been any fish scraps to be scavenged here for many years.

Curled up in the remainders of wood shavings under another bench lay a puppy, undisturbed by either the cats or the sea cows or Nellie's presence.

Poor thing. Was it sick?

But when she crouched, the puppy raised its head and wagged its tail. A sprinkle of sparks trailed over its fur.

Magic.

Nellie whirled around, only to hear more sea cow heads plop back under the water. A carrot rolled across the paving and then over the edge. It landed in the basin with a splash.

A puff of magic sparks trailed the water's edge. She had

seen those sparks before. *The dragon*. She knew for sure now. That was what had been spying on her.

Nellie rose. "Come out, there's no need to be afraid of me."

Her heart thudded.

There was no reply, but she could see a little spark of magic in the corner.

"Come on." She held out her hand.

Of course she hadn't thought to bring the box. Maybe now that he was hiding, the dragon would be happy go back. Who knew what dragons thought?

"All right, you can go and be silly. I am not happy with you because you gave us away and now we are in a lot of trouble. But if you want, you can make it up and help us."

The little trail of magic sparks oozed along the ground and disappeared under the workbench next to the cats. One of them batted a paw at it.

"Have it your way. But we are going to come here anyway."

This was the safe place to take the children.

CHAPTER 9

LATER THAT DAY, Nellie and Mina walked across town with the children. They wore all their clothes, and each carried a pot or a stack of chipped bowls or cups with broken handles. Nellie had told them to collect everything that was theirs and carry as much as possible with them. She didn't want to go back a second time. Guards were everywhere, and she had spotted one of the men talking to Zelda.

The children had asked where they were going, and whether they would see their mother.

Nellie couldn't bring herself to lie as Mina suggested. Koby and Ewout were old enough and wise enough to see through that. So while they walked, she told them about the shed and that it had belonged to the Queen's family, and when she said that sea cows were hanging around in the barn, Bas said, "Whoa! We can tie them to a boat and go anywhere!"

"Except we have no boat," Koby said.

And Mina added, "And there is nowhere to go. It's winter. The water is cold and there will be ice floating down the river."

But there were a few towns just outside the city, and Nellie had cousins in one of those towns. And what Ewout had said was true: they *could* catch sea cows and tie them to any boat. The barn even contained the necessary harnesses.

To get to the harbour, the group needed to cross the marketplace. As it had become a regular occurrence, many people had gathered around the bottom of the church steps to read the notice on the church door.

"What are all those people doing?" Anneke asked.

"The Regent has made a declaration," Nellie said.

"What is a declaration?"

Nellie and Mina looked at each other over the children's heads.

It would be easy to say something like *That is only for adults,* or *You'll find out later*, but that was a sure way for the children to know that something was up. The children were not crazy. They had lived in hardship for the past six months. Koby, especially, was almost old enough not to be considered a child anymore.

"The Regent is going to hold a court to see which prisoners are witches."

"Is Mama going to be there?" Jantien's oldest daughter Jette asked.

"Maybe."

"Our mother is not a witch," Ewout said.

"We know that, but the Regent doesn't."

"So he will see that she is not, and he'll let her go."

But if the Regent so determined, all of them would be witches, because all of them were there to be made an example of. Because how did they determine that someone was a witch? Men in power had many different ways, and some of them were as simple as deciding they didn't like the prisoner's face. There was no reason to believe the Regent would use genuine ways to determine witchcraft.

But Jette kept asking questions. "And after they say that mammy is not a witch can she come back to us?"

"I don't know."

And Nellie didn't, though she didn't think many people who were put into the prisons ever came out again. But she couldn't bring herself to tell the children any of this because she didn't understand the reasons either. Jantien had done nothing wrong.

Mina and Nellie gave each other another look. The situation was bad, and there was nothing except the extraordinary that would change anything.

Nellie wished she could fix the terrible situation. She wished she knew someone who could find Jantien and let her out, with the apology that it had been a mistake. She wished the dragon would come back and listen to her, and she could tell him to frighten everyone away, break down the doors to the prison and set the prisoners free.

The group walked to the end of the wharf.

"In here," Nellie said, opening the door to the sea cow barn.

To her surprise, a waft of warm air came out. A fire burned in the fire pit.

"You were mistaken that this is a safe place. Someone is already here," Mina said.

"We can ask if we can stay with them," Hilde said, and she walked into the barn.

"Hello?" Agatha called out.

There was no reply except the crunch of a sea cow grabbing a carrot from under the water. So who made the fire?

"Where did all these carrots come from?" Mina asked.

A whole bagful sat on the floor. The side of the bag bore an emblem: that of the city stores. What was that about thieves? By the Triune.

Anneke walked around the fire, holding her hand up as

if she was running her fingers along an invisible object. Her eyes were distant.

"It's because Boots is here. He's watching us."

"Boots!" her brother called.

They both looked at the ceiling. A faint trail of sparks crept over the underside of the beams that held up the roof.

But no matter how much the children called, the dragon wouldn't show himself. Anneke had even brought the little kitten which she picked up and held in the air so that its legs dangled down from her hands.

The sparks drifted closer. The kitten looked at them, but then one of the women said something in the storeroom, and the sparks scooted back up to the ceiling.

"He's afraid that we're angry," Ewout said.

"I think he's scared of the fire dog," Anneke said. "He doesn't want to come out, but he still wants to help us."

That might well be true, but then where did those carrots, blankets and other supplies come from?

But no matter how carefully they looked, they could find no evidence that someone had used this barn for a long time. It was almost as if someone had come here to set up the shelter with food and blankets just for their use.

Whether these items were set there for good or ill, the women could do nothing but use them. The storeroom was snug and dry, and the carrots and beans made a thick soup that kept everyone warm. For now, no one knew where they were.

❧

THE JUDGEMENT of the prisoners was held the next day.

After a brief cold snap, the snow had melted again, and now it was raining. The city looked grey and colourless. The snow had been reduced to large areas of slush. They were slippery and made for cold wet feet when Nellie and a couple of the women made their way along the deserted quay. They had left the children in the warehouse because they didn't need to see this.

A great crowd of people had gathered in the market-place for the open court session. During the morning, carpenters had erected an installation. Three chairs stood atop a platform. A strange contraption was placed at the front of the platform. The part she could see over the heads of the crowd consisted of a horizontal beam atop a pole. A chain hung down from one end of the beam.

The ornate chairs with red velvet cushions were still empty. A couple of guards stood at the bottom of the stairs that led up to the platform.

One of them was Henrik.

He stared over the square, his face unemotional.

An ugly wagon stopped in front of the mayor's house, pulled by a team of strong workhorses. The driver sat at a wooden bench at the front of the heavy wooden box on wheels, with a row of tiny windows near the top. It was the prison wagon.

Two guards opened the door at the back, and the prisoners were marched from the wagon like a flock of sheep.

There were quite a few of them, old men and women. Nellie recognised Emmie, Josie and Jantien helping Yolande, the old owner of the shop on the corner opposite the warehouse, and quite a few other people including the baker, the herb seller and others. She was glad that Jantien's children were still in the sea cow barn.

All the prisoners had been tied together with a rope around their wrists so that none of them could escape without tripping up all the others. They were dragged to the bottom of the platform and told to line up facing the crowd. So many of them were women. There were only a few men, including Wim, who used to work as taster in the palace kitchens. What had he done wrong?

Normally, when the Regent held an open court for serious criminals, people in the city would jeer, but everyone in the crowd was silent. That was the fear the Regent had sown into the hearts of the citizens.

The prison wagon left and was replaced with a shiny coach in the red colour of the Carmine royal family, but lacking the royal standard at the back. This was the same coach that Queen Johanna had used to travel around the city. It was disgusting that this self-important man now used it for this purpose.

When the coach came to a halt, the coach driver jumped off, walked around the side and opened the door after folding out the steps.

From where she stood, Nellie could see into the interior of the coach.

For a while nothing happened, and then a booted foot appeared in the entrance, followed by the ornate trouser leg of the Regent himself. Compared to the scruffy clothing of the townsfolk, his blue cloak looked magnificent. The Regent rarely left the palace, so it didn't get much use.

A few people at the front of the crowd gave a lacklustre cheer. He waved at them, but didn't look further into the crowd. The Regent was not a popular man, and he knew it. The guards at the front ordered people to applaud, but beyond the first few rows, few people could be moved to follow their example.

The Regent stepped stiffly out of the carriage, assisted by a guard, and made his way between the two lines of guards up the steps, before sitting down in the middle of the three seats on the platform.

The next person to come out of the coach was the Shepherd Wilfridus. He wore his full cream-white robes and used his shepherd's staff to assist his descent, refusing the help from the guards.

The crowd fell silent. Maybe, like Nellie, they remembered his wide-eyed, red-faced rant against magic and evil.

He walked straight-backed between the two lines of guards and sat down on the seat furthest from the steps. His face was blank, and he stared over the heads of the crowd.

Who would take the third seat?

Certainly not Madame Sabine? In the past Nellie could remember the spot having been taken by the mayor, but his mop of white hair that always looked windblown peeked up from the gathering of nobles to the side of the platform.

Someone else moved inside the coach. Nellie recognised the hideous blue trousers before the owner came fully out of the coach. It was the Regent's son Casper.

What was that brat doing here?

He emerged from the coach and strode between the two lines of guards with his head held up as if he owned the world. He climbed the stairs to the platform and sat down in the third seat, looking over the gathered crowd.

Nellie always prided herself on being a forgiving person. She didn't like to keep grudges and preferred to forgive people for missteps and move on, but the hatred that welled up in her when seeing that ill-mannered brat in the position where he would decide over the lives of people sickened her. That spoilt piece of—no that would be inappropriate language. She would not lower herself to using that when describing people.

But oh, she was angry.

One of the guards called the others to attention, and the town crier came up the platform. He faced the audience, ringing his bell. Then he held up a piece of parchment and read, in his pompous voice:

"Let the proceedings begin! The Regent announces that one of his personal guests in the palace was murdered through evil witchcraft. He has made it his mission to find and eradicate all peddlers of witchcraft and protect the people of this city."

A few people cheered, but the sound died away quickly.

He stepped aside so that Nellie could see the strange contraption at the front of the platform.

A platform hung from the chain, and the other end of the beam was attached to a second chain with a hook on the end. A couple of hessian bags sat to the side.

"By the order of the exulted Regent, we will be weighing these witches," the town crier said. "When they weigh less than two sacks they are obviously held up on this world with the aid of magic, and they will be proven to be witches. The shepherd and the Regent's noble son are here to be witnesses and the shepherd will make the final declaration."

The first woman climbed the platform. Nellie didn't know her. She must have been in the prisons for quite some time, because her skin was deathly pale, marked with red sores. She was thin as a skeleton and barely strong enough to hold herself up.

The guard lifted up the first sack and hung it on the hook. The platform wobbled. The woman grabbed onto the chain to stop herself falling.

When he added the second sack, the platform with the woman shot up.

The Regent nodded. Casper nodded, looking self-important.

People around Nellie gasped.

The town crier called out, "A witch! She is a witch."

The woman fell to her knees. "I am not a witch. I have

a husband and three children who need me. I have an old mother who is sick and I need to look after her. Please."

The Regent's face remained unemotional. He flapped his hand to indicate that the guards take the woman off the platform.

Two guards grabbed the thin woman under her arms and dragged her off, still wailing.

"What will happen to her?" a woman next to Nellie asked.

"Nothing good," Mina said.

"Yeah," the woman said. "The Regent will be making some grand announcement that we're all safe thanks to him. But she's done nothing wrong, that one. All she did was lose her husband and camp in the church because she thought *helping the poor* meant that the shepherd would look kindly on her. They'll be sentenced to burn on the stake, mark my words."

Nellie felt cold.

The next woman was much bigger. Nellie didn't know her name, but recognised her face from the markets. She was of sturdy build and quite tall. She took her place on the platform and crossed her arms over her chest, looking directly at the Regent and the others facing her. The Regent's son had jammed his hands between his knees and studied his feet. The Regent said something to him, and the boy straightened. But the woman was still staring at him and he turned his gaze down again.

The crowd was utterly silent.

The guard hung the first sack on the hook where it swung back and fro a few times before coming to a rest. The platform sat solidly on the ground. Surely the next sack would not come close to lifting the platform off the ground?

But as the guard hung it on the hook, Nellie noticed

that another guard was putting his foot underneath the platform where the woman stood.

With the tip of his boot, he lifted the platform off the ground. It floated briefly before settling back onto the ground.

"She is a witch!" the town crier shouted.

The woman stuck her chin in the air.

Several people in the crowd yelled out. The guards all sprang into alertness, including Henrik, who held his hand on his sword hilt.

He wouldn't turn on his own people, would he?

Nellie's heart thudded.

Mina next her said, "Did you see that? He cheated."

The blood roared in Nellie's ears.

But the crowd calmed, and the guards returned to their positions. The woman was taken off the platform to join the other one who had been weighed.

And so it went on with all the prisoners who had come out of the wagon. Big, small, young, old, man or woman, every one was declared a witch, even the ones who pleaded to the Regent for forgiveness.

Jantien, Josie, Emmie, Yolande and Wim all followed the second woman's example and remained stoic, but none of them were set free.

The shepherd looked on but only spoke once or twice. His face was determined as he watched people fall to their knees and plead for their lives, and he did nothing. He *had* to know that the guard at the platform cheated by putting his foot under the platform. Was he so blinded by his hatred for supposed magic that he would allow this to happen in front of his eyes? A man of the church that called itself compassionate and claimed to care for the common people?

Nellie could barely think for her anger.

All this was a farce. She bet it was done by the order of

Shepherd Wilfridus, who was a mean man. The Regent knew it and he played along with it. Maybe the shepherd told him that if he wanted to be king, he had to do what the church said. Casper knew it and also knew that if he lied as much as much as these men were doing at home, he'd probably cop a strap across his backside.

He still sat with his hands jammed between his knees, but stared ahead as his father ordered the women to be taken away. His expression was distant.

Henrik . . . she hoped to heaven that Henrik saw this and next time she met him, she would give him even more of her mind than she had last time and she would not be sorry about any of it. Or apologise.

When all the prisoners had been weighed and found to be witches or wizards, the Regent announced that they were to be drowned in the harbour as soon as there was enough open water for the final test to be carried out.

"Any person who floats is a witch and will be shot by our archers. Any who sinks deserves to die for scaring the populace and pretending to be a witch or consorting with peddlers of witchcraft."

The proceedings concluded, the Regent, his son and the shepherd rose from their seats and made their way into the waiting coach while rumbles of discontent rippled through the crowd. None of the protests were too loud but, away from the platform and out of earshot of the guards, Nellie didn't hear one word in favour of the Regent.

Nellie and Mina returned to the sea cow barn.

Now that the weather had turned warmer, they had just a few days to save the Jantien, Emmie and all the other people from certain death in the cold water of the harbour.

CHAPTER 10

WHEN NELLIE AND MINA walked back to the barn, it was getting dark. It had rained a bit, and already a layer of water covered the ice.

"There will be no ice left within a few days," Mina said, her voice dark. "The Regent can hold the witch drownings by week's end."

"What are we going to tell the children?"

Mina shrugged and shook her head. Her eyes glittered before she wiped them with the back of her hand.

Nellie said, "We'll tell them we will have a plan."

She had no idea where that came from. She didn't have a plan.

Mina turned to Nellie. "What sort of plan? What can we do? We're just a bunch of poor women. No one will listen to us." Her voice cracked.

"No idea yet, but we'll make a plan. We'll do something." Mistress Johanna had always done something even if the situation seemed dire. Nellie wanted to believe they could do something. They had to try at the very least.

"Do you believe it?"

"Coming here is part of the plan. We're safe for now, we're dry, we have food to eat. That was the first part of the plan."

Mina snorted. "I can't see how we can do anything at all that will defeat a bevy of heavily armed guards."

"We can't defeat them. We need to surprise them with something smart."

"I'm not smart. If I was, I'd have married a rich man and wouldn't be in this position."

"We have to think of something."

"I don't know what, and I don't know why you keep saying that."

Nellie tried to shut out Mina's whining. Yes, things were bad, but that meant they had nothing left to lose. That meant they could do something utterly reckless.

"We have a dragon."

"We don't have it. It won't do as we say and won't even show itself."

"We could use him to scare people."

"In all the ways we don't want it to. Look, I know that you can't help it, but Agatha is right in saying that we never had any trouble before you came. You helped us and that was good, but I think it's better if you went back to the palace."

"Do you really think I could do that?"

Mina looked at her.

"Do you think it's that simple? Do you think anyone who watched me being dragged out the door by that dragon is just going to forget about it? There are whole armies looking for that dragon. Everyone in the palace is looking for him. Some people say he has *killed* a man, and they want either the dragon, or me, to be guilty. I can't just pretend he wasn't there."

"What were you doing with it anyway?"

"I hope you don't mean that as it sounds."

"I mean it however you take it. If you were doing stuff with that dragon, then heaven help you."

"I wasn't. My father worked for the church and he knew the church bought that dragon box. Someone stole it from the church and I wanted to return it to its rightful owners."

"Maybe you should just stop worrying so much about what is right and think about the people you're with. If that dragon hadn't come out of the hayloft, then we would have been fine in the warehouse."

"So now it's my fault? I'm a horrible person?"

"I didn't say that."

"You implied it." Nellie let out a long breath. If it were possible, she *would* go back to the palace, since these people were so ungrateful. "The dragon is a creature with his own will. He's no more mine than he is anyone else's, except maybe prince Bruno's, if he's still alive. He cursed me with his presence. So stop blaming me for what he does. I'm trying my best, but no one here seems to appreciate what I do—"

"Nellie, please, we *do* appreciate what you do, but can you please agree with me that the dragon is dangerous to us?"

"Only if you can agree with me that I can't tell him what to do and I'm still not going to let that stop me from trying to do something for Jantien."

Mina shook her head and then smiled and hugged Nellie. "You're crazy. You have this thing where you'll tell everyone you're just a maid, but then you'll travel to Florisheim and serve the Queen and the next moment you're working in the kitchens, all without complaining."

"Well, I didn't ask for the kitchen job."

"No, but you did it, just the same."

"Because life goes on, and you make the best of it. That's how I was brought up. Complaining gets you nowhere."

They arrived at the barn where the others waited. Disappointment was clear on the children's faces that their mother hadn't come back.

But they had few questions. Maybe Agatha, in her great bluntness, had found a way to tell the children that their mother would probably never come back.

Well, that wouldn't be true if Nellie had anything to do with it, and the more she thought about it, the more determined she became.

If they blamed her for Jantien's imprisonment, she would try to free Jantien. If they blamed her for killing Lord Verdonck, she would prove her innocence. Because out of all the things her father said, one determined her very essence: *the truth always has the longest breath.*

No matter how bad the lies, the truth always won. Hopefully before people died.

They prepared a simple meal, but because it had been so busy in the marketplace due to the platform for the judges being set up, Nellie had not been able to go to the palace for the leftovers.

Dinner was nothing more than a dried out hunk of bread and soup made from the carrots that had been mysteriously left in the barn. Nellie knew she would be hungry in the middle of the night, and that it would be very cold.

Maybe she should open the dragon box to see if the dragon would show himself, for all the trouble it would cause. At least they would be warm.

Funny that now the dragon was no longer in physical form, she wanted him to return.

That so-called judgement in the market place today

made her so angry that she wanted to set him on the guards or the Regent or the shepherd.

That latter thought chilled her. She didn't want to harm people. She wanted to make a bright and bold plan, but she wasn't smart enough.

While the women sat by the fire discussing how they could earn money to maybe buy one of the prisoners out of jail, she went outside and stood in the last of the dusk to think about the plan she didn't yet have.

On the other side of the harbour, a couple of men arrived with a cart full of lengths of wood that they dumped on the quayside in front of the important offices. They laid four planks out into a square and began attaching lengths of wood over the top to make a platform. The sound of their hammering echoed in the stillness.

This installation would probably be for the carrying out of the sentence although she wasn't yet sure how it would work. Presumably they wanted to drop several people into the water at the same time. That was how they usually carried out hangings: all the criminals were led up to the platform and then the floor fell away under them. Seeing all the people drown one by one would not make a spectacle that the citizens would stay to watch. Too many people would get angry.

Nellie shivered.

Mina was right that there was not much chance that they, as a handful of ragtag women with some children, could defeat well-trained guards. But something outrageous, something that was so daring that no one would have thought of doing it, might accomplish their goal.

But what?

They had no authority to appeal to and no money to bribe with. No one in the city cared about a bunch of servants and poor women anyway. They had no weapons and no skill to wield them.

They had no possessions useful for fighting, deceiving or bribing guards, no skills other than cooking and sewing.

Nellie could ride a horse, badly, and she could use a sea cow team. They had sea cows and half a harness, but no boat.

So her thoughts chased each other through her head.

The last of the daylight glinted in the windows of the offices on the far side of the quay.

Silhouetted in the orange light lay the magnificent ship that belonged to the Guentherite order.

It was hard to believe the order preached modesty.

But the ship was there, only a few paces from the place where the carpenters were building the wooden construction.

Nellie wondered how many people were staying on board while the ship lay in the harbour, and whether the monks would be happy to look at an installation that would condemn people to death.

Nellie had seen the ship manoeuvre into the harbour. It required a full team of fifteen sea cows. She presumed the animals were well tended in one of the quayside barns.

Imagine what that ship could do if a larger team of sea cows pulled it.

Imagine what it could do if it were pulled by a dragon.

Yes, like that was going to happen.

She walked along the deserted wharf and along the quayside. It was quiet. Other than a fisherman mending his nets, nobody was in sight, and only a single cat scurried away. She walked past the harbourmaster's office to where the ship lay moored.

The gangplank was down, but she couldn't see any guards. For a ship of this type, especially one so pretty and from out of town, she would have expected someone to stand watch.

Nellie walked along the quayside, taking note of the places where the bow had hooks for attaching the sea cow teams. She remembered doing this, many years ago, when she fled with Mistress Johanna up the river.

The line of little cabin windows were all dark, and she wondered if the ship lay abandoned, because if there was someone on board, it was too early for them to be in bed.

From working for Mistress Johanna's family, she remembered that the captains would stay with the ships. Some would even have their families live aboard.

Did the order's ship have a captain? She couldn't remember anyone ever speaking of one.

Nellie grew bold.

She went up the gangplank and stepped onto the deck. Most river ships would have doors for the cargo hold up here, but this was a passenger ship, so she came out on a deck area in between two cabins. A few days ago, she had watched people unload barrels of wine from this deck, but now it was empty.

To the left was the captain's cabin, with windows out the front and sides. That area was dark.

She walked up to the cabin on the other side and knocked on the door.

"Hello? Is there anyone there?"

When someone opened the door, she would ask if he had seen a little runaway boy who was crazy about ships.

But the door remained very much closed. The ship appeared to be deserted.

Well that was odd.

It was getting dark very quickly, and by the last of daylight she went back down the steep gangplank onto the quay.

The fisherman still sat on the wharf. He had lit a

lantern and his breath steamed by the light as his gloved fingers darned the net. The gloves were old and displayed several holes.

"They never leave anyone on the ship when they're in port," he said, nodding at the Guentherite order's ship. "It's dumb, I know, asking for trouble if you ask me, but there it is. If you want to speak to the monks, you have to go find them in town. Guess they're all landlubbers to begin with." He chuckled. "A good captain would never leave his ship. I guess they're more interested in the banquets."

Nellie nodded at his net. "You still go out fishing in winter?"

"A man's gotta eat. The neighbour's wife sells the fish at the markets. The neighbour wants to eat, too."

"If you could save us some fish, I can fix those gloves for you."

"That would be swell. The wife's been gone a few months and I haven't picked up any skills in knitting."

"Give them to me, I'll bring them back in the morning."

"Not afore I fixed my net. I'll still be here in the morning. Come pick them up. I'll bring you some nice juicy fish in the evening."

Nellie bade him goodnight and kept walking. The seed of a bold, ridiculous idea was growing in her mind. She might need his help.

Inside the barn, they had everything she needed to set up a team of sea cows. There were enough of the creatures to serve as a team, if she could entice them into a harness. Most of these free animals had done the work before, and the promise of food was always a good one to get them to do the work.

All she needed was a boat.

The prisoners would be thrown into the water. She would be there waiting for them.

But supposing they could rescue the prisoners, there was no going back to hiding somewhere in the city, because the Regent would send all his men after them. Once they rescued these people, they should take the sea cows and the boat to a farm out of the city somewhere and stay there for the winter. So they needed a boat, and the fisherman might help with that if she was nice to him.

They could hide a boat inside the barn and race out the moment people were in the water. A light wooden boat pulled by a full team of sea cows would do the job. They wouldn't have much time, because it would be cold, but if they could rescue only some people, then it was better than none at all.

The other problem was that once this boat was out in the open, the Regent would order his guards to shoot at it, so the people aboard had to be protected.

There were many questions. What sort of boat would they use? How many people could go on it?

But straight away, she saw a flaw in the plan: if the boat needed to be big enough for all of them and the rescued people, then it would be heavy.

Some people would need to stay on the shore in safety. The children, most likely.

But then what would they do when the prisoners were rescued and all the guards would be after them and maybe shooting arrows at them? She wouldn't put it past the Regent to order his men to shoot at women and children. It might even be likely that the citizens would be too scared to show outrage about this.

So: the rescuers would be on the water in the boat, being shot at by the guards from the shore.

The rest of the group would be—no, that made no sense. When a boat came out of the sea cow barn to rescue the drowning prisoners, everyone from the party had to have left the building.

By that time, they already needed to be at the next safe hiding place, or on their way out of the city.

She eyed the Guentherite ship. Unguarded. Sleek and fast.

No one would expect this group of women to take off with it. They could hide the children on board during the day and then take the prisoners to the harbour side of the ship and have it ready to go.

That was an idea. It was a bold and scary idea that frightened her so much that it made her shiver.

Nellie went back inside the barn where the women sat around the fire, still talking about the daily problems of survival.

Nellie joined them, and Mina looked up.

"What have you been up to?"

"I was thinking. I would like to try to rescue the prisoners."

"So would we all, but the dungeons are well guarded, and they only have a tiny little window close to the ceiling, far too high to climb. How are you going to get anyone out of there? People have tried so many times already. They've dug tunnels, they've tried to chisel out the grate. I don't think it's possible to get people out of there, especially if you have no weapons."

"We won't do anything like that. We'll rescue them from the water."

"You mean once they've already been thrown in the harbour?"

"Yes. It would be the best time, and no one is expecting it."

"But how are you going to avoid all the guards with bows and arrows? To go out on the water, you'd be out in the open."

And Nellie explained about her plan. As she spoke, the women's faces grew more and more incredulous.

Agatha said, "You mean, you want to fish the people out of the water, steal a boat and leave town?"

"That's pretty much the gist of it."

"But we know nothing about boats. Do you?"

"I have handled a river boat."

"How long ago was that, though?"

"You don't forget those things."

"It sounds like a mad idea. We have children with us. We want them to stay safe. I can't see how going out there on the water will get us anywhere. It's cold, it's dangerous, we're out in the open. Those guards have no qualms about shooting women and children if the Regent orders it. I don't want to leave town, because it's cold and harsh out there, and there are bandits about who would just love to find a group of unprotected women. No, I'd rather stay safe."

"Don't you want to rescue our friends?"

"Yes, but not while risking the lives of so many more people with some madcap adventure. I can hardly believe I'm hearing this from you."

Nellie knew she would have to do a better job of convincing them.

They went to bed, all tucked up together in the storeroom where it was dry and the sleeping cats provided additional warmth.

As she lay in the straw surrounded by warm bodies, furry or otherwise, a trail of sparks travelled over the ceiling.

She said, quietly, "I know you're watching. Do something useful if you want to help."

The dragon did not appear to listen to anybody unless it involved the kitten. After he had fled from the fire dog, she had found the dragon in this abandoned barn looking after sea cows. He was fascinated by other animals. It appeared that other animals were fascinated by him. At least the kittens were, as were the sea cows. And children, he liked those, too.

They could lure the dragon out of hiding by having lots of animals and children around.

But, in this way, the dragon was already helping them.

CHAPTER 11

TO MAKE HER PLAN WORK, Nellie needed to pull out everything she had.

She spent a lot of the next day examining the bits and pieces left behind on the workbenches and the storage room.

There were two sea cow harnesses in the barn. One was complete, but held only nine animals. The other was one of the larger ones that held fifteen animals, but at some point, someone had dismantled the harness and one beam was missing. The straps were all broken, but there was a rope and leather to repair the harness, if only they had a beam.

How would she get a new beam?

Maybe she could "borrow" one from another barn.

She wandered around the wharf, trying to remember where else the other river traders used to have their barns. There used to be so many of them: the Nielands, the Deims, the Pietersens. Over the last few years, most of them had either closed up their businesses because of retirement, or had moved to more profitable harbours with less hostile rulers.

Their old barns used to be on the other side of the harbour, but it was likely that the Guentherite order used those for their sea cows, so it might not be such a good idea to spend too much time around there.

The warehouses next to the barn were mostly empty although one appeared to be in use as a place to store building materials.

Around mid-morning, she came across the fisherman again. He had just returned from a fishing trip and placed baskets full of fish on the wharf. Most of them were flounders, caught in the sandy beds of the delta that were free of ice.

"Good morning," he said, puffing on his pipe. "Still around? It's cold out there early, but I got some nice fish for you."

He gave her a couple of freshly caught flounders that were silvery and slippery. She took them—and the gloves she'd agreed to fix—to the barn.

Mina was most happy with the fish. "I'd been wondering if we could catch some ourselves, but I guess that's a lot harder than it seems."

Nellie collected the mending kit she always carried in her bag and sat down to fix the fisherman's worn gloves. With that done, she went back to the quay and gave the gloves back to him.

He gave her a broad smile.

"Why, thank you for this. I haven't had the pleasure of a woman's help since my wife died last year."

"I'm sorry to hear that. We're a group of women, and we can fix other things for you, if we can have more fish, or if you can help us with other things."

"Like what?"

"I'm looking for a boat the size of yours," Nellie said.

He gave her a strange look and then laughed. "You,

missy? All by yourself? What do you know about boats and fishing?"

"More than you think," Nellie said. But she was beginning to think maybe they needed more experienced people to help them. "But we're not fishing. We want to leave town, with a group of women and children. I know some farms where we might be safe."

"You'd be safer in the city. I heard the stories about bandits."

"Have you seen any bandits?"

"Me? No, but I don't set foot on the land. On the water, there are no bandits."

If they managed to get away with the Guentherite order's ship, they could live on the ship, too.

"We can handle bandits. They wouldn't dare attack a group of women and children."

"Never say never. Some of these men have no morals. I'd hate to see something bad happen to you."

"It's no longer safe for us to stay here with the latest raids."

"Some of you use magic?" he asked.

"Yes. We almost got caught last time. That's why we're sheltering here, because the guards are all over the artisan quarter." She left out the bits about people from their group already in prison.

"That declaration against magic is ridiculous. I don't know a single fisherman who doesn't use wind magic. If they don't, they're no good at catching fish."

"I wonder how the guards can tell that someone has magic."

"They can't. They use silly hocus-pocus and then it's all about whether they like your face and how much protest there will be and how much you can pay or whether they need you."

Yes, that could be why the guards had left Zelda alone,

because there would be trouble from the wayfarers if they arrested her.

"So it's not about magic at all."

"Not with the people they're picking up. If they want magic, they should be looking elsewhere. A creature's been prowling around here that looks like it's been made of fire. I first heard about it two days ago, but the old codger who mentioned it in the tavern is quite mad. But last night I saw it with my own eyes. And, no, I didn't have too much to drink." He shook his head. "I would be laughing if it weren't so damned scary. And what are the guards doing about that? Nothing!"

The fire dog. Nellie wished she knew who it belonged to. "Have many people seen this creature?"

"No, otherwise someone would be doing something about it. All those guards ratting out those poor peddlers because they use this or that magic trinket should be chasing this creature. But there's too few of us that've seen it, so they prefer not to believe us, because they can pretend what we say is unimportant."

"I've seen it."

He gave her an incredulous look. "The one that's made from fire?"

"Yes."

"It's an evil thing, don't you agree?"

"I think so," she said. "When the Fire Wizard ruled the city, he would just conjure these creatures up with a flick of his fingers."

"I know. I'm old enough to have seen it."

"Do you think he's back?" Nellie shivered.

"The Fire Wizard is dead. Queen Johanna encased him inside a willow tree."

The tree in question, a gnarled and misshapen willow, had stood in the corner of the marketplace until last year, when a storm had blown it over. Nellie remembered seeing that the wood inside the trunk was marbled with black. City guards had sawn it into pieces and taken it away. It had probably warmed the mayor's house that winter.

Was the dog perhaps a spirit that had escaped from the tree?

And why did the guards worry about petty magic when that thing was running around?

He squinted at her. "You seem to know a good deal about this magic thing. Do you know what else it could be?"

"The creature is a dog. I think fire apparitions normally belong to a magician who needs to conjure them. I don't know if any of these apparitions can live by itself. I have no idea who it belongs to, but it can't just be someone using wind magic. It has to be a powerful magician."

"So there is a powerful magician in town, even after the Regent has spent years banning all magic? Who would have thought?"

"Maybe the guards are looking for this magician."

He laughed. "Then they're looking in all the wrong places, and they're not asking the right people. They should be asking those trinket-sellers. Are you sure you don't have magic?"

"I don't, but several in our group do. That's why we want to leave town, to tell you the truth. My cousins will help us. We want to go there. I need a boat."

"You humour me. I'll help you. On the other side of this wharf is a big longboat that no one is using in winter. It's a cargo ship, and they can't go into the frozen canals. It's not much good going downriver, mind, because the sides are too low for going anywhere near the ocean. You'll want to go upriver."

"Yes, that's what we want. I think I can get a team of sea cows together. We need to fix a harness."

"Don't take it too lightly, mind. The river is swollen at this time of the year. There may be ice coming down, and you want shelter for when it rains."

"Oh no, this one is not for going far. We're going just out of town."

He frowned at her.

"Are you sure about all this missy? It seems to me that it's all very odd, and I don't know that you understand what you're getting yourself in for. It's not as though women like yourself handle boats a lot."

"I was on a boat with Queen Johanna when she had to flee. We did all the handling and steering ourselves. It was one of my tasks."

He gave her a concerned look.

Nellie asked him to show her the boat he had in mind.

It lay on the other side of the wharf, a sturdy low vessel that would transport heavy things across the harbour.

"It's very heavy," Nellie said.

"It's stable. If you have children in the group, their frolicking about won't upset the boat at all."

"It would be slow."

"And quiet."

But Nellie wasn't looking for slow. "I'm more after something like that." She pointed at a much lighter rowing boat.

"You can't use that. That's only for inside the canals. That little thing would capsize the moment you took it out of the harbour and it got hit by an ice floe. With all the will in the world, I couldn't let you take that thing out of the heads. I'm a good man, and that would be murder."

"I still don't want a heavy boat."

"That's madness. How many of you are there?"

"You have some magic, right?"

He frowned at her. "What's that got to do with it?"

"A lot. You're not on the Regent's side."

"By the Triune, no. Though I wish he'd plant his fat arse on the throne, so someone in Burovia or Aroden could be properly offended and send mercenaries to kill him."

"You must also be concerned about the Regent's order that no magic is allowed in the city."

"Not so much for myself. I got nothing left here. If they come calling, I get in my boat and sail off somewhere else. To Anglia if necessary. But yeah, I'm concerned for the folk who can't do that."

"Several people got arrested in the artisan quarter the day before yesterday. The Regent has decided that they will be drowned."

"I heard about that. That's foul business."

"We need the boat to rescue them."

His frown turned into a wide-eyed look. His mouth fell open. "But that is a dangerous thing to do. The harbour will be full of guards. They'll use crossbows."

"One woman is the mother of six children in our group. She's done nothing wrong."

He rubbed his chin with his hand. "That's not right, that is."

"We have to help her and the others."

"All right. I can help you with the boat. You'll be wanting to get across the harbour fast. There is a little barge on the other side that will do just that. It's a stable flat-bottomed thing, and useless for sailing, pretty useless all around, because it gets carried sideways in a current. I believe people used it to get peat. I can attach hooks so you can put the rig onto the front. I can help you replace your beam. I can even help you sell it. But I am not keen on weapons because those guards will have bows and arrows. I wouldn't count on the Regent not wanting to harm women."

"But what if we put up a shield?"

She remembered seeing building materials in one warehouse. Surely there was something they could use to protect themselves against any arrows.

He took her around to the other side of the wall where the peat ship lay. As he had said, it was a plain flat-bottomed thing, and she was a bit concerned with how flimsy it looked.

He showed her how he could fasten hooks at the front to attach a team of sea cows. Nellie told him she wanted to attach the big harness of fifteen.

"You'll have to watch those animals, because they'll be feisty."

"I need a lot of speed," Nellie said.

"You'll be dealing with young untrained animals. They might not stop in time. And what are you going to do when you've rescued these people? That little boat will be heavy, and won't be as fast when it's low in the water."

"I have a plan for that, too. That's why I need the second harness."

To her ears, it all sounded like a ridiculous plan. After all, what did she know about boats? But he didn't tell her so. In fact, he promised that he would help get the boat across the harbour and drag people into safety. *Because you will need a strong man's hands.*

He didn't ask her what she wanted to do after the rescue, and she didn't tell him about the Guentherite ship.

Next she needed to find something to use as a shield. She found a stack of wooden slats in the next warehouse. With the rope in the barn, they could be tied together into a flexible shield.

To get a new beam for the sea cow harness, she needed a carpenter.

The fisherman knew someone who lived one street back from the harbour, and he took her to the workshop where pieces of furniture stood in various stages of completeness, surrounded by wood shavings and sawdust. Two apprentices were sanding back a large table for revarnishing.

The carpenter listened to what she needed and said he could make another beam, but he wanted payment. She offered to fix his clothes, but he had a wife and three daughters who could do that.

"I have no money," Nellie said. "Is there nothing we could barter? I could bring you some ham."

It would mean asking Dora for an extra donation, and eating carrot soup for a few nights, but they'd survive.

"Hmmm. Ham and a cask of wine or beer would do."

Nellie didn't have either of those, but then she had an idea. "Gin. Would you accept gin?"

His eyes widened. "Would I accept it? That would be more than adequate."

Ham and gin it was, then.

"You surprise me, missy," the fisherman said while they walked back. "You'd not be the kind I expect to deal with gin."

"I'm not, but I know people who do."

"Tell me, once we rescue those people from the water, what do you plan to do?"

Since he was now in with the plan, she might as well tell him all. He might have useful and life-saving tips.

"I have another plan for that. You said the other day that there was never anyone at the Guentherite ship."

His eyes widened. "You're kidding?"

"No. We make sure we sneak the little ones on board and attach the second team to the ship before the rescue, and then when the rescue boat comes back, it will take the prisoners to the harbour side of the ship and we'll be ready to cast off."

"That is the most daring plan I've ever heard."

"It's all we've got."

"You'd need the large team on that ship," he said. "And the nine-animal team on the small boat."

"I thought the other way around. I wanted the large team on the small boat because we need to be faster. Then when we rescue the people, we take them to the order's ship and hook up both teams."

"So we'll want twenty-six animals?"

"That was the plan."

"That should do, but how are we going to get the sea cows? No one has that many animals anymore."

"They come into the old Brouwer Company barn. We have carrots they seem to like. Once we fix the harness, we'll try to lure the animals in. Most of them have probably worked before and will be used to wearing a harness, although the younger ones might be a bit feisty."

"You really *have* thought about this."

"I have—wait, earlier, you said *we?*"

"I have nothing left to lose. My wife is dead, my children grown up. I'm just existing from one day to the next, waiting for the Regent's men to come around and accuse me of having magic. If they're going to arrest me, I might as well give them a proper reason." He grinned.

"All right." Nellie was glad for his offer because he seemed capable and experienced in all the things she was not. "As long as you're happy to leave the city with us."

"I am, as long as there is water for me to go fishing."

"I didn't catch your name."

"It's Floris."

"I'm Nellie."

"Nice to meet you, Nellie. I've heard about you from a friend who used to work for the Brouwer company." He gave her a fishy handshake. "I was wondering if it was you. I knew your father. 'Nellie' doesn't sound right. You should call yourself Cornelia. A lot of the common folk are talking about you, because you're one of them. In some places they call you the Dragonspeaker."

Nellie laughed. "Well, if there is a dragon to be spoken to, it's sure not speaking to me."

Nellie wasn't sure that she was comfortable with so many people talking about her, but it was to be expected. Soon, few places in the city would be safe.

"You still have the dragon?"

"The dragon is not mine. I can't command him, but he follows me around when he feels like it."

But still, she chuckled to herself when walking back to the barn. The trail of sparks followed her along the quayside, and she had no means to call the dragon to return to his solid form; but to be called the Dragonspeaker—that was silly and impressive at the same time.

Nellie the Dragonspeaker.

CHAPTER 12

NOW THAT SHE HAD A PLAN, they had a few days to carry it out.

First, Nellie needed to secure ham for the carpenter. So the next morning, she went on another trip to the palace. It was risky, and she didn't need to go for leftovers because they still had the carrots and beans that had been left in the barn, and they now had a supply of fish, but there was no other place that Nellie could get ham.

She got up before the others, wound the shawl around her head and collected her basket with pots to disguise herself as a spice seller.

She stumbled through the dark barn to light the fire and turn up the wick to the old oil lamp and set a pot to boil so that there would be porridge and tea when she came back.

Two sea cows popped their heads above the water, and Nellie tossed them some carrots, which they ate with much crunching and slobbering, attracting even more sea cows. She guessed at least twenty animals called the barn home.

The number of cats had increased to six, the puppy still came to sleep under the workbench at night, and Anneke had pointed out that a handful of bats hung in the rafters during the day. The dragon's presence attracted other creatures.

Nellie made her way along the dark quay. Floris was still at home, his fishing boat tied up and nets neatly stowed on the deck.

In the palace forecourt a lone boy was walking a beautiful white and grey horse held by the reins. Those horses were Madame Sabine's. When she went into town, she would either ride one, or two of them would pull the coach. They were beautiful, tall animals with dappled grey fur, white manes and tails, white fetlocks and pale blue eyes. The stallion, which the boy was taking for a walk, had the reputation of being a cranky animal, but rumours also went that it was worth a lot.

When she walked past the stairs to the palace's main entrance, the sounds of angry voices drifted down from inside the foyer.

By the Triune, what was going on there?

Nellie looked over her shoulder. The guards at the gates had gone back to watching the market square. The stable boy was taking the horse back inside. Nobody could see her sneaking up the stairs.

Nellie stopped at the door, in the shadow of the porch, from where she could see into the palace foyer.

A surprising number of people stood in the foyer, especially considering the time of day.

The Regent's housekeeper was up at this time but he would be bustling about getting breakfast ready. The palace guards were up, but they'd be standing silently by the doors. The palace's domestic staff would be doing the washing and cleaning, not standing on the stairs and the edges of the foyer watching a commotion.

The centre of the attention was Lord Verdonck's son Adalbert.

The housekeeper was speaking. "And my master has assured us that anyone who has anything else to do with this dreadful affair will also be arrested."

Lord Verdonck's son said, "I don't believe you. None of the food produced here was poisoned. Someone came to my father's room and poisoned him, just him, no one else. Your suggestions that he was killed by a dragon are ridiculous."

"You haven't seen those scars," the housekeeper said.

"Rubbish. You speak lies. My father has had those scars for a long time, longer than you've been alive. You're trying to cover up for whoever amongst these pathetic nobles in this so-called court of yours has killed my father. If you continue to make no effort to unmask the murderer, I will withdraw my funding from this ridiculous excuse of a kingdom and you can all come to our estate on your knees begging for forgiveness and money. And let me tell you this: I'll take extreme pleasure in saying no to your fat, pampered faces."

"My master assures me we are hot on the trail of the dragon—"

"Stop your ridiculous suggestions. The dragon did not kill my father. The food at the banquet was not poisoned. The wine was not poisoned or if it was, your beloved monks would have something to do with it, and you wouldn't want to admit that now, would you?" The housekeeper stepped back. Nellie knew the man from her time working in the kitchen. He was a nervous, easily upset character and no match for the young noble's power of argumentation. He stammered, "The Regent has instructed the guards to arrest this person. Surely the Regent knows best."

Which person? Had anyone been arrested?

"It is nonsense. Just like your city raids are nonsense. The talk about the dragon is nonsense. All you will achieve is that you will sow discord amongst your people. None of the staff have done anything wrong, and your master knows it."

The housekeeper sniffed. "I will not take this treatment any more. I will complain to my master."

"Do that. I will enjoy arguing with him."

The housekeeper gave him a *rude prick* look, turned around and strode up the stairs, followed by the guards.

Adalbert Verdonck strode in the direction of the guest quarters, uttering a snort that sounded like, "Idiots."

The housekeeping staff dispersed and Nellie scurried down the steps before anyone could ask what she was doing there.

She sped past the side of the palace into the servants door to the kitchen.

The moment she opened it, several people gasped.

"There she is," Corrie said, seated at the table. "We were just talking about you, Nellie."

Dora stood at the stove, stirring a pot. "Quick, hide yourself before the guards see you."

Hide herself? "Whatever is wrong?" Nellie asked.

"The guards were just here looking for you. You're to be arrested to be accused of the murder of Lord Verdonck."

"Me?"

But Nellie felt cold inside. She had expected that this would happen at some point when no clear culprit could be found.

Corrie explained, "Yes, they say because you visited him in his room, and because you got herbs for him, you must have poisoned him."

"Well I didn't, but I guess that is no argument."

"No, and you must leave as quickly as possible. The

guards wanted to know if we had heard anything from you since your last visit. Apparently, they went to the warehouse where you were rumoured to be, and didn't find you there."

Nellie's heart jumped.

Had Zelda had been spying for the guards? Really? There was no way that the guards would otherwise have known where she was. The ones who had come into the warehouse had been city guards who didn't know her, and had enough to deal with, like a big dragon in the hayloft.

"I can see it's becoming dangerous. I won't come back here after today. At least not for a while, but I need to get some ham."

Dora laughed. "You're getting picky now?"

"I promised someone. It's a trade."

Dora went into the pantry and came back with a hessian bag full of bread and cheese. She put it on the table in front of Nellie.

"Here is your ham. I put in a little bit more than usual. If you let me know where you are, I'll try to come out there and bring it to you, or I'll send one of the young ones. We have to be very careful. They'll punish me if they know where I'm going."

"I understand. But we're fine for the time being. I may need to ask you later, when things quiet down. I'm looking after six children whose mother has been taken prisoner and whose father has fled town."

"How old are they?"

"The oldest is ten, and the youngest is just three. There is one set of twins. They were never poor. They used to live in a normal house and their father had a tailor shop when he was forced to leave town."

"Poor mites. Come with me."

Dora preceded Nellie into the hallway, and to the linen room.

This corridor was so familiar to Nellie. Just the thought that she could go to the end of the corridor and find her comfortable room still there disturbed her. Someone else might have taken it, but she didn't think so. She had wanted to collect her few remaining positions, but she knew better than to burden herself with unnecessary furniture when she had nowhere to put it.

It was dark in the linen room, and the smell of soap was achingly familiar.

"It's probably just as well you missed the big to-do here in the last few days," Dora said, after she shut the door. It was cold in here, and her breath steamed in the air.

"It is about the Lord Verdonck's son, isn't it?"

"Yes. The son demands an explanation for his father's death. He is invoking the unspoken rules that hosts of castles and palaces are responsible for the safety of those under their roof."

"So the Regent has been scrambling for someone to blame for the poisoning?"

"That's about the gist of it. First, they came and arrested poor Wim."

"But he did nothing wrong."

"No, and the Lord's son said as much. Then they came here to look for you because, apparently, you gave Lord Verdonck some herb concoction."

"I brought tea, which he was in no state to drink."

"And then, in another desperate move, the Regent said that Lord Verdonck had been killed by a dragon, and the son grew extremely angry. The Regent then said he would punish Wim, just to have someone to blame, and because he was the only person he could find who could remotely be responsible for the poisoning."

"Wim didn't do it."

"We know that. They know that. I think they wanted you, but they didn't know where to find you."

They were silent for a while.

"If they find me, would they release Wim?"

Dora's expression was horrified. "Oh, I don't know. Probably not. I wouldn't try that if I were you."

"I don't intend to."

"Good."

Few sounds reached this room, except someone must have come into the back yard, judging by the oinking of the pigs.

Nellie said, "The Regent wants to blame someone so he can get Adalbert Verdonck off his back."

"He wants to blame *everyone*."

"Adalbert Verdonck is not happy with the story about the dragon. I don't think he should be. The dragon didn't kill his father."

"They said he had scratches on his leg."

"The dragon didn't kill him, believe me."

"Have you seen the dragon lately?"

"No. He flew off. He's probably gone home."

Dora sighed. "It's not an easy situation. The guards have been in here many times. They also talked to some other kitchen workers."

"Not Els and Maartje?" Nellie's heart jumped. She had rescued the two sisters from a certain fate of becoming whores, and she did not want anything bad to happen to them.

"No, those two were smart enough to stay away. Haven't seen them for days either."

Els was smart. In fact, if she did not work at the palace, Nellie probably knew where to find her. And she also was not entirely convinced that Els had nothing to do with the poisoning. Especially not with her strange monk friend. But drawing attention to it helped no one.

So she was now under suspicion. She'd prefer that to pointing suspicion at Els and her young sister.

Dora had opened one of the linen cupboards and took out several sheets and some blankets.

"Here, put those in your bag. I will ask around for people to bring spare clothing for children, and if you let us know where you are, I can send someone to bring it to you."

"Thank you very much. I'll let you know once we're safe. I don't think I would still be alive without you."

"Don't be silly. Now, look after yourself."

But Dora's eyes glittered, before she took Nellie into a strong, soup-scented hug.

Then Nellie walked along the hallway to the side entrance of the palace, knowing she might not come back here for a long time, if ever.

While she had been inside the palace, there had been a change of guard, and one of the replacements at the gate included Henrik, who stood in the guard box, and could not be fooled about her identity, no matter how much she pulled the shawl over her head.

HE PULLED HER ASIDE, into the darkness of the box.

"What are you doing here?" he asked, his voice little more than a whisper.

"I only found out that apparently I'm supposed to have poisoned Lord Verdonck."

"You are risking your life by coming here. If I were you, I would run as far away from the palace as possible."

She didn't like his tone at all.

"You don't believe that I poisoned the Lord, do you?"

He glared at her. "I consider whatever proof we are given."

Nellie couldn't believe her ears. "So you believe these lies the Regent tells?"

"I look at evidence. We know who came to Lord

Verdonck's room. We know who was at the banquet. We know where the food came from—"

"But do you know which item was poisoned?"

He glared at her.

"That would be a start, if you knew that. Or you knew the type of poison and who has it—"

"Don't tell me how to do my job."

"Then do your job. Look at the most obvious possibility. Who supplied most of the food and wine? Who was there to help serve it?"

"You want to blame the church? What happened to you? Is that what your father told you? Your father left the church because he was disgraced. He attempted to overstep his boundaries as accountant, so he could dictate what the church bought, which should be the shepherd's decision. And it should be the Regent's decision. No one else can see their plan for this city. I don't need to remind you that the church keeps us safe from magic, and the Regent keeps us safe from the bandits that roam the countryside. He has made the city a safe haven. I don't need to remind you of how scarce imports from other lands have become. Produce can't come through. The traders see no more reason to stay in our town. The Regent has a plan to fix all that. The Regent is my superior. I don't always agree with what he says, but I have to listen to him, because he has the best interests of the people at heart."

"You genuinely believe that?"

"And you do not? You think he came here out of his own free will, just because somebody needed this job to be done? He had to be asked, and he agreed, and he did not want to come here, and especially his wife did not want to come here."

Well, he was right on that latter statement.

"He came here because—" and then she stopped.

There was no point in arguing with him.

He did not understand, he did not want to see the depth of deceit that these men were playing on the people of the city. There was nothing she, an old woman, could say about the situation that would make him believe it. She would have to show it to him another way, or not at all. Whatever their relationship might have been, whatever course it had been on, it was not to be. There was no point in pursuing any of this.

She yanked her arm loose.

"I'm leaving. You won't see me again, so don't even try find me."

And she walked out of the palace gates, but her eyes pricked.

She would show him.

Her father did not leave the church out of disgrace. And Henrik was wrong about the Regent. And he was wrong about who poisoned Lord Verdonck. She would show him and then he would have to apologise to her.

Walking across the market place, however, she realised that by fleeing, she as much as admitted her own guilt. If they suspected her of poisoning Lord Verdonck, the guards would hunt her forever. She could never come back to the city, and would live her twilight years in fear.

The only way of clearing her name was to find out who had poisoned him, right?

She was probably halfway to finding that answer.

It was time to find some gin.

CHAPTER 13

ON HER WAY BACK to the barn, Nellie came past the quay where the carpenters were taking a small break from erecting the platform where the sentence would be carried out.

The wooden platform sat half over the water, held in place by a couple of weights in the corners. Nellie assumed that when all the people stood on the top, these would be removed, causing the platform to tip. The men had coated the top planks with wax so there would be nothing to hold onto.

Apart from this simple mechanism, the carpenters had also built a second, lower, platform where she assumed chairs for the Regent and other important witnesses would be placed on the day. She wondered who would be present to watch this horrible spectacle.

SHEPHERD WILFRIDUS usually attended hangings of criminals to bless their spirits as they left the body.

Sometimes people would cheer when a man who had murdered his wife or a child was hanged, and would protest any suggestion of forgiveness by the Triune. The shepherd usually preached forgiveness.

But who was there to forgive if the very act of carrying out an unjust sentence was wrong?

A couple of men were standing near the work in progress, watching, with their hands in their pockets. The carpenters were giving them sideways looks. Oh, they knew many citizens in town disagreed with this verdict. This was not the hanging of a criminal.

Nellie delivered her booty to the sea cow barn where the women were sitting around the fire tying together the lengths of wood that would function as shields against the inevitable arrows.

The work was starting to look quite good, and they stopped for a brief bite to eat.

"Rumour has it that it will be the day after tomorrow," Mina said.

It wasn't necessary to name the event.

Agatha said, "I'm saying it will be the day after that. Certainly, the Regent will want to stick to the old king's rule that citizens have to be given at least two days to register their protest against any sentence being carried out."

"I don't see anyone traipsing up the steps to the palace to register a complaint," Hilde said.

"That's because they're too scared," Agatha said. "But he knows if he ignores that rule, it will be to his peril. Mess with food and punish people unfairly, and you have a rebellion."

All in all, the plan for their own rebellion seemed to be proceeding quite well. The fisherman was going to bring the flat-bottomed boat into the barn in the evening under the cover of darkness, so they could attach the harness and attract sea cows with the mysterious supply of carrots.

Nellie needed to be present for that because apart

from the fisherman she was the only one who knew how to handle sea cows.

The carpenter had already brought the beam. Nellie was surprised about that.

"When did he come to deliver the beam?" she asked.

No one knew. The women had been out when the beam had appeared in the barn.

"That was quick."

Nellie hadn't even paid him yet. She had the ham, but she had better arrange the second half of her payment to him.

But first, they needed to get started on training the cows to the harness. She instructed the others to tie the ropes that would be attached to the boat to the beam. Her hands still knew how to do the knots and how to tie the straps.

Then she told the children to drop some carrots into the water.

Attracted by the food, a group of sea cows came into the shallow area where the women then lowered the harness. This was a delicate operation, heavy and cumbersome as the thing was, and unused as the women were to handling it. But the beams floated so fortunately no one fell in the water.

"Put the carrots close to the harness so the cows know it means food," Nellie said. "Then hold out the harness until an animal comes, like so." She held the leather straps on the hook at the end of a long pole. A couple of the children also had these poles.

One boy managed to loop a leather strap around the body of a large female, and the creature let him scratch her fur.

"It's very spiky," the boy said.

A whoosh of sparks went over the water. The animals snorted and took off. The mature female was still in the harness and she pulled the rope with her, tipping the boy into the water.

With yells and shouts, all the women rushed to the water's edge.

While the mothers fished the boy out of the water, Nellie grabbed the dragon box and chased the sparks around the barn, all along the edge of the water and into the storeroom and back again.

She yelled at the dragon, "Come here, get into the box. You're not helping."

The dragon tipped over the bag of carrots and several rolled into the water before Nellie could pull it back up.

"Hey! That's our food for the trip."

She glared at the swirling sparks, breathing heavily. What did this dragon think he was doing?

Down in the water, the sea cows chewed on carrots with much slobbering and blowing bubbles.

Nellie set the box aside and went to help the women to keep hold of the harness while the animals darted over and under it.

Several times, she was tripped up by one of the cats.

Eventually, they were all wet and exhausted from chasing, and they still only had one animal in the harness.

"We have to try again later, tomorrow maybe," Nellie said.

She unlooped and unreeled the rope so that the animal could graze with the others.

"I hope that magic thing stays away," Mina said.

"Yes, it spooks the sea cows," Agatha said.

They were both looking at Nellie, but she had grown sick of arguing over the dragon and the suggestion that she could do anything to control his behaviour.

She also hoped the dragon could be enticed to go back into his box, but so far, he was ignoring her and she could do nothing about it.

No doubt the dragon would reappear at a most inconvenient time, but they would just have to deal with him. Hopefully, he remained interested in kittens and other animals and wouldn't turn on any of his human companions.

After a quick midday meal from the bread and cheese provided by Dora, Nellie left again. She had the ham, and now she needed to get the gin.

The commercial quarter where she had first gone to see Els and her monk friend produce illegal gin was in between the artisan quarter and the main part of town. It was quite a walk from the harbour.

Today, the streets in the artisan quarter were almost deserted, as both sellers and buyers were in short supply. Winter did not help matters. A lot of businesses were closed. Many displayed signs that they had run out of stock because of the troubles up the river. Many others were closed because the owners were gone.

Nellie spotted a sign in a window of a shop that was still open that said, *Because the shop owner has been taken prisoner, we ask that you support his family by buying our produce.*

Nellie had never felt quite at ease in this part of town, and her short time of living here had not changed that feeling at all.

With every step she took, she expected Zelda or some other wayfarer to come out and harass her. She expected that people were watching her from behind the curtains and that someone would call the guards on her. One of the alleys looked out onto the tents and wagons of a wayfarer camp on the edge of town.

Nellie found the side street and park where Mustafa the animal keeper used to have his exotic menagerie. That had been such a happy time, and she had not even realised how good life was.

On the other side of the empty lot were the two warehouses, one that built coaches for rich people, and one whose building had not even been finished, where Els and her friend plied their illegal gin trade.

Because it was getting cold and misty, the smell of boiling grain hung close to the ground. Once you'd smelled it, you'd recognise that scent anywhere.

Nellie went up to the front door and knocked.

For a long time nothing happened.

She wasn't sure if anyone was even in the warehouse, so she went to the alley, climbed onto a bin, and looked into the little window on the side.

She didn't see anyone, but the vats were cooking, issuing steam into the air. The inside of the window was fogged up.

She went back to the main door and tried to open it.

It was unlocked.

Well, that was easy.

Inside the warehouse, the smell was much stronger.

The place where she entered was a little hall, made up of wooden boards to act as the reception area to hang up one's coat or to shelter the activity in the warehouse from those who came to the door.

"Is anyone here?" she asked.

There was no reply, so she went into the main hall.

The floor was clean, and a couple of sturdy tables stood in the middle of the room. Rows of bottles were lined up on the tables, all cleaned, without labels. A box of corks stood nearby.

The labels were in a little box on a different table. They said *Sailor's Pride*, with a picture of juniper berries on the tree underneath.

Still, no one had come.

"It's me, Nellie. If Els is here, I would like to speak to her."

Her voice faded in the large room. She didn't believe there was no one there.

And then she heard a small scuffling noise. It could have been a cat, but a moment later a young woman came out from behind one of the cooking vats.

"Nellie?"

It was Maartje, the younger of the two sisters, and the less boisterous one. Nellie couldn't decide whether she looked happy or disturbed to see her.

She gave Nellie an uncertain smile. "How are you these days? How did you know where to find us?"

"The people in the palace kitchens told me you haven't been working there, and I happened to know where to find you, because I once spotted your sister entering this warehouse."

"I don't think it's that much of a secret anymore. Most of the sailors know where to find us."

"I came to look for your sister, because I want to ask her a question."

"She went out, but I think she'll be happy to hear from you. We heard you left the palace. She asked about you, but Dora said she didn't know where you were."

There were a lot of unsaid statements in the pleasantries. Nellie had left the palace because of the dragon, and Nellie, the paragon of virtue, had a dragon in her room—like that was something a kitchen maid just had in her pocket.

"I couldn't work in the palace anymore," Nellie said. "Apparently the Regent has been spreading the rumours that I killed Lord Verdonck, because I visited his room and he asked for herbs."

"Really?" Maartje's eyes widened.

"I *did* visit his room, and I brought tea, but he drank none of it."

"Then why don't you tell them so?"

"Because they won't believe me. Like they don't believe Wim and Jantien. Between us, someone will get the blame for the killing, whether they've done it or not."

"It could have just been his health. He was not a young man."

"Many people would like that to be the case. However, I saw him, and I know it was poison. We know that nothing that came through the kitchens was poisoned. We know the wine wasn't poisoned. It had to have been something else because no one at the banquet got sick either. Anyway, I'm here to get a small bottle of gin."

"You? I didn't think you drank gin."

"I don't. It's a payment for a favour by someone else. I thought it would be fair to ask because you two owe me some favours."

"All right. Wait."

She disappeared into a door at the back.

Nellie walked around the tables and installations, looking at, but not touching, all the equipment.

The fire under the big metal vat kept the huge space warm. Steam blew from a vent at the top.

Three lines of bottles stood on the table. They were all made from clear glass, but they weren't all the same. Some were round and plain, others more elaborate with a stamp from the maker. Others again were square.

Wait—she remembered seeing a bottle like that in Lord Verdonck's room. It had been empty and there had been a label with a goat on it.

The labels Els used were different, but no one had mentioned that bottle.

"Here you are." Maartje put a small round bottle next to Nellie on the table.

"Thank you so much." Nellie slipped the bottle into her basket. Then she hesitated. "There was a bottle of gin in Lord Verdonck's room. It was empty."

Maartje's eyes widened. "My sister doesn't sell anything to the palace. They only buy from the official distilleries. We don't sell bad gin either. If we did, all the sailors in the harbour would line up to kill us."

"Do any of the gin suppliers in town use a label with a goat?"

"I don't know. It's not ours, that's all I know. You'll have to ask my sister."

"Do you think someone could put poison in gin, maybe just one bottle?"

She looked at the bottles that stood on the bench.

"I'm sure that could be done. A lot of the poison tastes foul though, so you would have to mask the taste, and you'd have to use something that doesn't have a colour."

"Gin has a strong taste already."

She shrugged, uneasy. "I know little about it. My sister has been running this plant, and I'm just helping."

It sounded like half admission to Nellie, but she didn't want to press any further. Maartje was only thirteen and knew little of her older sister's machinations. And when Maartje said Els didn't sell to the palace, Nellie believed her. Oh, those two girls were up to their ears in mischief, but it probably had little to do with the palace.

"So are you still working at the palace at all?" This gin-selling business could go nowhere good. It was only a matter of time before the Regent's attention would shift from magic to the next thing to be declared illegal. Contraband gin was always a popular black sheep to target.

"We'll try to go back to work, if it's safe enough to return."

"But if you have nothing to hide, then wouldn't it be safe enough already?"

Once, Nellie had tried to do everything in her power to make the girls abandon this risky path. They had a whole life in front of them. They couldn't start it by doing illegal things. Before they knew it, they would be stealing and breaking in or whoring and then they'd end up in prison. But Nellie wasn't doing so well herself, so she had no right to tell others to do things she couldn't do herself.

Maartje hesitated, then her expression turned defiant. "I don't think it's safe. Wim had nothing to hide. He was just doing his job. It's just that someone didn't like him. As far as I understand he is in the palace dungeons. Should I return to a place where people get locked up for doing their jobs? Me, I'd like to stay as far away from those guards as possible. That's the safest place for us to be."

Oh, she sounded so much like her sister when she said this.

Thirteen years of age, and full of street smarts.

And Nellie would do best to stop telling her what to do. All she could try to do was be there when they needed help.

"Thank you for the gin. I can bring you some fish, or carrots or anything else, except money."

"If you can, bring juniper berries. Don't worry too much about giving something in return. You've done a lot for us, but don't tell my sister that I gave this to you."

"All right, I won't tell her." Nellie looked around. "Is this installation all hers, or is it someone else's?"

"Oh no, it belongs to the other girl."

"The one who dresses like a monk?"

"Something like that."

She didn't meet Nellie's eyes.

Nellie could ask many questions—about Els' relationship with Gisele, about Gisele's past, about her intent to go through life while pretending to be a monk.

"Look, I don't want to do either of you any harm. I helped you and offered you a job at the palace. But a man has died, and I am one of the people they may accuse of the murder. Like Wim, everyone who worked in the kitchens during the banquet could be a suspect. I visited the dead man's room to bring him tea, so I'm even more likely to be wanted for questioning. If I can, I would like to find out what happened, because the murdered man's son is determined to find out, and he's holding threats over the Regent's head. So if you happen to know who sells this gin with the goat label, I'd be happy to hear it."

"I said you'd have to ask my sister."

"When is she coming back here?"

"I don't know. She took some of her stock and went to sell it this morning."

"All right, I'll come back later."

But Nellie didn't have time to wait that long.

CHAPTER 14

ONCE SHE GOT to the harbour, Nellie was dismayed to find how many taverns there were. She thought she knew the one where Els' mother worked most of the time, but she had never been inside. This was not the type of establishment that respectable women entered. Unlike in some other places she had heard about, there was no official rule that women couldn't enter a tavern, but people thought poorly of those who did. She had to admit that the prospect of facing drunk men frightened her somewhat.

Although there shouldn't be anyone drunk at this time of the day, should there?

There were several visiting ships in the harbour, most of them moored on the far side of the pier. Nellie walked past the taverns a few times, thinking about an excuse to go in, but with all her might she could not think of one. Her newfound boldness only went so far.

She was cold, it was drizzling a bit, and if she stood here long enough, people would wonder what she was doing.

So she gritted her teeth and went up to the door. She pushed it open and stepped into the tavern room beyond.

The room was dark, and my, it smelled bad in here. No wonder these men were so unhealthy.

As she had already suspected, there were few people inside.

A man came out behind the bar on the other side, wiping his hands on a cloth. He raised his eyebrows when he saw Nellie.

"Good morning," he said.

"Good morning." Nellie's voice came out high.

"You look nothing like our normal customers," he said. "Which of the drunkard husbands is yours?" He laughed, showing a mouth with missing teeth.

Nellie looked over her shoulder. A man with grizzled hair and a couple of days' worth of beard was asleep on the table. She shuddered.

"I'm not married, thank you."

"Then are you here to buy a drink?" He laughed again.

"I'm here to look for someone who sells gin."

He smiled vanished. "What do you know about that? We don't sell any gin and we don't buy it from strangers either."

He seemed touchy all of a sudden.

"I said am looking for someone who sells gin. I was told that this person might be in here. I know nothing about gin, but I'm just looking for her, because she did a job at the palace, and we need her to come back."

"Oh." He smiled again, this time much more friendly. "I thought you were going to talk about the illegal gin trade for a minute."

Of which there was evidently a lot. "I know nothing about that. I didn't say I wanted to buy gin. Do I look like I would do that?"

"Well, could be that the guards are sending around anyone now."

An old woman was clearly "just anyone". No one had told him how to be polite to people.

He continued, "With what they've been doing in the rest of town, shutting down people's businesses, nothing surprises me anymore. I don't want any trouble. It's hard enough keeping the safe stuff from the magicked stuff."

"I know nothing about trouble. I'm just looking for this girl. Her name is Els."

Now he gave a big belly laugh. "Oh, that one. Yes she came in here, but she's probably in one of the other taverns." He winked. Nellie hadn't known how quickly she could leave again. She had to make an effort not to run past the sleeping drunk man. Even when she got outside, she still felt jittery from the experience. What an unpleasant, sleazy man. But she had learned something. Gin could not just be poisoned, but it could also have magic. Maybe she was looking for poison in the wrong place.

She clamped her arms around herself, walking through the rain. The man had said Els might be somewhere around here, but Nellie didn't feel like going into another one of those disgusting establishments.

Heavens, she might run into a whore. She would just have to go back to the warehouse to find Els later.

Nellie was about to return to the sea cow barn when a tavern door opened, and two young women came out chatting and laughing. It was Els and her sometimes-monk friend Gisele.

Both stopped when they saw Nellie, and an expression came to Els' face that she sometimes showed in the palace, that expression of looking guilty and having been sprung.

"Good morning," Nellie said, keeping her voice casual, but failing utterly.

"Good morning to you, Nellie."

She sounded far too cheerful.

Both girls carried baskets, but the cloth cover lay folded up inside, indicating that they had already delivered the contents.

"Are you out shopping?" Els asked.

"No, I wanted to ask you some questions," Nellie said.

"I don't work at the palace any more. I handed in my aprons and my dresses if that's what you're after."

Well, well, that was different from her sister's story. "I don't work at the palace any more either."

Els gave her a strange look. "What? Why not? Does it have something to do with that dragon?"

"It's long story, and I'll tell it to you, if you can find somewhere we can talk where it's dry."

Els exchanged a look with her monk friend. The girl nodded.

"All right. We know a place."

They walked silently along the harbour front.

It was kind of uneasy. Nellie had never been easy with Els, cunning as she was. That whole business with the juniper berries "for my mam" was still fresh in Nellie's mind. She'd wanted the berries because they needed them to start a new batch of gin and no supplies had reached the shops.

Whatever Nellie told Els was likely to be used in unusual ways.

They came to an alley in between two houses that led away from the quay and around the back. It was so narrow they couldn't walk next to each other.

Els went up the steps to the left and through a doorway.

The wood had once been painted green, but the paint was coming off. An emblem had once been painted in white at eye level. Most of it had flaked off, but the letters BR from "Brouwer Company" were still visible.

This used to be the old office belonging to Mistress Johanna's father. Even when Nellie came to work for the family, he barely used it, but the company had several employees who worked here, and he would sometimes use it when visitors came.

When Mistress Johanna had been queen and she and her father lived in the palace, they had sold this office to another river trader, who had occupied it until a few years ago when they had left town. Rumours were that the business had gone to Burovia.

The girls had turned the dusty space into a comfortable sitting room. There were four mismatched old chairs, a table with one of its legs missing, propped up by several bricks, and a metal barrel placed on bricks that served as a fire pit. Some half-burned logs still glowed, keeping the room at a higher temperature than outside.

"This is quite a nice place," Nellie said.

"The owner kind of allows us in here, because if we were not using this building, there would be people ripping up all the wood for fires."

Yes, that was probably true. Nellie remembered how Zelda and the others were getting their firewood from one of the old warehouses next door.

They sat down and Nellie told a simple version of the information she was willing to share about her flight from the palace. That she didn't control the dragon—true—that he had abandoned her once they reached freedom—half true—and that the women convicted of being witches were innocent. She also told Els that the Regent suspected her of killing Lord Verdonck.

"You? But that is ridiculous."

"I know, but they are desperate. Adalbert Verdonck demands that Regent Bernard find the killer. I'm a suspect, Wim is a suspect, the *dragon* is a suspect."

"The dragon?" Els laughed.

Her cheeks were turning red with the warmth from the fire that the monk girl had stoked and fed with some pieces of wood.

"So now you know my story. But why did *you* leave?" Nellie asked.

"There were just too many questions being asked there," Els said. "I have to protect my sister, because I didn't want her questioned."

"Why would you worry about your sister in particular?"

"Because she is too young for this sort of thing. If the guards ask her questions and they get insistent, she may well admit to something she hasn't done, just to please them. These men are very good putting words in people's mouths."

That was true, but Nellie suspected that Els was afraid her sister might give away things about her little illicit gin business here that might lead to her arrest. Which, all things considered, was fair enough.

"They've been scraping the barrel trying to find someone to blame for this poisoning. They're blaming the kitchens, because they haven't a clue. So we poor women will pay because we can't defend ourselves. That's why we left the palace. Not that I don't appreciate you, Nellie, but that's just how things are for people like us. If there is a crime that people can't solve, the poor people are always the first to be blamed. So if you're like us, and you're poor, and your mother is a whore and you have nine brothers and sisters from nine different fathers and there is never enough food on the table, then you learn to recognise the signs, and you get out of there. You get out before they can do anything to you or your family."

"It's always the same," the monk girl said, and it was the first time she'd spoken. Nellie remembered that her name was Gisele. "They blame the ones who can't defend themselves. They drag us off to the dungeons, they make out that we're witches, and then they banish us or they kill us or they sell us off to some slave trader or some other thing."

She had a distinct accent that Nellie couldn't place. Her hair was short, her face looked boyish—necessary when she was wearing a habit, which she was not today—but in her loose trousers and jacket she looked just as much a boy as she did in the habit. She was very skinny, and quite tall.

Nellie said, "I understand that this gin production is all yours."

"It is." She lifted her chin in the air as if daring a challenge.

Nellie wasn't sure what to think of this girl, unsure whether to trust her. "I'm looking for somebody who might have sold poisoned gin to the palace."

At the same time Els said, "We have no idea, I already told you that."

Gisele said, "You don't really want to know."

And Els turned to her friend, her expression aghast.

Nellie looked at Gisele. "Do tell me more about this."

"We only make good gin. If we made foul stuff, then there would be hundreds of sailors who would come after us, and we wouldn't see tomorrow morning."

That was true, and Maartje had also said that.

Gisele continued, "But once we sell the gin, there is no guarantee what other people will do with it. It is well known that in other countries, like Burovia, some monasteries poison wine to get rid of people they don't like, and therefore wine is always suspicious. Wine is dark and holds poison well. Gin, being clear, is trickier, because many poisons have a colour. Magic has no colour or smell and cannot be measured. People put magic in bread and in fabric. Nobody has yet tried it with gin."

"So is this why the Regent is so keen to get rid of magicians?"

"It's hard to say for sure. I don't think he knows much about it and I don't think he's received good advice. If he wants to solve this crime, it's likely he needs a magician. I have no great skill with magic, but I can point to some places where people from the palace have bought things that are suspicious."

"And those people would be?"

"For one, you would want to have a look at your beloved church."

"But the church is very much against magic."

"What they say and what they do is not always the same thing."

The artefacts in the glass cabinet, the ruby skull, the books filled with dark magic. Nellie nodded, slowly. There was also that occasion where she had felt betrayed when Shepherd Adrianus listened to his superior and had *not* stood up when the poor people were thrown out of the church. "I guess you know about what goes on in the church."

"Not in that way. Only the important monks do. Other than that, those churchmen are all the same. Once they know you're a girl, they are only interested in feeling you out, if you get what I mean. I have to protect myself, meaning I don't meddle in their business and don't cross their path."

"One day I saw you in the church."

"Well, I am a monk. I have to pretend, don't I?"

"But do you provide certain services to monks?"

"I try to avoid that, if I can at all, but one has to eat sometimes, doesn't one?"

"Does being a monk not feed you well enough?"

"I detest begging, but I have no rich family who sends me parcels of goods."

And begging was what monks often did. Despite the

obvious riches of the monasteries, many of the monks were themselves dirt poor, and Nellie had heard stories that monasteries liked to get sons from rich families who would then contribute to the upkeep of the building, while the men themselves would live in poverty, for the sake of living a simple life.

"What do you know about the books and other things they keep in the church crypt?" Nellie asked.

Gisele raised her eyebrows.

"My father was an account keeper for the church. He knew about all the stuff they buy. He didn't agree with much of it."

Gisele shook her head. "Oh, there is some disturbing stuff there. The church says it wants to keep this material so it doesn't fall into the hands of citizens who are supposedly unable to deal with horrific material."

She was sassy and probably also very smart, which was not a good thing for a young girl. She reminded Nellie of Mistress Johanna.

"Tell me what you have seen."

"Why are you so curious? My friend here tells me you're a church person, that your parents grew up in the church, and that you take the letter of the Book of Verses literally."

"I have not lived to the age of fifty by believing everything people tell me. I believe there is an essential good in the teachings of the church, but that its interpretations are not always well-intentioned."

"Well, you can say that again."

This girl knew a lot more than Nellie had bargained for.

"Did you know the church had a dragon?"

"There were rumours, although I live at the monastery, and I've never seen it. It was gone from the spot in the cabinet when I first came there. I asked what the octagonal spot in the dust was and they said it belonged to an important artefact that they were studying—that was the dragon that took you out of the kitchen, right?"

"I think so."

"The one that lives in a box?"

Nellie nodded. "Do you know why the box was no longer in the cabinet when you saw it?"

"No one ever mentioned it to me. Mind you, it was not as if I could ask these kinds of questions. But there were rumours that Shepherd Wilfridus himself was looking at it."

"Was it stolen from his study?" Nellie asked.

"From the library, apparently, a few months ago."

"Then wouldn't it be easy for the shepherd to track who came to the library?"

"Not every visitor signs the book. Not every monk is free of suspicion."

Also true. "And you believe it was a monk?"

"Not a monk, I don't think. But someone from the church."

"A bad apple," Nellie said, filling with hope. She didn't want to believe the church was evil.

Gisele said, "It is more than just one person. I want to take down these tyrants who call themselves the saviours of our souls and show the citizens what evil they sow. It's all a load of nonsense."

Nellie protested, "The church isn't evil."

"I mean not this church, I mean all churches."

"But then, are you a heathen?"

"I believe in the good of people. I believe they can be good regardless of their belief. If they feel they need a church to motivate them, that is good, as long as they do good things. But the moment this institution becomes a law onto itself, and frightens people for the sake of its own profit, that is wrong."

And Nellie could not disagree with that. It also seemed to have been something her father had realised and tried to express in words in his book.

While they drank tea, Gisele told Nellie about some things she had seen while serving as a monk. "In the monastery just across the border in Burovia, every farmer in all the surrounding land is brought in once a year, to deliver one tenth of their produce to the church. They do not get anything in return, except a promise that their souls will be saved. The church doesn't always even own the land. Sometimes the farmers come in purely out of fear because someone in the service has said the Lord of Fire will descend upon them if they don't obey. Woe the poor girls who become with child when a monk forgets that he's supposed to have sworn off the pleasures of female flesh. They are treated like they are the worst sinners, their families have to increase their contributions to the monastery and the girl herself can never marry well. In the crypt of the main church in your city here, the church keeps a collection of truly dreadful things. It is not the black skull with the ruby eyes that is disturbing, although people often talk about it, but it is all the books filled with the most terrible things that people can do to each other. And some of them are books of magic, but most of them are books of insane cruelty. It is also the place where if a monk or some other person in the church falls foul of the leadership, they will lock this poor person up, sometimes for years, sometimes until the end of their lives."

"You mean the church keeps these prisoners at present?" Nellie had seen no places where prisoners could be locked up. Although there was that large room with all the bottles she had not investigated very much. She only had so much time because it was dark and very dusty in the crypt and that large room looked to be a storage area for wine.

"Yes, that's right."

"And they lock people up for years?" Nellie couldn't imagine the horror of living in the dark for that long.

"There is a rumour of a boy," Gisele said. "I don't know how much is true, but they say a young boy lives in one of the cells and has been there for years. I've never seen him, but I've definitely seen people carrying food into that area."

Nellie's heart jumped. "Do you think the boy could be Prince Bruno?"

"Who is that?"

Nellie related the story of the misfortunes of the royal family, of the fact that the king could not have any children, that neither of his two children had been his, and that the younger one, who was the son of an eastern trader, was called Bruno.

"He's the owner of the dragon box. I used to work for the royal family. The box was given to him by his father, and he kept it on the shelf in his room."

Gisele frowned. "Did you ever see the dragon? Is that why it hasn't attacked you, but it has attacked everyone else who tried to open the box?"

"I don't think so. The dragon wouldn't know who I am. I never saw him back then. I only saw his father's dragon. Do you think they kept him in the dungeons because he's the only one who can use the dragon?"

Gisele looked disturbed for a moment. Then she shrugged. "Could be. I don't know if it's the prince. But someone definitely lives down there."

Nellie said, "Would you be prepared to check?"

"I have no idea how to get in there. The only way I got in was with someone else who opened the door for me."

Yes, but Nellie had the key.

CHAPTER 15

NELLIE DEBATED whether she should let Gisele know she had the key, but decided against it for the time being. She *thought* she could trust Gisele, as least somewhat, but if Gisele got desperate, who was to say she wouldn't trade the information that someone had the key for something she wanted?

She might want Gisele's help later, but she would only tell her that she had the key at that time.

So she asked Gisele and Els for information about how to poison gin. Had they ever seen or heard of gin that could be poisoned with magic?

"A lot of sailors talk about this," Els said. "When they go out to sea, they have no way of getting back at whoever it was who sold them the foul gin, so they prefer to buy only from people they know are safe suppliers."

"And I'm guessing you are a safe supplier?"

She smiled mischievously. "Reputation is everything. You have told me many times yourself."

"Who are they, then, these magicians who poison gin with magic?"

"If people knew, then they wouldn't live for long,"

Gisele said. "It's considered the lowest form of crime to kill someone in this way."

"But they would have to be a magician, wouldn't they?"

"Either that, or they would have to employ a magician to do it."

Nellie said, "What sort of magic would be involved? I know that people who have wood magic see things in wood, but they can't do anything with the wood, other than listen to it. I know that works the same with wind and water magic. People touch the water, or let the wind touch the face, and then listen to all the things it tells them. I think that is called passive magic. Artisan magic. If someone were to put magic in gin that would be an active use of magic." Nellie struggled to find the right words. She had heard some language used to describe magic when she was travelling with Mistress Johanna, but she was not well versed in the terminology that magicians used to talk about their skills. That, she realised, was the way Saardam had seen its downfall. It was because someone who had a dangerous amount of magic—the young princess—had been left untrained. And here was the church, who wanted to forbid the training of all such people, instead banishing them from the city.

It made sense, in an evil kind of way.

Gisele said, "Yep, that is active magic, and it's rare and dangerous."

"That means that there is such a magician in the city."

"Or somewhere outside, and the gin is imported."

"But gin is only made locally. Even a little distance up the river the monks prefer wine, and further still, they have all kinds of different liquors."

"That's true."

So, Nellie asked again. "Who else in the city sells gin? I know you don't like talking about your competitors, but we need to know, or several people will be put to death unnecessarily. Specifically, I'd like to know who sells to the palace."

"We don't sell to the palace," Els said.

"I know. You have already told me that."

Gisele said, "The Regent is from the south, and I don't think he likes gin."

"Would he not provide any for his guests?"

"Gin is considered a drink for uncivilised sailors," Gisele said. "I don't know that anyone sells it to the Palace. When I was serving there, I didn't see any."

Nellie didn't remember seeing any while serving, either. In fact, thinking back to her time working with the Regent, she didn't think she had ever seen gin in the dining room. "Yet there was a bottle of gin in the Lord Verdonck's room. I know because I saw it there. It was empty. I remember what it looked like because it was one of the square ones like those in your warehouse. The label was different, with a goat on it. I've never seen that before, but I'm sure he would have bought it somewhere in town."

"The gin that gets sold in the shops is made at the Oliver distillery," Gisele said.

"Do they use a label with a goat on it?"

"Their usual label doesn't have a picture, but they may do special batches for people. I don't know. I have to say I would be very surprised if someone who has a lot of magic would work there, so probably someone bought it there and then infused it with magic before giving it to Lord Verdonck as a present. They might even have changed the label."

That was another option, and Nellie's head was spinning with all the different possibilities. She wasn't sure she would ever find out who sold that bottle of gin, and she became less sure that the poisoning had been caused by the gin.

The distillery was one of the businesses that still operated in the street behind the harbour, and Nellie decided to go and have a look after she had said goodbye to Gisele and Els.

It was operated by the Oliver family, a well-respected merchant family in town. There were two brothers in the business. One had the distillery, the other ran the confectionery and special foods business that supplied the palace. It was a respectable business in a good part of town, and it had been there for a long time. When someone mentioned the name, she could smell the smoked ham, and the salty aged cheese that was so dry it crumbled when you tried to cut it. She could see the racks of bottles with exotic spices. There was a set of shelves containing bottles of gin, too, which came from the family business.

When she came to the distillery building, the doors into the factory hall were open. The familiar smell of boiling grain wafted out in clouds of steam. The setup was much bigger and better than Gisele and Els' operation in the abandoned warehouse. This hall had permanent tables, wash basins for bottles, drying racks and a giant pot hanging over a raging fire, where a man was stirring the contents. Another man was writing out labels and affixing them to bottles and then packing the bottles in crates.

A young man whom she knew as the son of the business owner came to meet Nellie. He wore a simple thin coat and his cheeks were red from the steamy heat inside the hall. "Can I help you?"

"I've got a strange question," Nellie said. "I was wondering if you could tell me whether someone from the nobility or the palace bought a small bottle of gin as a present for a visitor."

The man laughed. "We sell hundreds of bottles every week. Do you think I would remember?"

Seeing the size of the operation behind him that did not surprise her at all. "But you do sell to the palace?"

"Not very much, we don't. That foreigner insists on having his own foreign drink brought in as if we're not good enough for him."

Clearly not a supporter of the Regent. "Where do you sell to, then?"

"Many people. All the nobles, merchants, the church."

"The church?"

"Yes, they love a good glass of gin. Especially Shepherd Wilfridus."

With all the will in the world, Nellie could not imagine Shepherd Wilfridus approving of drinking anything like gin.

But maybe he gave it to his monks to loosen their tongues.

"So you don't remember anyone who bought a small bottle as a present? It could have been someone from out of town." She looked around him, but the labels the man at the table was sticking on bottles contained only writing, no pictures of goats.

"I'm sorry, but we don't have memories as good as that."

"Do you make small batches with special labels?"

"We sometimes sell bottles without labels, if clients want to use their own."

Well, this didn't help Nellie very much. What had she expected? To see crates with goat-labelled gin? What would that mean anyway? Probably that the poison hadn't been in the gin. She considered asking about the goat labels, but decided against it because it would only draw attention to herself.

She was about to go, but then thought of another question. "Can you tell me, is there such a thing as gin magic?"

"The making of gin is a craft. In our case, it has been passed down from generation to generation. If you want to call that magic, you are wrong. In this factory hall, we do not meddle in magic or other dark craft. What you see here is all honest work."

"I'm sorry to upset you. It was not my intention. But I know that when a baker makes bread, the best bakers have a kind of magic that makes their bread better than everyone else's. Someone told me you are the best gin maker in town."

"The only one." His face was prim.

"So I wondered if there might be a special gift involved in the magic of gin."

"It's craft, no more."

Whoa, he was defensive all of a sudden.

She thanked him for his replies and left again, with more questions than when she had come.

So it was possible that the gin in Lord Verdonck's room had been purchased at that distillery, and that someone else had put the goat label on it and infused it with magic. But it was a long shot, and who that person would have been was a mystery.

Then she had another thought. She already knew an accomplished magician was in town because the fire dog would not exist without a master. That person would have enough magic to do such a thing. But Nellie had no idea who that person could be.

She wasn't getting anywhere near solving who had poisoned Lord Verdonck, but she knew where she might find Prince Bruno. Because the more she thought about it, the more convinced she became that the boy was Prince Bruno. She also remembered that she had seen a drawing in a book in the crypt of a boy aged about ten who looked like Prince Bruno. If there was indeed a boy in the crypt, as Gisele had insisted, then it was Prince Bruno.

If the women were going to escape from the city, they should take him, because the thought of a young boy locked up inside the crypt horrified her.

She should tell the dragon she knew where his master was. If anything could entice him out of hiding that information would do the trick.

When she came back to the barn, the women were again sitting on the floor of the main barn tying wooden slats together with a thin rope to make a shield against arrows.

They looked up when Nellie came in. "Where have you been?" Agatha asked, her voice brusque.

No matter what Nellie did or said, she could never shake the feeling that Agatha disliked her.

"This is going really well," Nellie said of their handiwork.

"It's cold work," Agatha said. "My fingers are ready to fall off."

She held up her hands. Her fingers were red, the skin flaky.

Nellie was more concerned about Koby's fingers. The girl was quiet and didn't complain, but her hands and legs were covered in sores that never seemed to heal.

"I will come and help you soon, but I have some news I have to tell the dragon."

"What makes you think it will listen this time?" Agatha said and continued to talk about *some* people doing all the work while other people gallivanted about.

Nellie ignored her. At some point, she would figure out what Agatha's problem was, but that time was not now.

At the word *dragon*, the children in the corner of the barn stopped dropping pebbles in the water near the sea cows and watched Nellie.

She went into the storeroom where they slept and retrieved the dragon box from her bag.

When she picked it up, a puff of sparks exploded from the top shelf and drifted down to the mattresses that lay on the hay, and then back up into the air.

Nellie opened the box.

The sparks withdrew to the door.

"Do you want to get in? Are you afraid of this box?"

The sparks moved closer to her and back to the wall a few times.

"Come on, show yourself. We won't bite."

And then she had to laugh about that. Fancy telling a dragon not to be afraid. Dragons shouldn't fear anything.

She snapped the box shut again.

"Suit yourself, but if you don't get in the box, you will never see your master. I know where he is."

The sparks came a bit closer again.

"Do you know that he's alive? I learnt this today from someone who knows there is a boy living in the crypt. I think that's him. I think you know that, too."

Sparks came a little closer.

"Come on. I'm not angry with you. At least I won't be angry if you're nice and behave yourself and don't mess things up again."

Now the sparks went lower, to about knee level.

"So this is it, right? You feel sorry because you made a mess?"

The sparks went even lower.

Nellie kept talking. She wasn't sure that the dragon understood, although she would like to think he did. "I know you can't help it. That fire dog scared me, too. I don't know where it came from. I need your help to figure out who it belongs to. We need to make sure it doesn't discover us. Maybe when we have your master we'll defeat the magician who owns it, but for now we just need to be careful."

The sparks shivered.

Nellie bent down and pretended to pat them as if they were a dog.

Her hand and went right through, and she didn't even feel any pricks of the sparks.

"Come on, we could you use your help. I forgive you. We all make mistakes. I'm sure that the other women will forgive you too, as long as you now know to be quiet."

The sparks exploded outwards.

Slowly the space in between solidified. First a golden mist appeared that grew thicker and thicker until it formed into a deep golden dragon with shimmering scales. Not the same colour as before, because the dragon had been red, but still the same animal.

"Boots!" Anneke yelled from the door. She ran into the storeroom and spread her arms against the dragon's flanks.

"See, he came back. He was here all along. He loves us."

The other children also stood in the doorway, cheering. "Boots is back, Boots is back." This brought the adults to the door.

Nellie went to stand in front of the dragon and held out the box. He sniffed at the box, and then sneezed, blowing a gust of warm air over Nellie's hand.

"I hope this means you will behave, and you will go back into the box whenever we tell you. It's for your own best interest, and we do want you to come with us."

But in all honesty, she was happy to see the dragon again, because having him around would mean they had another weapon against the guards. If things went wrong during the escape attempt, having a dragon in your pocket was always a good thing.

With the dragon in the room, it was already much warmer, so at least tonight they would not have to bring coals into the room with all kinds of danger of fire.

The other women were all standing in the doorway.

"Look, mammy, Boots is back," Anneke said.

"As long as it doesn't get you kids into any more mischief," Agatha said, in a prim voice.

"We'll be very careful. We'll teach him to lie still and be quiet, won't we, Boots?"

Her mother sniffed and turned to the barn.

There was something familiar about her behaviour that made Nellie think of herself when she first came to work for Mistress Johanna. The little girl had only been a few years younger than Nellie, but Nellie was so very disturbed by the way Johanna used her wood magic to snoop on people. Because it was Not Proper, and One Didn't Do That Sort Of Thing.

And the church said magic was bad and therefore people with magic were bad, which she believed . . . until she met a person with magic, and it wasn't like that at all. Nellie had been afraid of Johanna at first, and her fear had manifested into telling Johanna not to do anything that brought her into contact with situations where magic might happen.

Nellie was scared of it, and she had been even more scared that her father would find out that the well-off, wholesome merchant family who employed his daughter had dealings with magic. Because she was sure her father would be furious and tell her to stay home. Nellie had *liked* the young girl and her father, and she *liked* living away from her home, so she had forced herself to accept Johanna's magic.

That made her realise: Agatha was scared of her daughter's ability.

CHAPTER 16

AT NIGHT, IN the storeroom, while listening to the waves slapping against the quay and the soft snoring of the dragon which again slept surrounded by the children, Nellie attempted to sort out the disturbed thoughts she had about the church.

She believed the church had collected evil artefacts with the purpose of keeping them out of the hands of unwitting citizens.

The past of Saardam was littered with stories of people who had acquired evil items by accident and had suffered for it.

So she accepted the good intentions of the church in keeping those items out of the hands of the public.

With no will in the world, however, could she justify keeping people prisoner. Not even the most evil of crazy people deserved to be locked up in the crypts of the church. She didn't think that most people in the church knew about this, because good, honest people would never stand for it. And most of the people in the church were good, she had no doubt about that.

And then, because it was dark, and at night everything

seemed different, the more she thought about it the more she doubted that there was a boy locked up in the crypts. Why would the church lock up people when there was a perfectly good prison for them to go to? A prison, which she should add, the Regent had no trouble using.

At night, when the world was dark and strange and sounds kept her awake, was when she needed her faith in the Triune to pull her through. All her life, the church had been her one shining beacon, the light that guided her through the dark waters, the home she longed for.

The church *couldn't* do something as bad as lock up a young boy.

Gisele *had* to be mistaken. She *had* to be.

But, as the fishermen woke up outside and she could hear them talking on the quay, and the light that peeped underneath the barn door slowly turned grey, she thought about the things Gisele had told her. Gisele would not lie about the things the monks did to her. She could blame the Guentherite order, but they were ultimately part of the same church, and if the church did something bad and the order covered it up, or the other way around, they were both wrong.

There was no way she could shape or bend it. If there was a boy locked in the church crypt, that was unspeakably evil.

She got up early, because pretending to be asleep was a waste of time, and started making the fire. She hung a pot over the fire to boil.

While she waited for the fire to spread across the chunks of wood she had thrown in the pit, she stared over the water. A couple of sea cows stuck their heads above the surface and looked at her with their sad eyes.

She felt utterly miserable. It had taken her all this time, since she had received her father's book, to realise that the world that was the foundation of her very essence was a lie. She had always believed kings and barons and dukes existed solely to enrich themselves, and that the church existed to keep them honest and make sure they didn't abuse the people. But they were all in bed with each other. They sat at the same table and shared the same wine.

There was a soft sound behind her. She turned around to see the dragon coming out of the storeroom. He did this by dissolving into sparks and reforming into a dragon once he got into the barn, because otherwise he wouldn't fit through the door. He came up to the fire and blew a gust of hot air over the flames, fanning them into a roaring inferno.

"That was useful, thank you. But be careful. We don't want to start a fire in there."

The dragon turned his head to her, with his ears flat against his neck.

Nellie patted the warm skin.

"You are a silly dragon."

He made a soft purring sound. Maybe he had taken too much notice of the kitten.

"You want to free your master, don't you?"

The dragon looked up at her, giving no sign that he understood what she said.

Nellie patted his warm neck, seeing the inside of the barn and the dragon's golden skin through a haze of tears.

Everything was broken. Everything she had ever believed in was gone. She had always found strength in her inner peace, and now even that was gone.

Was there anyone left in this place she could trust?

But she would give the truth one more chance.

Nellie hadn't seen Shepherd Adrianus since she had left the palace. In fact, she hadn't seen him since he had stood by while Shepherd Wilfridus evicted the poor people from the church. Since it had turned out that some of those poor people were not quite as poor as they looked and some were there because that was their way of life, Nellie could see some of Shepherd Wilfridus' reasoning.

The church was for worshippers. There were other places where homeless people could sleep. With so many of the houses in the city empty, it shouldn't be hard to find somewhere. It did not *need* to be the church.

It was just that . . . many of those, especially the women and children, were church people, looking for help and being turned away.

Nellie might *understand* it, but agree with it, no. Shepherd Adrianus wouldn't agree with it, either. To her, it felt like he might have known of some disturbing facts he was too scared to become involved in. That he was scared of falling foul of Shepherd Wilfridus, who was his ultimate superior.

She wanted Shepherd Adrianus to know that whatever happened in the next few days, she still loved the church and she understood and forgave him, and that she would continue to worship the Triune and carry out His word.

It was with a certain trepidation that she entered her beloved church, expecting . . . she didn't know what. To be banished? To be called a witch? To be asked about the dragon?

The muffled sound of her footsteps in the church vestibule, the achingly familiar smell of incense mingled with the musty smell of dust and dry stone made her eyes prick. She longed for the good times that she had come here during, times in which she had utter trust in this organisation.

Her footsteps echoed in the empty space when she walked down the aisle to the statue of the Triune behind the altar.

This statue looked a lot kinder than the one in the main church, and its faces, that were so contorted in the statue in the main church, were almost friendly. You could imagine the Father as an old man visiting your house, the Ghost as a patient friend who always stood behind you, and the Holy God as a shepherd who led the way.

There were no more candles in the box next to the altar, and she had no coin to drop into the donations box, but she went up to say a prayer anyway.

She prayed that the Triune would forgive her for all the things she would do. She prayed that He would see that her intentions were good, and that she was only angry with the selfish people who took the word of the Book of Verses and twisted those words to suit their own means.

She prayed that the Holy Triune would see that she only wanted to expose those powerful men who wanted to enrich themselves and used the church to do so. And this, incidentally, was one of the major accusations they had levelled at the Belaman Church.

She prayed that they would see their errors and return to the good intentions of the Triune.

She prayed that the church had a very good reason to hold someone prisoner inside the crypt. She prayed that the person down there wasn't Prince Bruno, but was a poor altar boy who had committed some transgression and that all the times that Gisele had heard about this person, it had really been a number of different people.

It might even be that being locked up in the dark for several days was part of an obscure ritual that the church liked to put naughty boys through.

She prayed that she had been mistaken, that she had misread her father's notes, and that everything could go back to normal, the prisoners would be freed and she wouldn't have to risk everyone's lives by carrying out that ridiculous plan.

When she finished her prayer, she got up, and walked

through the side door of the church to the courtyard, on the other side of which the shepherd's house stood.

It looked so familiar. She had lost count of how many times she had walked up these steps to find Shepherd Adrianus and his warm friendship. The clean windows, the neatly painted door, the slightly worn door handle: she could picture it all.

For moment Nellie thought everything would be as it was before. The shepherd would see her argument and would be able to convince everyone in the church she was right. The witch drownings would be cancelled and the prisoners released, because people were good, weren't they?

But when she tried to enter the door, it was locked.

She knocked. "Shepherd, it's me, Nellie."

There were some sounds from inside the home, and moments later the door opened. But the person inside was not Shepherd Adrianus. It was one of the deacons who used to work in the main church. Nellie didn't remember his name. He was tall and lanky, towering over her, and regarding her with a flat expression. His face was unpleasant.

"Yes? You knocked?" He sounded annoyed.

"Oh. I'm here to see Shepherd Adrianus."

"He does not live here any more." His voice was cold and the tone chilled Nellie.

"What do you mean? I was here just a few days ago, and he—"

"He doesn't live here anymore. Simple as that. This is not his house. It belongs to the church."

Yes, she knew that, but Shepherd Adrianus *was* the church. "What happened? Where is he now?"

"Believe me, child, it would be better for you not to worry about it. The shepherd needed some time apart from the church and the congregation, and he has gone away for a while. When he has finished his deliberations, he will be back."

"When will that be?"

"I can't tell at this point in time. The Shepherd Wilfridus has the final say over that."

"I just want to know what happened to him," Nellie said. "He's my friend. He's all right, isn't he?"

"He is in fine health," the deacon said.

"Then where is he? I want to see him."

"The shepherd has decided to relieve him of his duties for a limited time."

"He hasn't done anything, has he?"

"He needs to reconsider his position. Look, it's nothing serious. We all do this from time to time, to reconnect our bond with the Triune."

Nellie was really starting to dislike this man. Avoiding her questions and making out like Shepherd Adrianus had done something wrong. She knew she should probably give up, but she wanted to show that Shepherd Adrianus had supporters. She straightened her back.

"Well, I hope he comes back soon, because he's a very good man. He always looks after the poor people. We all like him very much."

"That's very nice to know, child. The church makes their own decisions, however. But I can ask the shepherd if he will take it into consideration."

And then Nellie left because there was nothing more to say. She had her answer.

If the church appreciated good men, they would not send shepherd Adrianus away.

She had no more excuse. She would need to act. And that meant a lot of things she dreaded doing, but they had to be done.

While walking through the city, she felt cold and inadequate. She was just Nellie, a kitchen maid, always a servant to someone else. She had put into motion this ridiculous plan, but did she really have the skill to carry it out? She knew she would have to do it, because many people had pinned their hopes on it. For one, Jantien's children deserved their mother back.

But inside she felt so small and useless. She was old, she was a woman, not even someone's mother. She had no family left in the city. She was utterly alone, and all the people who had tried to help her, people like Henrik and Dora, she had rejected.

While she walked, tears welled into eyes, blurring her vision.

She would *not* cry. She would *not* give in. She would come back and clear the suspicion that hung over her.

She jammed her hands deeper in her pockets, trying to keep the emotion inside.

The bottom line was, she was no hero. She was just Nellie, who would serve the dinners and clean the rooms and pick up everybody's laundry and hang it out and take it inside when it rained and feed the pigs and the chickens and whatever else needed to be fed.

That had been her life.

This thing called freedom didn't sit well with her.

While she walked, she noticed from the corner of her eye that a trail of sparks followed her.

Had the dragon turned back to his magical form?

When she looked at them, the sparks vanished. And then when she kept walking, they reappeared.

She stopped in the entrance of an alley between two houses.

The sparks crept up the wall next to her.

"If you're going to follow me around, can you at least do something useful?"

The sparks detached from the wall, twirled through

the air and settled on her coat. Nellie tried to brush them off.

What was this?

But then the sparks touched the bare skin of her hand and filled her with warmth.

The dragon couldn't speak. But because she had forgiven him, he wanted to help her. He seemed to want to let her know that he cared and would be there for her.

Fate had brought them together, and he hadn't forgotten that he had regained freedom because of her.

She had to be strong.

When she came to the market place, a crowd of people stood at the steps to the church door.

Someone had affixed another declaration to the door of the church.

Nellie already knew what it was before she could hear the yelling and shouting. Sixteen people were to be drowned in the harbour in two days' time for engaging in witchcraft.

"They're almost all women," a man shouted. "How dare he drown mothers and daughters and wives?"

"What about giving us the time to prove their innocence?"

"It's the mayor's fault."

"Down with the mayor."

Nellie wrestled her way through the crowd until she could read the names on the list. They included Jantien, Josie, Emmie, Yolande and Wim.

Behind her, the crowd in the market square was getting more agitated. A couple of guards had come in, and people yelled at them.

"My son was accused of stealing," a man called out. "He's done nothing wrong."

Others agreed and added their grievances.

This was getting nasty. These people would be talking to each other in the taverns and they would organise themselves into angry mobs that the guards would have to deal with unless they could bring in enough men to scare the citizens.

When the sentence was carried out, there was sure to be a large crowd watching. That could be a good thing, or they could get in the way.

In the barn, the women had attracted a few more sea cows to the shallow part of the water so that they could lure them into the harness. This required one person to stand in the water. One of the children was attempting to attach the harness to the creatures while another fed them carrots.

"How is it going?" Nellie asked.

"We've got three so far," Mina said, standing at the quayside with a handful of carrots.

That was better than last time, but still not enough. They had two days to get this part of the plan in order.

With Nellie's help they managed to catch another two more animals. Nellie also helped pack up some oiled sheets they would use to cover themselves. The shields were all ready, and Floris the fisherman would bring the boat around tonight.

Some of the children had been watching the Guentherite order's ship, and had found that people visited it during the day to deliver or pick up things, but that there was generally no one on board overnight.

"But one thing you haven't yet mentioned," Mina said. "Where are we going to go after we escape?"

"There's a farm on the other side of the delta," Nellie said. "I know some people there who have an apple orchard. We can offer to work in return for staying in their barn."

"But that land floods all the time. I know, I have a cousin who lives there, and they sometimes have to move out and can't get to the house for weeks. Winter and spring are the worst."

"If the weather is bad, we might go up the river," Nellie said. "There is a village where my cousins live."

Now Hilde said, "Last I heard, that area was unsafe, because of bandits."

"Yes," Agatha said. "I don't want to escape the city just so we run into bandits. They are not nice people."

Mina said, "You win prizes for stating the obvious."

"Well, it's true," Agatha said. "This adventure is already the most ridiculous thing I have taken part in. I don't want to make it any more ridiculous by putting ourselves and the children into any more danger than necessary."

"I will find a way to see which place is safe." Nellie said. Add that to the long list of things she had to do.

"How are you going to do that?" Agatha said. Her voice sounded suspicious.

"I will ask some people."

"People with magic."

"Yes. Do you see another way?"

She snorted. "Magic got us into the trouble we're in. If there hadn't been any magic—" She glared at the door to the storeroom where presumably the dragon lay sleeping. "—then none of this would have happened. I've tried to shield my children from magic so that they don't become victims of this witch hunt, and you're undoing all my efforts."

There were many things Nellie could say. That Anneke was born with magic and it would come out whether Agatha shielded her or not. That she needed a magical person to talk to her about it, not to be shielded from it. But unless Agatha could see that for herself, Nellie would be wasting her breath.

She knew. She had been like Agatha for much of her life.

CHAPTER 17

BUT WHO SHOULD Nellie see to ask about safe places?

She didn't care much where they went after they escaped. She had dealt with bandits before. They usually moved in small groups and were easily distracted. If the plan succeeded, their group would number more than thirty, which made it too big to be an easy target for cheap thieves.

But she understood that Agatha wanted assurance—which could only be given by a magician.

There was a time that Nellie had known a wind magician. He used to work for Mistress Johanna's father, then he had become a shepherd of the church and last she heard he had left the city to study religion in the holy southern city of Senoza, which was the most holy place of the Belaman Church.

Nellie didn't want to go back to Mistress Julianna if she could avoid it because the old woman frightened her. She would talk about predictions again and imply that Nellie should hand the dragon over to people who knew what to do with him, and try to make her feel guilty for not giving him up.

Most of the other people who had magic had left town.

So she went to see Gisele because she might know other people with magic that Nellie didn't know about. She needed to talk to Gisele anyway.

She found Gisele at the table in the middle of the warehouse, busy filling bottles with clear fluid from a metal jug. She looked up when Nellie came in.

"Oh, Nellie. This is a coincidence. I wanted to come and see you. You remember when we last talked about poisoned gin?"

Nellie nodded, although that seemed such a long time ago.

Gisele continued, "I was just handed a bottle that has contained a magical substance." She set down her jug and picked up an old bottle that sat on the side of the table.

Nellie recognised it. It was the old square bottle she had seen in Lord Verdonck's room, complete with the goat on the label.

"That's the one. Who gave it to you?"

"It came from Mr Oliver, who sells to the palace. Every week, he collects empty jars and bottles so he can refill them. He puts the ones that are not from his business in a crate out the side door of his shop. We get a lot of our bottles there."

Yes, it was definitely the one.

"So, if the goat label doesn't belong to him, then whose is it?"

"That's the strange thing, because it does belong to him, I found out. I saw a bottle of wine in one of the taverns, and I asked the owner whose it was, and he said the label belongs to the Guentherite order and they get Mr. Oliver to handle the bottling and labelling for them."

"Then why was the bottle out in the box?"

Gisele shrugged. "A mistake?"

Or they knew this bottle was trouble and wanted to be rid of it. But then they could as easily have smashed it, or at least taken the label off.

"How do you know there was magic in this bottle?"

"I found a test in an obscure book that says how quicksilver is repelled by magic."

"And you have quicksilver around?" Nellie thought that was the domain of the alchemists.

"It's an ingredient in some of the things we use."

Nellie was tempted to ask what things and whether she was an alchemist, but the time for these sorts of silly games of judgement were over. Her father had been very strong on judging people according to a set of rigid rules, only to find his core belief shaken.

So instead of all the things she could have asked, she said, "How true is this test?"

"Do you want to see it?"

Without waiting for the reply, Gisele brought a shallow porcelain dish that contained a small amount of silver liquid that jiggled and shimmered as she moved. Nellie looked at it with fascination. She had heard of the fabled quicksilver, but had never seen it.

"Don't look at it like that. It's not scary, it's just a metal, but it's liquid. Like water is hard when it is frozen, and then you make it warmer and it becomes a liquid."

"Does this quicksilver ever become solid so we can build things out of it?"

"Some of the great alchemists say quicksilver is the base of all metals and that it can be formed into any other metal, but Rinius says their structures are different. He refers to the silver mines of Senoza where people use quicksilver to get the silver out of the stone, and that this may be the basis for the rumour. He says that, like all substances, quicksilver will become a hard material, but it may need to be so cold we couldn't survive to see it."

And now it dawned on Nellie. "You're a student of Rinius."

"Well, not him, because he's been dead far too long, but he had some followers, most of all his son, Fabrice, who is maybe even brighter than his father. They have a house south of Lurezia where the greatest students of nature, men and women, live and study to figure out how things work by experimentation. Some people will call this magic, but really it is not, because magic depends on the ability of people, and this does not. They call it science. You might know about it."

Nellie had heard the word science, but her knowledge went little beyond that. "Aren't magic and science the same thing?"

"No. Magic is part of science but science is much more than magic." She walked to the other side of the bench to collect the glass bottle. "Anyway, look at this."

She set the bottle in the middle of the dish with the quicksilver. And all the silvery liquid crept to the sides.

Nellie frowned. "Why is it doing that?"

"Magic repels quicksilver."

"How do you know that magic is doing it?"

"Well, if you didn't believe me, look at what happens with this bottle."

She took the bottle out and put one of the ones that stood on the workbench in. The bottom of the glass dipped into the silvery liquid.

"I guess it would be on my say-so that this is caused by magic, but you would have to agree that the two are different, right? They're both empty bottles."

Yes. "They're both made of glass?"

"Better than that, they were both made by the same glassblower who has a business in town. We can ask him because he is one of the few craftspeople who have not left. He makes bottles, simple objects, and does not use magic for his craft."

Nellie looked at the first bottle with the goat label, wondering how this would stand up as proof that the poison had been in the gin and that it was magical poison, in a country where magic was forbidden. No one would believe her, an old woman, who didn't even have any magical ability herself.

"How does one put magic in gin?"

"You can do it in a couple of different ways. You can infuse gin with a magical object, that is, if you have an object that's powerful enough and small enough to fit inside a container so you can cover it with gin. Or you can distil the gin with magical herbs. Since Mr Oliver's brother made the gin, he definitely didn't do the latter, so someone has infused the gin with a magical object after they bought it at Mr Oliver's store. Before you ask, no I don't know what kind of object. It can't be too big, obviously, but it also needs to be powerful. I guess an amulet or relic of some description. Mind you, you might need to ask a magician."

"You mean you're not a magician?"

"I guess I'm something close to a magician. I'm an anti-magician. I can feel and see magic, but I don't have any of it."

She also had a very good memory.

Nellie had started out distrusting Gisele because she was so strange and unlike any woman she had ever met before. But now she was finding her very useful.

She took a deep breath before starting on the second reason she had come here. "I have to ask you something."

"Oh?" Gisele's eyebrows flicked up.

"You said someone lived in the crypts, and I'm pretty sure that it's Prince Bruno. I want to free him."

"You? How? First you'd have to—"

"I have to tell you something. I have a secret. I didn't tell you before because I didn't know whether you would betray me."

"That is always a good position to take for people like us."

"People like us?"

"People interested in unmasking the wrongs of the world, no matter how powerful they are."

Yes, Nellie thought with trepidation. That was her new situation. And then she realised that there was another word for people like Gisele: heretics. And that filled her with even more trepidation. Especially since these appeared to be the only people who, while the men of the church were fighting for power, appeared to be doing something for the good of all.

So, although it frightened her, she was stuck with these people and the fear the shepherds liked to spread about them. Nellie wasn't a heretic, because those people had lost their belief. She had lost the belief that the current leaders of the church were good people. That was different from being a heretic, wasn't it?

"Last time when I saw you, I asked you about the things that the church hides in the crypt."

"That was because of your father, wasn't it?"

"Yes, it was, because he worked for the church. But there was one thing I didn't tell you. When I got my father's box with his book of notes just recently, there was a key in the bottom. It is in fact the key to the metal door in the grate at the end of the crypt. I went in there. I saw the things they keep down there, so I knew you were speaking the truth about them, about the ruby skull and the octagonal space in the dust."

Gisele's eyes widened.

"Well, I'm with a group of women and children who

are planning a quite ridiculous operation, when you hear all about it. But we want to leave the city afterwards, and it makes sense that we take as many people as possible. If it's true that the young Prince Bruno is locked up in the crypt, I would like to take him. Then I can return his dragon to him."

Gisele started laughing and didn't stop laughing for nearly a minute.

Nellie felt increasingly embarrassed. She was already sorry that she had mentioned this. "If it is such a ridiculous idea, I will carry it out myself."

"No, it is one of the most amazing ideas I have ever heard. If you can carry that out, it will be the best thing ever. I would love to see the looks on the faces of the Regent and the shepherd."

"Does that mean you'll help me?"

"Of course I will."

"Then come with me tomorrow night and we'll go into the crypt."

Gisele agreed that she would do that, and they made arrangements.

Then Nellie asked, "Since you know about things that happen in the church, do you know what has happened to Shepherd Adrianus?"

"Many people are talking about it." Gisele's expression was dark. "I've only heard the rumours. He was said to have disagreed with the Shepherd Wilfridus and was punished and sent away from the city. Someone else has taken his church."

"Yes, I went to see him, but he was no longer there. Where is he?"

"I presume he has been sent to a monastery somewhere outside the city to pay for his sins."

"But he was only trying to protect people."

"That is not how these men of power think. Anyone

who threatens their position is an enemy, church or not. If anything, it is even worse in the church, because people don't expect it and don't look for it. But all these monks and all these priests are constantly at each other's throats. Mind you, they have nothing else to do. If they don't see the whores, and a lot of them truly don't, all they can do is fight with each other and attempt to enrich themselves at the cost of the others. To be a monk can be a hard life. Some of these monasteries are doing very well, and it is not because they're being nice to anyone."

Nellie felt ashamed for having judged her father badly because he had seen what was happening. "And I am guessing that one of the things they do is dabble with magic?"

"I haven't personally seen this, but I'm sure you're right."

"Then why do they tell the Regent to get rid of everyone who has magic?"

"It's simple, really. It is so that they can control the most powerful magicians in this area. This city is like a blank canvas. There has never been much magic here, only a few people who dabble in it, but things are changing. Magic lines are never stable, and they're moving into this region. And a lot of people want to make sure they get their share of power once magic moves into Saardam."

"Is that why the church put the Regent in place?"

"It's why they chose him. There were a lot of other contenders for the position, but the church chose the one least likely to pose a threat to their power. Now they are using him as a tool to get rid of anyone who can point out the hypocrisy of preaching against magic while also learning magic."

"Didn't they make the excuse that in order to learn about a thing, you need to study it?"

"That's their official excuse, but many people aren't

buying it anymore. Anyone with magic knows it's a blatant ploy to get rid of all magicians in the city. To what aim, we can speculate, but *to keep the city safe* is certainly not one of the possibilities."

"Which is why it's so hard to find a wind magician. I need to know which is a safe place to hide after we leave the city. People say there are a lot of problems with bandits upriver."

"Not half as much as they make it out to be."

"What do you mean?"

"I travelled down the river."

"On that beautiful boat?"

Gisele laughed. "No, that's only for important people attending the banquet. We came with a coach and horses from the monastery. It's a good two-day journey."

"You didn't see any bandits?"

"The only ones I've heard of are small groups of youths that are not terribly harmful. They will steal things if they can get away with it, in particular horses, but they're not interested in occupying land or killing people. The threat is much blown up by people who have an interest in keeping the citizens in the city."

"But I still need to tell the women in my group that the river and the riverbanks are safe. I need someone who is a wind magician, and the local magicians have all left town."

"Oh, there are still some good ones. Some of the people in the Science Guild are magicians. There'll be a meeting of that group tonight. Feel welcome to come as long as you can keep silent. The meeting will be of magical and non-magical people, and they mostly talk about science. But there will be someone there who can answer your questions and I'm sure they'll be happy to see you there as a true child of your father's."

"My father?"

"He was one of the founding members of the Science Guild. I presumed you knew."

No, she didn't know. Her father never told her or her mother anything. With the book she had received, a universe about his life had opened to her.

Walking back home, Nellie thought she had finally dug through all the layers of her father's message. Having thrown himself into church life in his younger years, when the Church of the Triune riled against the display of riches and the cruelty of the magic of the Belaman Church, her father had seen the new church become just as cruel and corrupt as the organisation it sought to replace. The break between the Church of the Triune and the Belaman Church was not as complete as people suggested. They shared many beliefs and customs. People went to Senoza for pilgrimage and study. In fact, they even still shared some of the monasteries. The Guentherite order accepted young men from both churches.

So her father became disillusioned when the shepherd showed more interest than he thought was wise in old church relics and obscure, forbidden books. The virtue that mattered most to her father was honesty and transparency. None of this secret, hush-hush stuff. He loved numbers because numbers never lied.

Her father had become a heretic which, finally, made her understand why he had so angrily refused visits from anyone from the church in his final years.

CHAPTER 18

GISELE TOLD NELLIE where to go for the Science Guild meeting that night, and Nellie was nervous. It sounded all secret and mysterious.

Nellie's apprehension was not made any better when she heard Gisele would not be going. She had monk duties to fulfil. "I already spend so much time doing other things. I need to attend the weekly service for giving thanks. If I'm not at the church, there will be talk."

Nellie understood, but it didn't make her feel any easier about meeting a room full of strangers by herself.

Gisele told her the names of some of the people who would be there, but Nellie didn't know any of them personally, and there were even some people whose names she had never heard. They sounded like important businessmen.

As to what they normally spoke about, Gisele said, "They report on experiments with new knowledge and techniques. The people of all the low countries were very much upset back when the Eastern Traders came into our harbours with their iron ships. But they have to be careful because the Regent forbids magic and science is closely related to magic. The people in the guild are in search of the ultimate truth. The iron ships are not powered by magic. They consist of parts that can be made to work when they are put together in the right way. The Science Guild is about finding this way to make better machines."

Nellie knew about the iron ships. She had been there when the ugly square ship with the fat masts that belched smoke came into the harbour. She remembered how everyone wanted to buy those ships, but the eastern traders weren't selling anything except the produce they carried. So everyone tried to build their own ships, and this led to disasters more often than not.

"But magicians will come to the meeting?"

"Not all of them will be magicians, but some will be."

The meeting was to take place in a house in the artisan quarter that was a block away from the main street, and not too far from where Mistress Julianna lived. In fact, to get there, Nellie had to walk past Mistress Julianna's house.

She wondered if people like Mistress Julianna would be members of this group, because she still didn't quite understand what they did. And her father had been a founding member?

As she came near the house, she noticed a number of other people walking in the same direction.

All of them looked like ordinary citizens, and she even recognised some of them. They were shop owners and craftsmen who plied trades. One man she knew was a carpenter, and he was in the company of the very carpenter who had made the beam for the harness.

HE GREETED NELLIE. "I wasn't expecting you here tonight."

"A friend said that I should come."

They went into a narrow alley that led past the back of the houses. In a little alcove at the end of the alley was another sight that Nellie knew well. A horse stood tied to a fence post. But it was not just any horse. This one was a beautiful grey stallion with dappled fur, a long white mane and fetlocks, and blue eyes. She knew this horse. It belonged to madame Sabine.

"Is the Regent's consort here?"

"She is our most influential member. Didn't you know that?"

Nellie didn't. She hadn't asked, and Gisele hadn't told her. She hesitated at the top of a flight of stairs that led to the door into a basement room where the stream of people were entering. The carpenter went ahead and she lost sight of him.

Did she still want to go to this meeting when the only person who knew that she had stolen the dragon box was in attendance? Of course, Madame Sabine could easily have betrayed Nellie. She hadn't, because it would mean admitting that she or someone working for her had taken the box from the church in the first place. She hadn't, because it would shine the light on her own activities that no one knew about, which no doubt included coming here, because there was no way the Regent could know about this. If he did, he would never keep quiet about it.

Which meant it was probably safe to continue.

A group of people walked past her, down the stairs into the house. Nellie followed them.

The room looked like it had been a servants' kitchen in times past, but it had been a long time since any respectable family lived in this house. The wallpaper was peeling from the walls, and in parts the plaster had come off to reveal the brickwork underneath. Dark stains marked the ceiling, and the tiles felt gritty under her feet.

But there was a warm fire in the hearth, a wooden table stood in the middle of the room and several people sat around it on a collection of mismatched chairs, hard benches or wine barrels. In the low light, most of them were mere silhouettes, but Nellie recognised none other than madame Sabine, her round-cheeked face gilded by the torchlight. She wore her hair tied up at the back of her head and had again dressed in men's riding trousers and a man's shirt.

When Nellie came in, she looked up, met her eyes and smiled. Nellie wasn't sure whether it was a friendly or an evil smile.

There was some banter between the people in the room and the new arrivals, and someone directed Nellie to a place on the bench.

As soon as she sat down, madame Sabine got up and walked around the table. She came quite close, leaning over Nellie so she could almost feel the warmth of her body and was enveloped in the smell of her perfume.

"Fancy seeing you here."

"I was invited."

"Is that so?"

Nellie straightened her back. "Just in case you don't know, Cornelius Dreessen, who I've learned has started this group, was my father."

Madame Sabine's eyes widened briefly. "So that's where you get your impertinent nature."

"I'm not interested in playing games. I want only the truth."

Madame Sabine laughed. "Still so naïve. Where is the dragon?"

"I let him go."

"You—what?"

"I opened the box and set him free, so that he can go back to the east, where he belongs."

"So that its power is lost to all of us? You *stupid* maid."

"The dragon is still around, but he isn't interested in letting people experiment with him."

"You know *nothing* about it."

"I know that he flies well."

Madame Sabine grabbed the front of Nellie's coat. She met Nellie's eyes, nostrils flaring. "I know you still have it. We have other ways of getting what we want."

Nellie coolly yanked her coat out of Madame Sabine's grip. "You can't treat me like that. I am no longer your servant."

"I will remember that. In my book, servants of the court are afforded protection by the family they work for. I will be happy to acknowledge that does not apply to you."

"You could have told your husband some story that 'proved' I stole the dragon, but you didn't. To me, that means you're hiding activities you don't want him to know about. Does he know you're here?"

"How dare you talk to me like that?"

"I respect people who are worthy of respect. Like my father. He wasn't a very *nice* person, but he never did anything dishonest."

Madame Sabine gave her a hard stare but made no reply. She whirled around and went back to her seat.

The man next to her quickly turned away from her to mask the fact that he had been staring at the interaction between her and Madame Sabine.

Her heart was still thudding. It was obvious: she had become more than *just* Nellie the maid. People knew her and watched her. It was a scary and exhilarating thought.

Nellie looked around.

She was surprised that she knew a lot more people than she thought she would. She recognised the faces of a baker, and the two carpenters she had seen before, a tailor, the cheese-maker, and many other people who provided trades in the city. Many of them she had not seen for a while because they had stopped coming to the markets.

A few more people came in after Nellie did, and more chairs were being carried in from somewhere deeper within the house.

The man at the head of the table was Master Beck, a tall grey-haired man who kept counting the people in the room. He was the head teacher at the city's College of Knowledge, a place where nobles and rich merchants sent their sons to be taught to write beautifully and without mistakes, to manage a company's accounts, the basics of the Burovian language and other things that noble sons needed to know.

Eventually, Master Beck was happy that everyone was present, and he began.

"Welcome to our meeting tonight. As you see, we have a visitor here today, invited by our friend Gerard who unfortunately couldn't make it tonight. Why don't you introduce yourself?" He looked at Nellie.

Nellie gulped. This didn't fall under *keeping quiet*. Had Gisele known this would happen? Did these people even know that their *Gerard* was a woman?

She steeled herself.

"My name is Nellie. I lived and worked with Queen Johanna since she was a little girl. You will be familiar with my father, Cornelius Dreessen."

There were several gasps around the room. A few people looked at her with an interest they hadn't shown before.

Madame Sabine gave her a foul look.

"It is an honour to have you here," a man across the table said. His hair was white and his eyebrows were fashioned into horns.

Nellie thought he was an account keeper with one of the major importing companies.

"Your father was a dear friend," another man said. Nellie remembered him vaguely from a time he and she had been much younger.

Several people who hadn't noticed Nellie before turned to her and nodded or greeted her.

Madame Sabine said in a prim voice, "Nellie has made a bit of a name for herself, because she left the palace in the company of our elusive dragon."

Several people nodded. The gossip about her had obviously spread.

Had the dragon been part of this group's experiments? Had Lord Verdonck been a member, too?

"You didn't bring the creature?" Master Beck asked, meeting Nellie's eyes.

"He's not mine. He doesn't obey me."

"It's dangerous."

"Not if you don't try to harm him, or the things he cares about."

A man laughed. "Whatever does a dragon care about?"

"He likes children and animals. He will protect those."

"That's the most ridiculous thing I've heard." The speaker was an old man with a big bushy beard.

"Who should he listen to, then?" Nellie asked him.

He missed the cynical tone of her voice. "It will obey a proper magician. A dragon is a strong magical creature. You will need magical artefacts to control it."

"You speak as if you know everything about dragons. Do you have experience?" She thought of the scratches on Madame Sabine's back.

"I have studied dragons in the literature."

"With a real dragon?"

He gave her a what-do-you-think look. "They're dangerous creatures."

"They are dangerous only if you try to harm them or the things that are dear to them."

The man snorted.

Nellie said, "As I have already said, the dragon doesn't listen to anyone. He does as he pleases. I believe he may only obey the rightful owner, but none of us."

Now the man turned to her, his expression somewhat annoyed. "Do you have any magic of any kind?"

"Of course I don't." Nellie's cheeks grew warm.

He spread his hands. "Well, there you have it. That's why the dragon won't listen to you. If you were to pass it to us, we could make it obey."

"The dragon chose to stay with me. He hasn't tried to attack me or the children or any of the animals that we have with us. I can give him to you, but it is up to the dragon to accept a master."

It was Prince Bruno's dragon, and of course he would never listen to just anyone who said they owned him by paying money for the box.

Master Beck said, "I would strongly urge you to let us try to gain control of it. If you showed us where it is, one of us could accompany you to entice the dragon to come with us. We, the entire city, are in dire need of it, now that the fire dog prowls the streets at night. We can cope with the guards and their raids to obtain every little magical trinket in this town, things that were never much use to us anyway. But now we have bigger concerns, and we should use everything in our power. We need this dragon to fight evil."

There were and a lot of nods around the room.

A feeling of frustration came over Nellie. No matter how many times she said that the dragon didn't listen, they still believed that they could control him. Well, look at what had happened to Madame Sabine when she tried.

She was sick of these people. Science Guild or Church,

they were all the same: only after fame and riches for themselves, over the head of a dumb kitchen maid. But, if they didn't want to believe her, maybe they should learn their own lesson. This kitchen maid was not going to take this without getting her own fair share of the bargain.

She said, "Much as you will be surprised to hear this, I have no use for a dragon. I am happy just to take my friends to safety. If you can help me leave the city, I am happy to hand the dragon on to you, providing that you will look after him and that he will be treated properly."

Madame Sabine's eyes widened. Oh no, she didn't buy it.

Master Beck asked, "So what do you want in return?"

"I live with a number of women who have lost their husbands, and children who have lost their parents. We have very little, especially for the children. We could use food and winter clothing and blankets. I also want the advice of a wind magician."

"For what?" a man asked. His voice sounded suspicious.

"We're planning to leave the city as soon as the weather turns warmer and the roads are open. I want to know where the bandits are."

"Is that all?" Master Beck said.

Madame Sabine shot him a furious glance. Oh, she wanted that dragon, just as badly as Nellie wanted to keep him out of her hands.

And Nellie grew even bolder. "We could use a cart and a horse, and a crate of liquor, wine, beer or gin, to bribe the guards."

"That's asking a lot. The horse and the cart, I hand you that, but getting the guards to look the other way? That amounts to treason."

"Someone else has made that offer to me."

His eyes narrowed. "Who, if I may ask?"

"I bet it's that witch Julianna or her wayfarer friend,"

someone said behind Nellie. "I heard a story that a councillor's wife got the most terrible skin rash from a concoction that was said to have been made with dragon excrement."

Oh, the glory. Nellie had suspected that Julianna and Zelda might be friends. Here was her evidence.

"She didn't say her name," Nellie said.

"And you would give a magical creature to someone who doesn't give you her name?"

"I didn't say that. I said I'd had an offer. I have to think of the women and children in my group and I'll take the best deal. I don't think you can handle the dragon anyway, but if you will give me things in return for a free creature, then I'll take the best deal."

"We want the box, you stupid woman," Madame Sabine said.

"The dragon is not in the box."

"Give us the box, and the dragon will come."

"I don't have it with me. I can bring it when I see you fulfil your side of the bargain."

"How do we even know it's the real box?" the man opposite Nellie said. "She could be trying to lead us all astray."

"Heavens, she is Cornelius' daughter. Will you lay off it?" Master Beck said. "Or would you rather that she gives this treasure to the witches who will do goodness knows what with it?"

Silence. A few men shook their heads.

"What do you intend to do with a dragon?" Nellie asked.

"Study it, and use it to fight the fire dog. And learn about magic because that study has been sadly neglected in this city."

Despite the greed in this group, Nellie trusted Master Beck's intentions. It was tempting to agree, because a rogue dragon might cause all kinds of problems for her, but there were many reasons she couldn't give in.

She asked, "What do you think these witches would do with him?"

"It's hard to say. There are many possibilities. Already, one of them has been peddling 'products' based on the dragon. They might continue to extort people who have money and really should know better, or they may do a range of other things, including selling the box to people we definitely don't want to gain control over it."

"Such as?"

"King Leopold, Baron Uti's family."

No. Nellie shuddered, thinking of the round-waisted, big-bearded baron, who already had far too much dark magic at his court. If she had to pick between giving the dragon to him, or to Master Beck or Zelda, there was no choice. But the dragon wasn't hers to give.

A merchant said, "I could bring blankets and child's clothing. I have no more use for those now that my children have grown up."

"I can spare a cart," said another.

Oh, they wanted this dragon. Their naked greed was ugly.

Then another man said, "If you had any wind magic, you'd know that the stories about bandits are highly exaggerated. Yes, there are some rogues, but not nearly as many as the palace wants us to believe."

Nellie found the speaker at the other end of the table. "Are you a wind magician?"

"I am. I can tell you which places are the safest."

Another man said, "With regard to this dragon, I have a worry. I say we keep everyone relating to the creature within the city walls, including this woman. We will give her some food and blankets and shelter them if they want, but I am not happy to let them leave the city. We may need her later on."

A few people made noises in agreement.

Nellie hated how these people kept talking over her head. "Excuse me, but what would you need me for?"

Master Beck said, "Do you know anything about dragons?"

"Aside from having lived with one?"

"Do you know about their biology? About their needs?"

Nellie's cheeks grew hot. She hadn't even figured out what the dragon ate.

From the other side of the table an older man said, "We cannot judge her like this. She's unaware of the knowledge we have." He looked at Nellie. "In the lands in the far east, dragons appear in times of great need, when towns are threatened by evil. There are many stories of towns and even great cities saved by the appearance of a dragon. Each town has a dragon magician who can use dragon stones to summon the beast to the defence of the people."

Nellie was wondering where he got this information. These learned people always seem to be so certain of themselves.

As far as she understood, dragon magic was a type of artisan magic, just like wood magic or water magic. And children with magic in the east received a box which they then filled with a magical object, like a tree or a dragon. And as far as she knew, the thing in the box only protected its owner in extreme need.

These people were just full of nonsense. They made it sound like they knew what was going on, but if there was any science in this group, it had long since been overtaken by politics and scheming.

They didn't know what dragons were for. Whatever

Madame Sabine had done to the dragon, it was not how dragons were meant to be treated.

These people wanted to keep her here, because they were afraid of handling the dragon, and they wanted control over him at the same time.

These people knew nothing.

She thought of just giving them the empty dragon box in return for food and clothing, but that would be deceitful, and she did not like that at all. In the end, they could flee the city without extra food and clothes, and she had the information she needed. She left them with the illusion that she was desperate for their help, and sat quietly while the members of the group discussed the uses of a dragon against the fire dog—seriously, did they really think that spreading "dragon stones" around the city was going to help? These stones looked suspiciously like river pebbles.

Nellie said she'd think about their offer. She had the information she needed about the safety of leaving the city, and no one had yet offered the horse she had asked for, although Master Beck said procuring it wouldn't be a problem.

Soon enough, the conversation moved to different subjects.

A woman set a wooden box on the table and proceeded to hand out little satchels to all the members. This happened without many words, and without discussing the contents.

Nellie asked her neighbour what the satchels contained, and he said they held pills that kept the mind clear when one was threatened with magic.

One of the men had travelled to Lurezia to study some phenomenon of the sky and gave a lengthy talk about it. He set a wooden box on the table and unpacked a selection of instruments from it and explained how one could use the instruments to determine the position of stars in the sky.

The talk was rather boring. Nellie was tired, and it was stuffy in the room. She had trouble keeping awake and wished she could leave.

CHAPTER 19

IT WAS GETTING LATE, and people were still talking.

Nellie's eyes were gritty with fatigue. She was looking for a way to leave the gathering, because she had the information she needed, she wanted to avoid making any further agreement about giving the dragon to these people, and she had quite a long way to go back to the barn. The talk about the fire dog prowling the streets had made her nervous. She wasn't normally prone to seeing things in the dark, but she had seen this creature before and knew it wasn't a trick of her mind.

In the middle of a discussion, one man in the group got up. He walked to the window and looked out. Because they were on a level below the street, the window existed for little more than letting in light from a tiny sunken courtyard.

He then went to the door and opened it. A blast of cold air came in.

Several people shouted at him to keep the door shut.

"Whatever is going on?" Master Beck asked, casting an annoyed look at the door.

"I thought I heard something," the man said.

He left the basement—still leaving the door open—went up the stairs to the street level. A moment later, he called out, "Come up here. Look at this."

A couple of the men ran to the door and up the stairs.

Nellie looked for her coat. It was really getting cold in here.

Voices drifted down from the street.

Most of the people now left the table and were putting on their coats, grumbling about the cold air streaming into the room.

The fire roared in the hearth, making Nellie realise how stuffy the air had been.

More people went to the door. Nellie followed, having put on her coat, wondering what all the fuss was about.

She was halfway up the steps outside when the most terrible screeching howl echoed over the city.

Men in the street shouted.

A number of people came running down the stairs. They were men who had been at the meeting and other citizens, trying to get into the safety of the basement. The press of bodies swept Nellie down until she most fell. A fierce orange glow came from the right.

Someone shouted, "It's the fire dog!"

People screamed.

Madame Sabine's horse let out a screaming whinny, followed by a snap and the thundering of hooves.

Nellie scrambled inside the basement in the throng of people trying to get to safety. The last person shut the door and bolted it.

Someone put the damper over the fire, and the moment it went out a waft of cold air went through the room.

Another person blew out the candles, so they were sitting in the pitch dark, not knowing what was going on.

No one spoke.

Nellie sat at the table. She listened for sounds from outside, but it was quiet as death.

"Has it gone?" a man asked after a while.

"Sounded like the horse has bolted," someone else said in the dark.

"He will come back." That was Madame Sabine.

Someone opened the door, showing a faint strip of light coming in from a street lamp outside.

Nellie said to the man next to her, "Isn't anyone going to fight this creature?" Some of these people were magicians. If anyone could fight it, they could.

"Fight it? Anyone who tries would be defeated straight away. We need someone who is more than an artisan magician. But there are none left to defend the city."

"It's time to call an official end to this gathering," Master Beck said somewhere in the darkness. "We should all go back home and keep our families safe. We'll investigate this woman's dragon, because it alone has the power to defeat the fire dog."

Except the dragon was afraid of the fire dog.

The door opened further and one of the men went up the steps again, and a moment later voices drifted in from outside.

"Who is he talking to?" someone asked.

A man came in carrying an oil lamp from elsewhere in the house and used it to light a candle.

"There are guards out there," a man said in the dark part of the room where Nellie couldn't see him. "I doubt they're here to take on the fire dog. They probably haven't seen it, and are still in their ridiculous quest to find small time magic while the big magic has free rein."

Another said, "I would love to see them try. They would be burnt to a crisp."

"They would be running for their mothers," another man added.

And someone else said, "That will teach the Regent that he will need magicians to protect him."

Madame Sabine got up. "It's time to go home."

"Be careful of the guards. They arrested a lot of people around here."

"They wouldn't dare to touch us," Madame Sabine said. "They are my husband's men, terrified of me, and to be honest, most of them are not very smart."

She went into an adjacent room where people had dumped their winter coats.

A couple of men's voices sounded outside, and the next moment a group of men came down the steps into the cellar. They were city guards, at least ten.

One of the guild members quickly whipped a book off the table and stuck it in his pocket.

"Good evening," the patrol leader said.

There were some nods, but no one replied.

"We're looking for any magic or magical objects in this building," the patrol leader continued into the silence.

"We don't have any," said a man.

"Why don't you check the magic beast that just crossed us in the street," the merchant said. "We were having a business meeting here, and all of a sudden there was this terrible sound outside. We went to check, and found a giant dog, completely made of fire like the fire demons of old. You would be wise going after that thing and trying to catch it. It's going to set the entire city on fire."

"We didn't see it and haven't heard of anything like that. Trying to mislead a member of the guard with the intention to deceive is a criminal offence."

The merchant spread his hands. "I'm telling you the truth! I saw it."

A few men tried to shush him.

One of the guards walked to the table where the box with astronomical instruments still stood from the earlier demonstration.

"Show us what all these items are for."

He upset the entire box of instruments. Metal stands, lenses, boxes of dials and calculus frames clattered over the table.

"Hey, careful with that!" The owner lunged after a metal tube that was in danger of rolling on the floor.

"Show us what magic all this stuff does."

"That has nothing to do with magic," the man said. "These instruments are to watch the stars and to plot their course through the sky."

"We already know the course of the stars through the sky. All the stars and celestial objects appear in the east at night, and they set in the West, just like the sun except that they're on the night canvas. There is no need for all this ridiculous stuff. This is alchemy and magic."

"I can assure you, it's not. I can explain what we're all doing, but it's late, and that creature that is out there is not going to be friendly if it finds any of us by ourselves on the street."

Several people had moved to the door, but the guards blocked the way out of the basement.

One shouted, "In the name of the Regent everybody stay inside."

"In the name of what Regent?" came Madame Sabine's voice.

She emerged from the other room, where she had retrieved her coat of thick, light-grey fur with a luscious cover that sat snugly around her neck. She looked positively regal compared to the frumpy merchants who wore many layers of clothing like stuffed sausages.

Nellie expected the guards to be surprised, but they

were not. They didn't even show any sign that they had recognised her.

"What is all this about?" Madame Sabine asked.

The patrol leader said, "We have it on good information that meetings take place here every week about magic and heresy."

"Well, just the fact I am here proves those rumours wrong, doesn't it?"

"That man over there explained to us what exactly you were doing here. Those who doubt the existence of the sky canvas . . ." He looked around. "A number of people in this room are known to us as being less than trustworthy."

"That is news to me. Where did you get this information? I am merely doing business, helping the merchants of this city get access to the newest discoveries. When the time comes that the neighbouring kingdoms and baronies are convinced that they can take Saardam without much resistance, they will come with machines that fly and move by themselves, and if we don't have those machines as well, then we'll have no way to defend ourselves."

Oh, she was so good at acting the prim lady.

"We have orders from your husband. You're deflecting our questions." He addressed the gathering. "Now, all of you, if you have any magical objects at all, give them to us, and we'll view your case with leniency. If we are forced to search you, and we find any magical objects you have hidden on your person, we will not view that in a positive light."

He waved his hand and two of his men sprang into action.

Madame Sabine said, "Wait, wait. Who says you can search these people. They're my business associates. They are carpenters, they are fishermen, they are merchants."

"What sort of business is going to be conducted then?"

"It is a council of business people and we discuss

matters relating to the most terrible export conditions that our country has ever seen, and the dwindling of supplies."

He seemed to agree, almost, because at the last moment he said, "In that case, if that's true, none of you will have any objections whatsoever to being searched."

"To the contrary," Madame Sabine said. "These people are my friends and trusted contacts. They'll consider it rude to be subjected to any form of searching. The suggestion that they conspire against my husband is preposterous."

"It's the Regent's order."

"My husband only orders this so he can humiliate me."

"We have reliable information that there is magic and heresy practised in this meeting. I don't care whether you call yourselves innocent business people or not. We will search you before you can leave this building, and if we find any items of magic, then you will be taken to jail."

"Which liar told you that?"

"You would like to know that, huh? So that you can use your magic on them."

"I have no magic. You are not searching any of these people. Go back; leave this room now. Come on, out with you." She flapped her hand at the two men who had started going around the table, asking attendants to the meeting to take everything out of their pockets. Nellie was glad she hadn't brought the book or the box.

The men glanced at their superior, but he told them to keep searching.

"I order you to leave us alone," Madame Sabine said.

"We take orders from your husband. You're obstructing our task. Stand to the side, please. My men won't be long."

"I tell you to get out! I'll talk to my husband about this."

"He'll be most amused." His voice sounded belittling, and sent a chill through Nellie. Because no matter how well a woman married, if a problem occurred, she was still worth less than her husband's male guards.

"How dare you talk to me like that."

"Get out of our way. Search everyone. Leave no one undisturbed."

At a gesture from the patrol leader, two guards came from either side and grabbed Madame Sabine by the arms. They pulled off her pretty fur coat.

Madame Sabine screamed, "Keep your hands off me!"

A guard drew his sword and swung it around. It caught the light of the fire.

Someone screamed.

Nellie held her breath and brought her hands to her mouth.

She couldn't believe what she was seeing. Was he really going to mow down a defenceless woman in front of these people? No less than the wife of the Regent. Had the Regent ordered this?

Nellie couldn't watch this. She closed her eyes.

But instead of—what sort of sounds even came with someone being cut with a sword? Nellie didn't want to know—there came a great ripping sound.

Madame Sabine—obviously still unharmed—yelled, "What do you think you're doing? You boor. How dare you do this?"

Nellie opened her eyes.

The guard had cut right through the back of Madame Sabine's overdress. Parts of the rich brocade fabric lay on the ground.

Madame Sabine wrestled to get free, but the guards were much too strong.

They peeled off the dress and then the soldier cut

through the laces of the corset without bothering to undo them.

Master Beck said, "Hey, I don't know what your orders were, but you don't do that to a lady. Have some decency, man."

The guard then grabbed Madame Sabine's thin under-dress in both hands and ripped the back open.

"Ha!" He forced her to turn around, so that her pale, soft back was exposed to the light. The red scars showed up clearly.

The patrol leader laughed. "What did you say about magic? What creature do you think did this?"

People in the room gasped.

"This woman is a witch." The man threw Madame Sabine her tattered dress. She pulled it over her shoulders. She didn't protest, and didn't say anything. She kept her chin in the air, regarding the guards with disdain.

Nellie wondered: how they'd known about those scars? The only person who might have known was the Regent, but Madame Sabine had told Nellie he didn't care about her anymore. They slept in separate rooms.

And if she'd acquired the scars long ago, they obviously had never been a problem in their relationship before.

Why now?

The only other person who could have known was the healer witch Graziela, but she had left town long ago. Or was she somehow still passing information to the Regent in return for her freedom?

But then she had another thought: Zelda. Madame Sabine had been looking for a healer in order to look after the scars. Zelda was well-known amongst the nobles as someone who sold remedies. She had betrayed Madame Sabine as she had betrayed Nellie and the other women.

A number of other guards had lined up on the stairs and tromped into the room.

One by one, they went to all the people who had attended the meeting. They asked them to take off their coats and jackets and shirts. They searched the trouser pockets, they searched their socks and their shoes, they searched the pockets of their jackets and coats and their bags. A small pile of items grew in the middle of the table.

Nellie didn't recognise many of the strange devices, except to know that some of them had been used in the talk about stars and the sky—little looking glasses on stands and models of balls on arms revolving around each other.

Some of them looked like they might have been made by the same people as the ones who made all the magical artefacts in the cabinet in the church, but they were objects with clear functions like measuring how far the stars were from each other and measuring distance at sea. Because, as the man had explained in his talk earlier that night, this was a constant problem that people faced when they went out onto the ocean where there was no land in sight.

The speaker of that presentation protested when one of the guards shoved all these items in a bag.

"No, you can't have my instruments. They're not magic but they're rare and I paid a lot of money for them. I have no problem with you having a look at them, but I absolutely have to have them back, because this will be the future of sailing."

The guards ignored his protest. They told him to stand next to Madame Sabine and wait while the other people in the room were searched.

Nellie was glad that she hadn't brought any of her magical items. The only thing the guards found in her pockets when it was her turn was a dirty handkerchief.

Then the guards were done.

The patrol leader faced the merchant and Madame Sabine.

The merchant's face was contorted with naked anger, but it was Madame Sabine's cold eyes that made Nellie shiver.

The man said, "We arrest both of you in the name of the Regent. You are hereby charged with witchcraft."

"Don't be ridiculous," Madame Sabine said.

"The Regent has ordered us specifically to investigate you. You are further charged with conspiring to overthrow him, with the murder of his close advisor, and conspiracy against the church."

At this time, the severity of the situation began to dawn on madame Sabine's face. "He wouldn't dare."

But obviously the Regent did dare, and Madame Sabine had no one who would stand up for her.

"I will give the Regent a piece of my mind as soon as I can see his ugly face."

But the threat sounded hollow.

CHAPTER 20

THE GUARDS FORCED Madame Sabine and the merchant up the stairs and disappeared from sight. After their footsteps had faded into the distance, and the clatter of the wheels of the wagon had gone, they left behind a deep silence.

"What sort of man would do that to his own wife?" Master Beck said.

"A man whose hand is forced by others," a merchant said. "Evil can be a necessity for those who are struggling to survive. Especially when the struggles are financial. People will understand if someone needs to defend themselves or their families with a sword, but they don't understand the power of financial ruin and the fear it strikes in the hearts of those who have money. Money is an evil thing."

"That's easy for you to say. You inherited a successful business. All your customers were handed to you by your father."

"I could be made to disagree with you on that, but that's not the discussion at hand. We need to free her."

"I am not terribly inclined to argue with those guards."

The rich merchant said, "No, that wouldn't be the way to do it, anyway. I am happy to ask for an audience with the Regent about this. He depends on my business. I know he is financially in a difficult spot, and I can threaten to withhold my services from him."

Master Beck nodded. "Someone understands the power of money. There is no need for weapons or any of that ugly, primitive business when you have money to work with. I'll come with you. I know things about Sabine that Bernard would be wise to heed."

So the agreement was made that Master Beck would ask for an audience with the Regent and demand that Madame Sabine and the supplier of lenses was freed. He would explain the science and what they could do with it, and maybe the Regent would be interested, because he was always interested in schemes that made money. What he knew about Madame Sabine, however, remained private knowledge.

It was time to leave. It was getting late, and it was dark and cold outside.

Other people were also leaving the house, and Nellie followed closely behind them. She walked with a group of men going in the direction of the marketplace but kept looking over her shoulder. Not that she could do anything to save herself if the fire dog returned, but in her memory she kept seeing the terrible creatures that the Fire Wizard unleashed over the city.

In the dark, all kinds of terrible thoughts took hold of her. They had cut down the tree that the wizard had been imprisoned in. Had that freed him?

If nothing else, this evening had made one thing clear to her: Mistress Johanna used to say people with magic had to be taught what to do with it. She had even started classes—which were quickly abandoned after she and the king had been killed by their own daughter. But stopping the classes had been wrong. They needed *more* classes. To defeat a magic threat, only one thing was useful: the understanding of magic.

Nellie had no understanding of it. She didn't think the *science* group had much understanding either, but they, at least, understood the power of knowledge and wanted to gain it.

These were dark days for Saardam.

Nellie had to walk by herself the last part of the distance. The streets were dark and lit only by the occasional street lamp.

The platform at the quayside where the punishment would be carried out was barely visible against the blackness of the water. It was lit by a single street lamp that cast a golden glow over the macabre installation. It lay ready. The carpenters had removed the spare wood and their tools.

Nellie hugged herself at the sight of the dreadful thing. A couple of sea cows followed her in the water as she turned towards the disused wharf and walked along the empty warehouses. Their soft splashes were the only sounds in the still night.

In the barn, the women sat around a fire, and the smell of soup hung in the air.

To Nellie's surprise, there was also a horse in the barn. It stood against the far wall, its beautiful headpiece tied to the workbench with a piece of rope. Madame Sabine's grey and white horse.

"It just turned up at the barn door," Mina said. "It was spooked and nervous, but we let it in and gave it some carrots, since we have plenty."

"I think it's Madame Sabine's horse," Gertie said. "Someone will be along to pick it up, and maybe they'll give us some money."

As with all animals, the horse had probably been drawn here by the dragon's presence.

Nellie now noticed a couple of bags of vegetables that stood underneath the workbenches.

"How did you get all those?"

"I don't know. We were away, picking up fish, and we traded some eggs, and when we came back, all this was here. I thought it had something to do with you."

There were bags of carrots and beets and parsnips, and a bag of beans.

"That's strange. I talked with a couple of merchants who wanted to speak to the dragon. They were prepared to give us supplies in return."

Mina laughed. "Good luck to them."

"I don't think they're coming. We never reached an agreement. The negotiation was interrupted." Yet the supplies were here anyway. It was very strange indeed.

"Where is the dragon?" she asked.

Mina jerked her head in the direction of the storeroom.

Nellie looked inside. The dragon lay in the hay, and all the children were sleeping against his flanks. Madame Sabine must have done something bad to cause it to attack her.

Nellie went back to the fire, pulling along a tin to sit on.

She accepted a warm bowl of soup from Mina. They still didn't have any salt, but the children had caught some fish and traded one fish for two eggs and all of that had gone into the soup. It was the best meal Nellie had eaten in days.

She told the others all about the meeting. Several women gasped when she told them Madame Sabine had been arrested.

"But why would the Regent arrest his own wife?" Mina asked.

"She never wanted to come here in the first place. They distrust each other. I heard them have an argument. Not a healthy family life by anyone's definition." Nellie told them how she had first gone to visit Madame Sabine, seen the scars, and found the dragon box in Lord Verdonck's travel chest.

"Might the Regent be outlawing magic just because he is trying to make her life difficult?" Agatha said. "Because he hates her so much? I wouldn't give a husband any favours if he cheated on me."

Hilde nodded sagely. Her husband *had* cheated on her. Agatha had been none too fond of her own husband.

Nellie was going to say the Regent wouldn't let the whole city of Saardam suffer for his poor marriage but, being a noble, he probably would. This might well be part of the Regent's reason to chase magic: because he knew his wife had stolen the dragon and dabbled with magic.

And because Adalbert Verdonck was breathing down his neck, demanding that someone be punished for the death of his father.

Neither Wim the taster nor Nellie appeared to be high profile enough to make a satisfactory culprit, so why not blame your unfaithful wife? That solved two problems at once.

Madame Sabine could either confess her affair or accept the blame. Either would destroy her.

Because of the mysterious appearance of bags of carrots and parsnips in the barn, Nellie did not need to go to the palace for leftovers the next morning, and for that she was glad.

Mina cooked soup straight after breakfast, filling the warehouse with a smell so delicious that the puppy brought a friend and the number of cats swelled to over twenty. None of them were afraid to enter the storeroom where the dragon lay in the straw.

Despite being much bigger, the dragon let the cats climb on his back.

Nellie was busy.

Tomorrow was the big day, and the group's supplies needed to be brought to Floris' boat, since he had agreed to help take their things to the Guentherite ship and hide them below the deck.

Nellie needed to go to Gisele's gin distillery to pick up a monk's habit that she would wear on their adventure into the church crypt tonight.

When she left the barn, there were a lot of guards on the streets, and she hated to think how alert the guards at the palace gate would be. If she went to the palace, she might even run into Henrik, and she wasn't sure any more that he would not betray her. She had a fleeting thought that *he* might have told the Regent's guards about Madame Sabine's scars, except she was sure she never told him about them.

More guards than usual stood lined up in front of the door of the council building to the side of the market-place. A big group of people were standing in front of the building, held back by the line of uniformed men, where they were waiting for something.

NELLIE STOPPED at the edge of the group so she could listen. A woman behind her was giving a younger woman— a cousin or neighbour—instructions on how to use rabbit bones for making soup. A man on the other side said, "Don't let anyone hear that your son is trapping rabbits illegally."

And many people shushed him up because illegal trapping was the only way they could survive.

"I think the Regent has finally heard our plight," a woman said.

Another snorted. "I'll believe it when I see it."

Nellie couldn't restrain her curiosity. "What are you all waiting for?"

A man next to her replied, "The Regent's giving out food from the stores. He says he understands life is hard for us. He says that it's better than to have people steal the food, which is happening anyway."

The woman in front of him turned over her shoulder. "Those people need to be hanged."

A lot of people agreed, and many had their own opinion on it.

A man said, "I heard they come at night."

"Cowards."

"My neighbour says the guards get distracted and then, when they come back, the door is smashed in and some bags are gone."

"Are those men calling themselves guards? In my day, we were taught: one person stays with the door you're guarding, no matter what happens."

"There is no defending a door against evil magic."

"They're dark magicians."

Another woman butted in. "Foreigners. They don't know manners. They take what they see and think it's all theirs."

"Yeah. Long live the Regent."

The line shuffled forward.

Nellie didn't really want any food, nor did she want to wait for that long, but she had a strong suspicion that she knew who the thief was. And it was not a human. She had wondered for a long time what dragons ate and remembered the stolen carrots from the kitchen. Dora had complained about it. The dragon had already been in her room, and clearly he had helped himself to some contents of the kitchen pantry. And those bags of supplies that mysteriously appeared in the barn? She had a strong suspicion that she knew where they came from. Dragon poop was orange, after all.

She could see the dragon frightening the guards at the stores and helping himself to whatever he wanted.

But giving out the supplies seemed too radical a solution.

They were only at the start of winter. If the Regent gave out all the supplies now, there would be nothing to give later.

There had to be another motive.

She walked past the long line of waiting people until she got to the entrance of the building. People were going in, and others were coming out with bags and buckets full of parsnips and cabbages and carrots. Some people also got beans and flour, and they carried all this back to their homes, chatting happily.

But as people went into the building, they had to go past a table where a man was writing names in a big book.

A scruffy man was standing at this table, in a heated argument with the guard who stood behind the table. Nellie recognised him. It was old Bert, who used to sleep in Shepherd Adrianus' church. Mad Bert who had gone completely grey. His face was red and blotched and his coat had seen better days. She wondered how he was doing, living in the poorhouse.

"Why do you need our names? Why our addresses? Why do you want professions?" he yelled at the guard behind the table.

The man replied in a dry voice, "We need to make sure that every person in the city who is eligible only gets one lot of supplies."

"There are other ways you can do that. You can mark our hands with ink. You don't need to do the scribbly

scribbly scribbly on the paper and write down everything about us. Yes you can have a name, but why do you need people's professions? Why do you need to know where they live?"

"The Regent has told us to collect this information."

"The Regent wants to know which of us have a trade, so he knows which people to come after in his stupid quest to find magicians. I want my share and I'm not giving you my name or telling you where I live."

The guard replied with a straight face, "I suggest you apply for an audience with the Regent, if you want to protest against that. I need your profession and address, otherwise you get no food."

"Fine."

And Bert turned around and stormed out of the building.

Several people in the waiting crowd gave him strange looks as he made his way down the street.

"What was that man saying, mammy?" A little boy asked.

"Don't worry about him. He is just Bert, and he's mad. Everyone knows that."

"Is the Regent still going to give us food?"

"Of course he is. He's a good man."

But it seemed to Nellie that the only thing wrong with Bert was that he didn't know when to shut up.

This appeared to be the Regent's latest venture. The Regent wanted to be king. He needed support from the people. He had sensed that he wasn't popular in the city, so he opened the city stores—and damn what would happen at the end of winter when they needed the food—and he got the citizens' professions at the same time. She felt sick at the thought that people would fall for it so easily, but knew once she would have done the same. In fact, she had been grateful for her position at the palace because the palace gave her food.

Of course, the Regent had been doing the same thing to the nobles for a long time. That was the function of the banquets, so aptly sponsored by Lord Verdonck, and now under threat of having funding withheld by Adalbert.

So he turned to the common people, because it cost him little to give out food from the city's stores, since that food was all part of taxes paid to the city anyway.

Under the guise of giving people food, he was making a register of everyone who lived in the city so he could send his guards around to target any he didn't like.

CHAPTER 21

NELLIE HAD TO WAIT around until it got dark before she could carry out the next part of the plan: to rescue the boy—who she was reasonably sure was Prince Bruno—from the crypts.

Meanwhile, she helped the others pack up their supplies, ready to be carried to the Guentherite order's ship.

During the day, the children, and especially Koby, had kept an eye on whether anyone visited the ship, and had concluded that the monks sometimes came to pick up things or deliver goods that had to go back to the monastery, like a chest full of books, but that no one was permanently at the ship.

After dark, Floris would come with his rowboat and they would take the supplies across the harbour and heave them on board the ship. They would hide the bags and barrels underneath a sailcloth the women had found in a nearby warehouse.

Mina and Hilde would stay on board the ship to guard the supplies.

At dusk, Nellie met Gisele in an alley behind the market square.

She was dressed as a monk today, with the hood of her habit over her head so it only showed the lower half of her face.

She asked Nellie, "Have you got everything?"

Nellie nodded and felt for the key in her pocket.

She had also taken a handful of carrots and a small bag of beans from the stock, in case they need to bribe someone.

Gisele gave her a bundle of fabric. Nellie recognised the brown coarse weave of a monk's habit.

"Put that on when you get a chance," Gisele said.

Nellie took it from her with a heavy heart. She had always respected the monks and didn't like pretending to be one. Even though she knew some people in the church were not good people, she still didn't like deceiving them.

She went onto a porch and pulled the habit over her head.

The inside of the garment smelled musty, and Nellie was surprised how heavy the fabric was. It was quite long and hid Nellie's stockings and shoes. The hood went all the way over her eyes and would only stay up far enough to see the ground immediately in front of her.

"It's even got pockets," she said when she rejoined Gisele in the street.

"Of course it does. Where else do you think the monks put their prayer books and rosary beads?"

Gisele held her own pocket open. It contained a hammer and a knife in a sheath.

"Prayer books," Nellie said, her voice flat.

"You *do* have a sense of humour."

"You better make sure you don't accidentally cut the string for the rosary beads, because you won't be able to strangle someone with them anymore."

Gisele gave a broad grin.

To be honest, the girl frightened Nellie a little. She wasn't quite sure what Gisele wanted or expected from this expedition.

But for now, she would be useful, because the monks and the shepherds knew her and trusted her.

They set off through the streets. It was bitterly cold, the moon was clear, and the first stars were already coming out in the sky. Nellie's breath steamed in the cold air. There would certainly be frost tonight.

When they arrived at the church, Gisele went inside first to check if anyone was there, and she came back to say that the church was empty.

So they went up the church steps and in through the heavy doors.

It was very dark in the church vestibule. The altar was a pool of golden light at the end of the aisle and seemed to float in a sea of darkness.

In her mind, Nellie spoke a brief prayer to the Triune, whose terrible statue stood behind the altar, overlooking the church with its contorted faces and water stained bodies. She prayed for forgiveness for what she was about to do.

Not a single sound disturbed the silence. It was so cold that even the mice and rats had gone quiet.

Nellie followed Gisele down the aisle to the altar. She kept stepping on the hem of the habit, which was really annoying. When she tried to tie it up higher at the waist, the hood kept falling over her eyes.

Gisele crossed in front of the altar and opened the door to the crypt.

The door to the staircase opened into pitch darkness.

"Urgh. The candles are out. Hang on." Gisele went back to the altar and lit a torch from one of the giant holy candles that stood on either side.

Nellie followed her down the steps into that stifling darkness, trying not to trip or be disturbed by the strange shadows of the flapping flame from the torch over the stairwell's curved walls.

Down in the crypt room Nellie could almost feel the eyes of all the past kings and queens who were buried here. She was doing this for the good of the city. She was doing this because neither the Regent nor the church should get their hands on objects of power. She was doing this because if people were kept prisoners down here, that was wrong and the Triune would never agree with that.

They reached the end of the burial room and now it was Nellie's turn to do her part. She dug in her pocket, took out the key and opened the little door in the metal grate.

"How often have you been here?" she asked Gisele.

"A few times. The shepherd keeps his supply of good wine in here, and there is also a cabinet full of various other concoctions. He uses both on different occasions. He has a bad stomach sometimes."

Nellie remembered the cabinet with the bottles she had seen on the previous visit. Most of those had been extremely dusty.

They walked along the corridor with the cabinets stuffed full of strange, wonderful and dangerous objects that Nellie still didn't have the time to look at. She suspected there was more than a lifetime's worth of study in these cabinets.

"Look at this," Gisele said.

She held up the torch.

Out of all the splendour she could have chosen to highlight, she focused on a dusty, fire-damaged cabinet. Once it had possessed a glass front, but the pane had been smashed long ago. The bed of velvet inside was empty.

It was such a dour and dirty thing that Nellie would

not have given it any attention during her previous visit, but there was some familiarity to it. She had seen this cabinet before.

Yes, it used to stand in King Roald's office—which he never used—and it held the crown and sceptre—which he intensely disliked wearing. The maids would come in once every so often and polish the glass and shake the dust off the velvet.

"Why is this here?" And then the next question. "Where are the crown and sceptre?"

"That's a good question, isn't it? A rumour goes around that after the chaos where the King and Queen died, somebody came into the king's office and took the crown and sceptre for safekeeping."

"Somebody?"

"No one knows exactly who it was, but it's believed to be someone from the King's Guard."

This, Nellie remembered, had been a group of experienced guards whose task it was to make sure that the laws and agreements were obeyed by both citizens and guards. They had ceased to exist when there was no longer a king.

Gisele continued, "It's also believed that this person either denied that they had the crown and sceptre or outright refused to hand them to the shepherd when it came to the task of appointing a successor. The law says that in order to be accepted a monarch, the prince or princess must accept the crown and sceptre."

Nellie continued, "But because they don't have the crown and sceptre, they can't appoint a king."

"That's apparently part of the reason."

"The people were told that it's complicated to find out who has the most right to the throne. It's even more complicated to make it look as if the people you don't want to get it don't have the right."

Gisele chuckled. "I'm sure that's also part of the reason."

They continued into the cellar where the casks of wine were lined up. There were not quite as many as before. Evidently, many of them had been taken to the palace for the banquet.

"The room with all the books and the ruby skull is over there." Gisele jerked her head to the side.

Nellie knew about that, too.

She shuddered at the thought of the books she had seen.

If there was ever any case for books to be burned, this was definitely it, although she had no doubt that this collection was worth a fortune.

Gisele led the way across the cellar, over a worn tiled floor that felt gritty and uneven underfoot. Nellie had to watch her step, with the too-long habit getting in her way.

The wall at the far end of the low-ceilinged room sported a number of doors, all with heavy metal bolts on the outside.

Gisele handed Nellie the torch. "Here, hold this."

Nellie grabbed the wooden handle.

Gisele went up to the first door. She pushed up the bolt with a squeak of metal on metal. The door was so heavy that she needed both hands and all her weight to open it, and the dark maw beyond was most uninviting. Gisele stepped inside and came back. "This one is empty."

She tried the next door which turned out to lead to some sort of pantry with many bottles of strange substances, most of them covered in a thick layer of dust.

The next door however released a wall of foul air when Gisele opened it. Phew.

Gisele didn't step into the cell, but remained at the door. "Is anyone in there?"

It was too dark to see anything inside except for a

small patch inside the door which showed a floor covering of dirty straw.

Something rustled inside.

For a moment, Nellie was afraid that some terrible animal would come out. A big, mean black dog that would turn into the fire dog and escape this cell at night.

But instead, the face of a boy appeared in the opening, like a pale oval in the darkness, his eyes dark, his hair dark and dishevelled. His eyes were wide, and he held his legs bent so that he could run or duck when someone tried to grab him. My, he was filthy.

"Who are you?" Nellie asked.

This boy did not look anywhere near the way she remembered Prince Bruno. The boy she knew had olive skin that browned easily in the sun. His hair was sleek and black. He would smile a lot.

This boy was pale as death, his expression haunted. He was skinny and filthy and didn't look big enough to be fourteen years old.

He looked around with frightened eyes, and then he dropped to his knees and moaned.

"What's wrong? Are you hurt?"

But this appeared to be part of an act although Nellie didn't understand what he was trying to do.

Gisele pulled his arm. "Come. We're taking you out. You're free."

First, the boy did not want to get up. Did he even understand her?

Gisele pulled him up by the shoulders. "Ugh. He stinks."

She got him to his feet, but then he would not walk and it was clear why—his legs were shackled with metal bands, which chafed the skin.

Well, that would complicate matters somewhat.

"Can you talk?" Nellie asked.

He looked at her. A deep feeling of dread went through her. If he had been locked up for all those ten years, would he have turned into another mad prince?

"We don't have time for this," Gisele said. She picked the boy up and slung him over her shoulder. "Let's get out of here."

Gisele led the way out of the crypt, leaving Nellie to carry the light and shut the little metal grate behind them. She almost had to run to follow Gisele through the burial room and up the stairs.

Nellie was amazed at how strong Gisele was, but she hauled casks of wine and pretended to be a man.

At the top of the stairs, Gisele stopped so abruptly that Nellie almost crashed into her. She said some words that were most unmonk-like.

"What's wrong?" Nellie asked.

Gisele jerked her head in the direction of the altar.

Nellie peeked around the corner.

A man stood at the table behind the altar, turning the pages in a book by the light of flapping candles.

He had his back to her, but Nellie didn't need to see his face to know who he was. Out of all people who could have been in the church, Shepherd Wilfridus was the worst.

He held his hands up and muttered inaudible words as if practicing a sermon.

By the Triune, what now?

He hadn't seen them, so they might have to run. Gisele would have to go first and Nellie would either have to pull the hood right over her head and pretend to be a monk or, better, discard the habit and ask the shepherd some innocent question.

Nellie went a few steps down to put the torch back in the sconce at the top of the stairs. Then she took off the habit and draped it over the boy who clung onto Gisele's shoulder, shivering.

"I'll go in and talk to the shepherd," Nellie said. "You run when he's distracted."

If he asked, she could come up with a reason to have been to the crypt, because she used to serve Queen Johanna and she would have a valid reason to visit her grave. If he asked, she could even make up something about why she visited at this time of the day. But the thought of having to deceive the shepherd struck fear in her heart.

She stepped into the church. From the corner of her eye, she could see Gisele sneak away in the shadow of the outer gallery.

Slowly, Nellie walked up to the statue of the Triune, in the same way as when she came here to pray.

She shivered under her clothes. That habit had been so hot, and now the biting cold air touched the sweaty parts of her skin.

The shepherd still had not seen her. But he was accompanied by two altar boys who had definitely seen her. Neither of them said anything; they just stood behind the shepherd holding some objects.

Nellie kneeled and pretended to pray.

She glanced at the statue and its stained face, remembering how King Roald used to hate this thing so much that he wanted it out of the palace garden. She listened for sounds that Gisele had left the church. How long did she need to sit here? How long did it take someone to run the length of the church? She tried to look over her shoulder, but it was too dark. Maybe she should make a run for it anyway.

By the Triune, one of the boys was holding a bottle that looked like it contained gin. And the other held a bowl. As she watched, the shepherd snatched the bottle and emptied it into a dish on the table. Then the dipped his hand into bowl held by the other boy. He lifted his hand and let a stream of small things drop from his clenched fist. They looked like dried beans.

Then a glow of light emanated from the dish.

And a man's laughter echoed through the church.

An evil glow of red light consumed the shepherd's form. Red flames licked at his robe and his hair.

The two altar boys retreated, white-faced, until they stood with their backs against the wall. Both covered their mouth with their hands.

Shepherd Wilfridus dipped his hands into the dish where he had just poured the gin and dropped the beans. He lifted something out and turned around. In his outstretched hands, he held that horrible relic of the ancient church, the ruby skull. Its eye sockets glowed vivid, pulsing red.

He raised the skull and laughed a high, maniacal laugh.

"Look at this!" he shouted. "Look at this." His voice echoed through the cavernous space.

Then he noticed Nellie. His eyes widened for a moment and then he came towards her, holding the terrible thing.

"You thought magicians from other lands could control us? You thought the dragons and the demons they have sent would be strong enough to defeat us? Look at this."

He laughed again. By the Triune, he had gone mad.

In the back of her head, Nellie heard Gisele's words *someone has infused the gin with a magical object like an amulet. It can't be too big of course . . .*

Yes it could be big. If you poured out the gin and used a big bowl, you could infuse all kinds of things with evil magic.

The shepherd continued, "They all think we have no power. They all think we are powerless and so they can come in to possess, besiege and disown us. No, I shall be the ruler of this land, and I shall rule all the adjacent lands. There will be no ridiculous fat king with ill-behaved sons and a whore for a wife. There will be no council of pampered nobles who cannot decide because they're too afraid of their neighbours, their cousins, their brothers and half-brothers and the whole inbred lot. It's a wonder they don't all have six toes on every foot. Saardam will be a centre of knowledge. People will come from all the lands to learn about the historical rules. This will be a second Senoza. It will be better than Senoza. I have this power."

With each sentence, a glow of light pulsed out from the skull.

He had not only gone mad, but he had somehow found a way to control magic.

How else could he do that apart from being a magician?

And not just one of the artisan type, but a really powerful magician?

Nellie scrambled to her feet and retreated into the aisle.

He laughed. "Yes, run, child. Tell the world we will suffer no more fools. No more weak nobles, no more priests trying to curry favour with the masses, no more banquets for the stupid nobles. From now on, I will rule this city."

He laughed.

A burst of fire erupted from the ruby skull. It leapt into the air, uncoiling as it went, until it landed in front of the altar on four paws. The fire dog.

Nellie ran.

She hadn't run for many years, didn't know she still could. But she ran as fast as her legs would carry her, down the aisle, through the pitch darkness of the vestibule, into the biting cold of the night.

Gisele waited outside on the porch underneath the arched entrance. She had set the boy down to catch her breath.

Nellie ran out of the church. "Quick. Quick, it is not safe. We must go."

CHAPTER 22

THE DISTANCE FROM the church to the harbour was short but, in the darkness, while carrying the boy, covering it seemed to take longer than ever.

He didn't attempt to walk for himself; he just whimpered and hung onto Gisele's neck.

Nellie kept looking over her shoulder to check if the fire dog was coming. But it wasn't. The shepherd seemed to have been so engrossed in whatever magical victory he had achieved that he hadn't even noticed that somebody had removed the prize prisoner out of the crypt.

But now she wished nothing more than to reach the safety of the barn.

She had never done anything like this in her life. Disobeying the shepherd, stealing things from the church, sneaking around after dark. Not wearing a bonnet outdoors. All things she would have despised even as recently as a few months ago.

She was doing this to let truth and justice prevail.

She was doing this to prove her father was right.

And to prove that neither she, nor Madame Sabine,

nor Wim or anyone in the palace had killed Lord Verdonck. Here was the magician powerful enough to put magic in gin. Shepherd Wilfridus would have visited the palace often enough to know Lord Verdonck loved his gin and needed only have placed the poisoned bottle in his room. The shepherd hated Lord Verdonck because he stood in the way of the church's influence on the Regent.

The shepherd had chosen the Regent not as someone who would not upset surrounding nations, but as someone just strong enough to hold the position but weak enough to be controlled and replaced when the time was right. Replaced by someone from the church, just as the Most Holy Father Severino was not only the head of the Belaman Church, but ruled the city of Senoza.

The harbour was unusually quiet. The platform stood ready for use tomorrow, seats and benches all ready. The boats lay moored along the quay, dark and silent, with not a breath of wind rippling the water.

All the women came rushing to the door when Nellie and Gisele came into the barn.

Gisele put the boy down in the straw in the barn. He stared at the dark water.

The women all gathered around him, making comments about how skinny he was.

Hilde said, "Is that him? Is that Prince Bruno? He doesn't look like much."

"Oh my, he is filthy," Agatha said.

"Let me take those shackles off first," Gisele said.

She extracted the hammer from the pocket of her habit and with a few deft blows, dislodged the metal pin that held the two halves of the metal band around his ankles together. They fell apart with a clang.

The skin underneath was raw.

Nellie shivered. How could anyone do this to a young boy?

Gertie got a bucket of water from the rain barrel at the back of the barn. She came back followed by the white horse.

At the sight of it, the boy scrambled up, his eyes wide.

"Don't worry, we won't hurt you."

"Give him something to eat," Nellie said.

Koby ran to the table and cut a chunk of the bread.

She reached out to the boy. It struck Nellie that the two were similar in age, but Koby looked so much healthier, even if she had been without a proper home for most of her life.

He seemed hesitant at first, reaching out for the bread, but not quite touching it. Maybe because of their similar ages, he seemed to connect with her.

She pushed the bread to him. "Come on, it's yours."

"Me?"

It was the first word he said. Nellie was relieved that he spoke. She'd heard horrible things about children mistreated for most of their lives.

"Yes, take it."

He snatched the bread out of Koby's hands as if he still couldn't believe it, and bit into it as if fearing someone would take it away again.

What had been done to this poor boy?

"How long did they lock you up in there?" Nellie asked.

But he looked at her with a hazy expression, as if he didn't understand what she was saying. He was busy chewing.

"If I were locked in there, I wouldn't be able to tell the time," Gisele said.

True. From the way Gisele crossed her arms over her chest, and from her guarded expression, Nellie wondered whether she'd had a similar experience. Nothing about Gisele's life was simple or nice.

They all watched while the boy demolished the bread and then ate another piece.

While he ate, the uncomfortable silence lingered. What could you say to someone who had been so mistreated for so long and who clearly didn't remember Nellie from when she had helped look after him.

She asked if he wanted tea. He gave her a blank look, but water, he did want. He drank awkwardly, with water spilling over his cheeks.

She told the women, "Get him clothes, get him cleaned up."

While the other women scrambled around to find him something suitable to wear, Nellie sat down next to him on the mattress.

He was obviously much older than the boy she remembered, but now she noticed familiar features in his face, the set of his eyes, the fullness of his mouth. He had the eyes of his eastern trader father, but the nose and freckles of his mother, Queen Johanna. A chill went through her again. This boy's life had been stolen from him. His mother was dead; his father had fled.

"I'm Nellie," she said.

He turned around and looked at her, his eyes searching.

"Do you remember being in the palace when you were little and the woman who looked after you and took you into the garden? That woman was me."

He frowned.

"We had a lot of fun together, walking in the garden and catching frogs."

Nellie thought of those wonderful days, and she had often wondered about what she would do if she could go back and live it again, knowing how close they were to disaster.

"Nellie," he said.

"Yes, that's me." She wondered if he remembered those days at all. He'd only been four. "And your name is Bruno."

"Bruno," he repeated, his tone empty, as if he didn't remember his own name.

Who knew what the monks had called him for most of his life.

If he had spent so much time in the bottom of the crypt, the days in the palace with his family must seem very far away. Maybe he had even convinced himself that it was all a dream. After all, he had been only four when all these terrible things happened.

"YOU'RE FREE NOW. We will look after you."

And because she didn't know what else to say, she put her hand over his. His hand was cold as ice, the skin dry and flaky. She spread out her free arm, as if she wanted to enclose him in an embrace.

He didn't move to hug her. He didn't withdraw his hand either. He looked small and lonely and frightened.

Gertie and Hilde came back with some clothes they could spare and helped him to clean himself up and get dressed. He was so skinny and shivered so much that he couldn't put his shirt on, and he didn't seem to know what to do with buttons.

While all this was happening, the children had been sleeping in the storeroom. The dragon was in there with them. Nellie had expected it to show up, but it was still snoring.

Nellie went to the corner where she slept, found the dragon box, and gave it to him.

At first he just sat there with it on his knees. His face showed no emotion.

"It's yours. Do you remember?"

He ran his fingers over the smooth wood, a small frown on his face.

Was it because he remembered something?

"Open it," Nellie said.

He ran his hand along the crack between the lid and the rest of the box until he came to the fastening. He hesitated.

"Open?"

"Yes," Nellie said.

He slowly lifted the lid.

The box was empty, of course, and revealed only the beautiful silk interior.

His frown deepened. He put his fingers inside and felt around in the corners, as if he knew there should be something in it, but couldn't remember what it was.

"What?"

"It's yours," Nellie said. "Your father gave it to you. It's a box of magic."

He snapped the lid shut, dropped the box and scrambled away from it.

"What's wrong?"

"Th—th—there!" He pointed across the barn.

The dragon, which only a moment ago had been asleep with the children, poked his head out of the storeroom. He noticed the boy and seemed to freeze.

This was the time of truth. If any chance remained that this was not Prince Bruno, the dragon would know. He took a step forward.

Bruno whimpered. He retreated few steps.

The dragon came another step into the barn.

Bruno turned around and ran for the door.

"Hey, wait!" Nellie said.

He froze, one hand on the latch.

"He is friendly," Nellie said. "Let him sniff you."

To demonstrate, she walked to the dragon and put her hand on his warm and dry flank.

Bruno looked at her, eyes wide.

His mouth moved, but no sound came out. His eyes were so wide that the whites showed on all sides.

Nellie walked forward with the dragon. Bruno pushed himself with his back against the door.

"There is no need to be afraid. The dragon is yours."

"Magic?"

Sweat pearled on his forehead.

By the Triune, what lies had these monks and deacons told this boy?

One thing was clear: he couldn't control the dragon or perform great feats of magic with it.

Nellie might have hoped that he would command the dragon to help them, but in this current state the boy was no use to the group. Only a burden. Magic was a curse unless trained. She of all people should have realised that.

She said, in a calm voice, "Just let him sniff you."

The dragon came even closer. The creature was curious, more curious than he had been about her or any of the others.

Bruno pressed himself flat against the door, his hands clawing the wood. He would run if there was anywhere to run.

Nellie took his hand, guiding him forward. The skin felt clammy, and he pulled in the other direction.

"Why are you afraid of Boots?" came a small voice.

It was Anneke. When had she woken up?

She faced Bruno, her head cocked, holding the blanket around her. There was straw in her hair from sleeping in the storeroom.

"Koby says that you're Prince Bruno. You don't look like a prince."

"Anneke . . ." warned her mother.

The boy just stared at her as if he had never seen a child.

She repeated, "Why are you afraid of Boots?" She patted the dragon's neck. "See, he doesn't do anything. Except if he doesn't like you, then he goes all *wraaaa* and he spits fire."

Agatha said again, "Anneke, leave him alone."

"Why? I just want to show him that Boots is friendly."

While Anneke had been talking, the dragon slowly bent his head down and arched his neck, while continuing to look at Bruno. It was a strange position which Nellie assumed meant subservience.

Bruno had stopped trying to run away from the dragon.

Nellie figured that if magic was visible, it would surround both the boy and the dragon.

He held out his hand.

The dragon reached up to the outstretched fingers with his snout.

At the moment the dragon touched him, the creature exploded in a ball of sparks.

The women screamed. Agatha grabbed Anneke by the arm and dragged her away. Hilde ducked under the bench along the wall. The other women ran to the door into the storeroom.

The boy stood in the middle of the barn, with his hand still outstretched. A couple of sparks lay in his open palm. He stared at them, his mouth gaping. Slowly other sparks joined them, casting his pale hand in a golden glow.

"Give him the box," Nellie said in a low voice.

Gisele picked up the dragon box and held it open.

The flurry of sparks zoomed across the barn and snapped inside the box.

She calmly closed the lid.

To Nellie, this was a final proof that this poor, frightened, emaciated boy was indeed Prince Bruno. A feeling of fear and chilling importance overcame her.

If the citizens of Saardam knew this, they might view the Regent differently. They might demand he step down in favour of the prince.

Did the Regent know about this? Had the church kept this secret from him? Or did the shepherd see the prince as a rival who he might still need to control the dragon, but whom he would otherwise prefer to kill? A rival he had tried to destroy by locking him up? Was this boy even adequately sound of mind that he could rule?

Mina and Agatha came out from the storeroom, followed by Anneke, who was crying. Nellie wondered what her mother had said to her.

Hilde was still huddled underneath the bench, trying to be sure it was safe to come out again.

Prince Bruno, because she should now call him by his name, stood astonished in the middle of the barn with the box in his hand.

Gisele was a foreigner, so she had possibly no idea of the importance of this moment.

The horse continued to stand placidly in the corner. It had gone to sleep.

And tomorrow, they were planning the dumbest rescue mission ever, which could put them all in danger. Gisele had said she was coming, too—it was as if the enormity of what she had done in helping to free Prince Bruno only hit her now, and she'd grown nervous, especially after Nellie told her what she had seen in the church.

The smart thing to do was to get onto that ship and disappear now. Everything was ready, the sea cows were all in the barn, the harness was complete, the ladders lay ready, the shields were ready, the supplies waited in the hold of the Guentherite order's ship. There was no need to stay, except for that one thing.

Nellie couldn't live with herself unless she did her best to rescue their friend and the mother of the six children. And she didn't want to leave without attempting to save the other innocent people from certain death in the cold water of the harbour. The conviction of witchcraft was nonsense and everyone knew it.

And it was already time for the last preparations for the rescue before too many onlookers arrived at the quay.

Nellie and the women used carrots to entice the sea cows into both harnesses. They would attach one to the peat barge, the other to the longboat.

Once the barn doors opened both ships would go out, and one would make for the platform and the other, the longboat with Floris and the children, would make for the Guentherite ship. The children would climb the harbour side of that ship and wait there with Mina and Gertie until the others came with the rescued people.

Then both teams of sea cows would be tied to the ship and by that time Gisele would have cast off on the harbour side and everyone would jump on board.

The plan was risky and crazy, but it was all they had. Nellie grew nervous waiting, worrying that things might go wrong, because when they did, she would not survive. And then Saardam would be truly lost, and the dream of restoring the royal family would be forgotten.

Shepherd Wilfridus would claim all power to himself and everyone would suffer.

CHAPTER 23

THE NEXT MORNING dawned silent and misty, and for a while Nellie despaired that they might not be able to carry out the plan, because surely the Regent would postpone the punishment if people couldn't see what was happening. The whole point of punishment was that everyone in the city watched it and knew the Regent was serious about it.

The women waited anxiously, peeping through a crack between the barn doors to check for any activity on the quay.

Prince Bruno wandered around the barn. He was still insecure on his legs, the skin on his ankles raw from the chafing metal. But he was eating well and carried the dragon box with him everywhere, even if he jumped every time someone opened the main door, and he wouldn't let anyone touch him, not even to comb his hair, which looked like a bird's nest.

Nellie didn't want to wait any longer, because every day they had to stay here increased the chance that someone would discover them or the dragon, or their supplies on board the Guentherite order's ship, or Madame Sabine's horse in the barn.

But by mid-morning, the mist cleared and people started to gather on the quayside. A couple of palace guards appeared near the platform.

It seemed the proceedings would go ahead as planned.

Nellie packed all her possessions into the bag she had taken from the palace and gave that to Floris who stacked it in the longboat that would take the children to the Guentherite ship.

They held discussions about who would steer that ship. Floris and Gisele needed to be on the rescue boat because they were the strongest people in their group. Nellie said she would take the longboat, and then Agatha argued that because Prince Bruno would be on board, she didn't want her children to be in the boat, because *he will attract magic*.

In the tenseness of the preparations, Nellie snapped.

"What is your problem, anyway? Haven't you considered that your daughter might have magic? Can't you see that this might be useful to us? Don't you understand that she needs your love, not your rejection?"

"Oh, she has seen enough, with that sneaky bastard of a father of hers, that's where she gets it. She knows that he's no good. I'll not have *my* children associate with magic. They will *not* go on this boat that's going to be a target for trouble."

"And you say this after all the work we've done on making shields."

"If there is one thing I know about magic, it's that it doesn't care about any damn shields made from wood."

"You've been nothing but a pain since we started this plan. You know what I think? Someone betrayed us to the Regent. Somebody told him about the dragon. I think that someone was you."

"How *dare* you say things like that about me? What are

you, anyway, blow-in from the palace? You don't anything about living in poverty."

Mina stepped in Nellie's field of vision. "Calm down, calm down. Stop this, or we will *all* be doomed."

Agatha snorted. "We should just quit this stupid plan while we still can."

Mina held up her hands. "Agatha, if you don't want to come, then don't come. You're free to stay here. I won't think any less of you."

"Yes, you will, because madam over there says I betrayed you." She glared at Nellie.

Lise said, "Can we please stop fighting? Please, Agatha? My life is not worth living if I don't do the best I can to free my mother."

"And Josie," Hilde added.

Gertie said, "And those poor children need their mother."

Anneke said, "Mammy, please? We want to stay with Boots. He looks after us."

Agatha snorted again, thunder on her face. "Fine." She pulled her arms closer about her chest.

"Thank you, Agatha," Mina said.

"As long as she apologises. I did *not* talk to anyone from the palace. Do you think they would listen to me if I tried? Agatha from the street who was dumb enough to marry a loser magician?"

"You're not dumb," Nellie said.

"Ha! You *think* I'm dumb. You think I'm a bad mother for the children—no don't even open your mouth, I've heard it all before. You think I'm a bad mother."

"Stop it, Agatha!" Mina said. "We need everyone to make this plan a success."

Agatha gave another snort. She leaned against the workbench, her arms crossed over her chest. How much fun this expedition was going to be.

Nellie suspected that Agatha had always had a brusque personality, and that she didn't really want to leave the group. She was a strange woman, and Nellie felt sorry for the children, who repeatedly suffered the threat of having the things that brought them comfort yanked away from them through their mother's obstinacy.

The Triune help the poor mites.

On the quay, the guards had cordoned off an area where the proceedings would take place, and placed two seats on the spectator platform for the Regent and the shepherd to sit in.

The first people had already arrived for the spectacle.

Floris attached the first team of sea cows to the long-boat. Nellie climbed in and helped the children down the ladder. Jantien's youngest two were far too small to understand what was going on. She put them in the back of the boat and left Ewout and Jette, the oldest two, to keep an eye on them.

Bas and Anneke came next, watched like a hawk by Agatha.

"Be nice to Nellie and Mina," she told Anneke. "Listen to what they say."

"Yes, mammy," Anneke said.

Nellie looked up into Agatha's worried face. "Thank you for entrusting me with their safety," she said.

Agatha was a strong woman, so she would go in the boat that would try to rescue the prisoners.

Mina would come with Nellie, and she got into the boat next so that she could help Bruno down the ladder, because he was still quite weak and awkward, not in the least because he was clutching the dragon box so hard.

Nellie then got all the children to sit on the bottom of the boat, and she spread a sailcloth over them.

"Phooey, it stinks in here," came Bas' voice from under the cloth.

If they were lucky, the bad smell would be all they needed to deal with.

Nellie then put on her coat, tucked away her hair under her shawl and met Mina's eyes. "You're ready?"

"As ready as we'll ever be."

They watched as Floris, Gisele and Agatha climbed into the second boat. Floris sat at the front with Agatha and Gisele on each side next to the rolled-up shields.

The remaining women, Gertie, Hilde and Lise, watched from the side.

Koby was at the barn doors, giving updates on the happenings. She would go with the women. After some talk, they had decided it would be her task to climb the Guentherite ship from the quayside and cast off the ropes. Gisele had given her the spare monk's habit, and in the crowd, she would pass as a skinny monk.

They waited, listening to Koby's relays as the quay filled up, the mayor arrived, and the guards freed a path through the onlookers.

Then she said, "The Regent's coach has arrived."

That was the sign.

Hilde and Lise opened the barn doors.

Nellie sat on the driver's bench, unlooped the sea cow reins and flicked them up so that the leather straps splashed in the water.

The nine animals jumped into action and the boat shot forward. Nellie almost fell backwards. Whoa, they were very keen indeed.

The children giggled under the cloth. Mina told them to be quiet.

It was still a bit misty and from her position low on the water, Nellie couldn't see much of what was happening on the quay, but the sound of many voices carried over the harbour.

They must have arrived at the part where the guards

asked for three cheers for the Regent because half-hearted shouts of "hurray" came over the water.

The second boat had also cleared the shed.

Gertie, Hilde and Lise shut the barn doors again and walked along the quay in the direction of the platform. Nellie hoped they could get through. The quayside looked really busy.

Nellie let the sea cow team swim at their own pace but occasionally pulled one of the reins to correct their course. Floris had a harder time getting the second team—with the younger and stronger animals—to stay behind. Sea cows lived in small herds and always wanted to follow the other animals.

They made good progress across the harbour. Already, Nellie could make out the rope ladder Gisele had hung from the harbour side of the Guentherite ship last night.

It was going well.

Not much later, they reached that ladder, and the sea cows even stopped when she pulled the reins. Mina tied the boat to the bottom of the ladder in case the animals changed their minds, and Nellie climbed up the wobbly ladder.

It brought her to the deck of the ship in between the two cabins.

Since she had been here last, someone had swept the deck and left the broom leaning against the railing. There was also a bucket and a box with tools and bottles of oil, paint or cleaning substances.

Across the deck she could see the top floor of the harbourside offices. She couldn't see the quay and the people who stood there. But she heard them shouting. They were not happy shouts.

She was about to turn to the ladder to tell the children to climb up when there was a squeaking sound and the door to the large cabin opened. A middle-aged man in a monk's habit appeared in the opening. Before he stepped onto the deck, he brought his hand to his pocket, frowned and turned back inside. He'd forgotten something.

Nellie scooted to the side of the cabin, but to her horror, the ropes at the top of the ladder were moving, indicating that someone—one of the children probably—was climbing up.

The monk could not be allowed to see her, or the children.

She grabbed the broom. She could always distract him and pretend to sweep the deck, nonsensical as that would be.

No, he would still see whoever was climbing up.

He now came through the doorway again, closing the door with his back to her.

In her panic, Nellie lifted the broom above her head.

And then, before he could turn around, she swung it high and brought it down with all her strength.

The heavy part of the broom hit him on the side of the head before glancing off onto his shoulder. Nellie tripped and fell backwards.

He turned around, slowly, his eyes unfocused. And then he collapsed against the wall of the cabin.

Oh no, oh no, she'd hit a monk!

Nellie crawled over. He lay sideways on the deck. His eyes were closed, his mouth open. He mumbled some inaudible words.

What to do now?

In the box next to the bucket, she found a handful of rags, which she used to tie his hands and feet together and over his eyes and mouth. The latter not too tightly because she didn't want him to be harmed.

By the Triune, what were they going to do with him?

Bruno, Ewout and Anneke had come onto the deck. They stood watching with wide eyes.

"Is he dead?" Ewout asked.

"Heavens, no. Only asleep."

"He doesn't look asleep to me. I can't hear him snoring."

"Come this way, children." Mina had come onto the deck. She shepherded the children into the cabin while staring at Nellie with wide eyes.

"What did you do to him?" she mouthed, standing at the cabin door while the children filed in.

"I couldn't help it," Nellie said.

Mina shut the door. "What are we going to do with him?" she whispered.

"I don't know. Hide him first and then take him?"

"Well, we can't leave him here. That looks untidy."

Nellie and Mina grabbed the monk by the feet and shoulders and half-carried and half-dragged him across the deck into the captain's cabin.

From within the darkness of the cabin, Nellie could see the crowd on the quay through the windows.

To her relief, Koby was already on the deck. She couldn't see Gertie, Hilde and Lise, but they were sure to be nearby.

My, there were a lot of people out there. There were people watching even from near the empty warehouses, from the other ships, from the upper floors of the quay-side offices.

A wagon arrived. It was a heavy square thing, like a solid wooden box, pulled by four horses. The guards gathered around and a couple let down the back of the wagon, revealing the prisoners crammed together inside. When the back hatch opened, several shielded their eyes against the light.

The guards yelled at them to get out.

None of the prisoners wore shoes and several had

trouble walking. They were all tied together with rope—presuming so as not to waste good iron on them.

Nellie recognised Wim. Jantien was also there, and Yolande from the corner shop, helped down the ramp by Josie and Emmie. She hoped that none of the children were watching this.

The last person to come out was a woman with brown curly hair and thick fleshy arms. She was dressed in rags even though she was no commoner.

Nellie couldn't believe her eyes. Was the Regent going to kill his own wife?

A ripple of disturbance went through the crowd. People elbowed their neighbours and pointed. A woman clamped her hand over her mouth.

The citizens had no love for Madame Sabine. People spoke of her as being out of touch, a foreigner, aloof and selfish, but all of them recognised the horror of the Regent's actions.

No one cheered as Madame Sabine came down the ramp. No one clapped. No one said a word.

The deathly quiet of all those people was disturbing.

The guards who had come with the wagon led the prisoners to the wooden platform that had been built on the side of the quay.

From her position on the deck of the ship, Nellie could see Floris, Gisele and Agatha in the small boat. The water churned where the sea cows fidgeted in their harness, waiting for the terrible process to begin.

The Regent rose.

"Today, citizens, we gather for a sad occasion. These people you see before you are practitioners of magic and witchcraft and they endanger the fabric of our city and society. We gave them the opportunity to leave, but they chose not to do so. Today, they will end their lives in shame."

Somewhere in the crowd, a man yelled. Nellie couldn't hear what he said, but a scuffle broke out in the area. As some guards moved towards him, Nellie saw Henrik, dressed in his shiny uniform, standing to the side of the area where the Regent and shepherd sat.

She was filled with a wave of anger. How could he support the Regent in this cruelty and still sleep at night?

The shepherd, too, was looking on with a hard face, devoid of emotion.

The guards apprehended the man who had yelled and added him to the group. He put his arm around one of the female prisoners. Her husband or brother.

That, more than anything, was a sign of how unhappy people were to let these cruel men kill their families. If they had to die, they would die with their family members.

Now the shepherd rose.

In his left hand, he held aloft an object covered by a black cloth that he pulled away with his right hand.

Nellie knew what it was before the object had been fully uncovered: the ruby skull with red pulsing light glowing from the eye sockets.

Many people would never have seen this fabled object although everyone had heard about it. Those who stood close to the shepherd tried to push away, screaming.

A man yelled at a young woman next to him, "Stop this nonsense. It's only trickery!"

But people knew what they saw, and it *wasn't* trickery.

The shepherd yelled, "Quiet!"

The crowd went silent as death.

Many citizens stared at the ancient relic as if it demanded their attention and wouldn't let go.

Magic.

Shepherd Wilfridus started speaking in the preaching voice he used to speak of hell and damnation in church services, the voice that would echo through the vast hall and give her the chills. "Today, we make an example of those who disobey the scripture of the Triune. They have sown evil in our community and fear in our hearts. After today, these people will not bother us any more and our hearts will be free of fear. May the Triune be with them and may they be admitted to heaven to atone for their evil deeds."

At the quayside, the guards ushered the prisoners up the platform.

They were all tied up together, so there was no way that any of them could escape. Once they were in the water, even if one of them could swim, the others would still make sure everyone drowned.

The crowd became very quiet.

Across the harbour, the boat with Floris, Gisele and Agatha was getting ready. The water rippled where the sea cows strained against the harness, keen to get going.

The people on the platform stood in a tight group, holding onto each other, shivering.

The last person onto the platform was Madame Sabine. The rags she wore showed part of her pale-skinned, dimpled thigh. She kept looking at her husband all the time, not saying anything but making sure she did not lose eye contact with him. Her back was straight and her chin in the air.

Nellie now also noticed the Regent's two sons behind the upstairs window of the harbourmaster's office.

Casper was looking straight out the window, while Frederick wiped his cheek with the back of his hand.

She would like to know what they felt. At this stage she wasn't sure their father had not thoroughly convinced them that their mother was evil.

She would like to think one of them would come to their mother's aid, but they did not, and in all honesty, what could a sixteen-year-old and a fourteen-year-old do?

They stood frozen while, one by one, the palace guards cut the ties that held the platform in place. Henrik was standing to the side of the Regent's seat.

It was too far away to see his expression.

The guards began to cut the last rope, which strained at the bollard and looked like it would soon either break or rip the bollard out of the ground.

After a few hacks with the guard's sword, the rope broke with a snap that echoed across the harbour.

Slowly, the platform tilted. A woman screamed, and then another one screamed and tried to scramble to the high side of the platform, but the planks were too slippery because of the wax covering the boards. The platform tilted more and the first woman hit the water. Across the harbour, the peat barge raced full speed out of the barn.

CHAPTER 24

A **LOUD WHINNY** came from across the harbour.

Madame Sabine's white horse ran along the wharf, mane flying. Several people had to duck out of its way.

Nellie spotted Gertie, Lise and Hilde in the crowd.

"The others are here!" she called into the cabin where Mina had settled the children in the benches.

Mina and Nellie helped them up. Nellie sent Lise to Koby at the bow.

Gertie frowned at the monk who lay tied up on the deck. He was wriggling and trying to shout, but there was no time to pay any attention to him.

The peat boat with Floris, Agatha and Gisele had reached the group of people in the water.

Floris and Agatha were pulling people into the boat while Gisele stood at the bow with the reins. The animals had spread out amongst the prisoners. They gave the people something to hold on to.

The shields were up, held by the first prisoners to come out of the water, but the guards were occupied with the chaos on the quay caused by the panicked horse and trying to keep people away from the Regent and shepherd.

Nellie had lost sight of Henrik.

The peat barge came in the direction of the ship. The little boat was so full of people that there was barely room for them to sit. The water reached to a mere hand's width from the boat's rim.

Floris called out for the passengers to sit still and hang onto the shield over their heads if they sat on that side of the boat.

The peat boat came alongside.

Koby caught the rope Floris tossed her.

Then Gisele jumped onto the ladder. "Koby! Get the mooring ropes."

"Already done," Koby called back.

Floris was undoing the sea cow harness to transfer the team to the big ship. The first prisoners were coming up the ladder and Mina and Gertie stood at the top to pull people up. Nellie was relieved to see Jantien's face.

"Mama!" Lise called to her mother.

Emmie smiled at her, tears welling in her eyes. She was wet and dirty and still had the rope around her wrists.

The prisoners were coughing, crying and shivering. They needed blankets and dry clothes.

"Nellie!" Jantien stumbled across the deck and hugged her. She was crying. "Oh, thank you. I thought we were all going to die. I thought I'd never see my children again."

"Go inside and join them. We're not out of trouble yet."

Jantien opened the door and was met with shouts of *Mammy!* when she entered the cabin.

The next prisoner to climb up the ladder was Madame Sabine. The expression on her face was cold, and she didn't show any signs of hardship. But the lash marks on her arms must hurt.

She met Nellie's eyes and nodded, once, as if publicly thanking her rescuer caused her physical pain. Then, chin held high, she walked across the deck into the cabin.

There was work to be done. Nellie went to the other side of the ship and the scene of chaos on the quay. Guards were trying to keep the people away from the platform with the Regent and the shepherd, and the people on the quay were shouting and cheering at the empty peat boat , which Floris had pushed off with the shields still up so that people couldn't see that it was empty.

Several guards aimed arrows, but they fell short. Nellie couldn't see Henrik in the crowd. A few other guards surrounded Madame Sabine's horse which kicked at everyone who tried to grab hold of the rope attached to the headgear.

The mooring ropes were indeed loose.

Nellie pulled up the gangplank with all her weight. Oof, that thing was heavy.

The riverboat moved. People on the quay noticed it.

"The monks are getting too hot!" a man shouted.

A couple of people jeered.

Another man yelled, "Those are not monks!"

"Get inside, everyone!" Mina shouted. She and a few others were ready with buckets, in case there were any burning arrows.

Nellie looked over the quay. She was curious what had happened to Henrik. She wanted to see the look on his face when she realised that she had outsmarted his exulted Regent.

People around the order's ship were cheering. Guards couldn't reach the ship in time. They were protecting the Regent on his platform and the rest were dealing with the wayward horse.

In the middle of the chaos, Shepherd Wilfridus still stood in front of his chair holding the ruby skull. His mouth moved and his eyes were closed. Nellie didn't doubt that he had seen her and understood what had happened.

His face was red from shouting incantations even if there was so much noise on the quay that she couldn't hear his words from this distance.

He pointed the skull's eyes at the boat.

"Quick," Nellie yelled to the last remaining people on the deck. In a moment the fire dog would come out.

Someone called, "Nellie!"

And then she saw Henrik. He was pushing through the crowd in the direction of the boat. He called out, "Nellie! Wait!"

No, they weren't coming back.

He reached the edge of the quay, pushing people aside. "Let me come with you!"

Come? Him? So that he could be the Regent's puppet and betray them?

The sea cows were pulling the boat, but the ship was so big that it took a while to get going.

Henrik ran along the quay, shouting, "I'm sorry. I had to pretend that I didn't believe you."

What?

"Please, I'll tell you all about it. Throw me a rope."

The boat pulled further away. The strip of churning water between the hull and the quay grew.

Nellie didn't have a rope. She dropped to her knees, holding on to the railing with one hand and reaching out as far as she could with the other.

But the boat had already moved a good distance away from the quay. Henrik was not going to get there in time. He was not . . .

He jumped.

His warm hand latched onto Nellie's, almost pulling her over the side. He grabbed the railing with his other hand and swung himself over onto the deck.

"Henrik! I thought you—"

But in a few jumps, he climbed on top of the cabin, pulled two arrows out of his quiver, set the first to the bow, aimed and released it, while holding the second arrow with his little finger.

The arrow flew across the water and before it had even reached its destination, he shot the second arrow.

The first arrow hit the Regent straight in the chest and plunged deep into the flesh. The Regent's eyes widened. He looked down at the arrow protruding from his pretty shirt, surprised, and collapsed to the side of his chair.

The second arrow hit a bright glow of magic mere steps away from Shepherd Wilfridus' head. It burned in a ball of flames.

A man yelled, "Magic!"

People on the quay screamed. Everyone was pushing in all directions. People sheltered under the Regent's coach to avoid the crush of bodies. One man was pushed into the water in the scuffles.

"Holy heavens!" Henrik jumped off the cabin. "He's a magician."

"Quick, hide yourself," Nellie said.

But Henrik took a bucket out of Mina's hands. "You go inside with her and look after the poor prisoners."

Complete mayhem had broken out on the quay.

The guards still loyal to the Regent were shooting flaming arrows at the riverboat, but any that reached the ship glanced off or stuck uselessly in the hull after Henrik extinguished them with the bucket. The strong teams of twenty-four sea cows had already pulled the ship almost out of range.

Nellie held her breath. This risky adventure was over. They had made it.

But then an orange glow erupted from the quayside.

Nellie knew what it was before she could see the fire dog running over the water.

She sprinted to the cabin entrance and yelled into the opening. "Everyone! Come up here! The fire dog is coming!"

The ship would be burned with everything inside.

Mina and Agatha came to the deck first. Someone else was with them. A skinny boy on the edge of manhood, dressed in rags with the chafe wounds from the shackles still marking his ankles.

Prince Bruno.

As he had done for the past day, he clutched the dragon box to his chest.

"Open the box!" Nellie called.

He just looked at her, so she ran to him, pulled it out of his hands and opened the lid.

Bruno protested. "No! Mine!"

But it was already too late. The dragon erupted in a shower of sparks and immediately assumed its solid form.

Mina and Agatha ducked back into the cabin.

"Go!" Nellie yelled. "Whatever power you hold, defend us, or we'll all be dead, including your master. Go! Go!"

Whether it understood what she said or she frightened it, the dragon jumped into the air and flew off, so close that the whoosh from its wings ruffled Nellie's hair.

It soared low over the water.

The screams from the panicked crowd on the quay reached fever point. More people had fallen into the harbour, and others were throwing ropes and pieces of wood to help them out. Guards gathered around the Regent, easing him onto the ground. The front of his white shirt was covered in blood. He wasn't moving.

Shepherd Wilfridus had climbed on his chair and waved his arms.

The dog and the dragon clashed in the middle of the

harbour in a giant burst of magic that exploded with a bang. The water was whipped up into waves. Boats bobbed violently on their moorings. In some places, the waves were so high that water washed over the quay, dragging more people into the harbour.

The dragon and the dog fought each other in a glowing ball of bright magic. Sparks rained over the surrounding water and the boats that lay moored there. It made the water bubble and boil. Clouds of steam rose in the air. Sparks exploded in all directions. From the deck of the Guentherite riverboat, part of the harbour was obscured by the rising clouds.

The dragon that flew back to the riverboat was only the size of a cat, and he obediently went inside the box when Nellie held it up. There was no sign of the fire dog.

She closed the box and gave it back to Prince Bruno.

He gave her a wide-eyed look.

Meanwhile, the sea cows pulled the ship through the mouth of the harbour.

The last thing Nellie saw disappear behind the headlands was Shepherd Wilfridus on his chair, screaming that the Lord of Fire was going to curse them.

CHAPTER 25

ONCE THE BOAT was out of the harbour on the open water of the delta, the peaceful silence that surrounded them was unbelievable. The only sound was the rippling of water against the side of the boat.

Nellie and Henrik leaned against the outer wall of the Captain's cabin. Nellie was half expecting a call for help from Gisele, Koby or Floris at the bow of the ship, but it didn't come.

She expected smaller boats to follow them, but it took time to get a boat organised and collect a team of sea cows who were unused to a harness.

"We're free," Nellie said to herself as if she still couldn't believe it.

"That was amazing," Henrik said.

"No, you were amazing. I've never seen anyone shoot two arrows in such quick succession."

"It's a skill learned with age."

Nellie chuckled. "I guess you won't be going back to the palace now."

He laughed, the sound sad and hollow. "I'd longed to do that for years. Every time that gluttonous bastard would order us to run his foul errands, I'd wanted to tell him what he could do it himself."

Nellie couldn't imagine Henrik doing that.

"But you know, being a guard is about respect. I respected King Nicholaos and King Roald and their wives. I never respected Regent Bernard very much, although I respected the *position* of regent, because the shepherd and the Regent were looking for a more permanent solution. But I finally lost the last shred of respect for the Regent when he was going to kill the mother of his sons before the boys' eyes. As a father with children and grandchildren, how anyone could do that is beyond me."

"What about the shepherd?"

"That man is evil and I knew it the moment he stepped into the palace for the first time. The Regent was his puppet. I've been forced to listen to conversations where the shepherd forced Regent Bernard to do his will, and meetings where the Regent argued that he should be made king and the shepherd telling the man repeatedly that he was stupid, that everyone in town hated him and that he would never amount to anything unless he listened to the church. A truly evil man."

"The shepherd had a hand in the killing of Lord Verdonck."

"Of course he did. He saw Lord Verdonck as a thorn in his side because he was trying to talk sense into the Regent about letting himself be controlled by the church. Whatever happened with the poisoning, it was all of Shepherd Wilfridus' design, which was another reason the Regent was so keen to blame someone from the kitchens as quickly as possible."

"I saw him infusing his magic into food. And I know the magical poison was in the gin."

Henrik frowned. He said in a low voice, "And he was blessing the food at all the Regent's banquets."

"By the Triune." Nellie raised her hand to her mouth. "You're right."

Did that mean Shepherd Wilfridus could have poisoned all the people who came to these banquets?

Her mind raced.

Were there magical poisons that changed people in other ways, such as making them agree to be quiet and support a ruler they wouldn't normally support?

Had he poisoned Lord Verdonck because the gentler kind of magic hadn't worked very well on him? By the Triune, she *had* noticed that Adalbert Verdonck never ate the food provided by the palace.

Had Lord Verdonck known this and taken a remedy and made a mistake in assuming that the gin was safe? Or was the poison in the gin extraordinarily strong?

If there was some kind of magic that made people agree with the Regent, the common citizens wouldn't be affected because they never came to the banquets, and they had never been influential enough to worry about. But now the Regent was going to distribute food from the city's stores to them, no doubt under orders of the shepherd.

And who ordered it didn't matter anyway, because the Regent was dead, and the shepherd could appoint another puppet noble as temporary leader and make this person behave so badly that the people begged for the good shepherd to save them.

That was the true reason the shepherd wanted a regent.

While they watched the shore go past, Nellie explained these thoughts to Henrik, who nodded at every sentence and didn't contradict her once.

When she finished, he said, "That's a pretty good summary of what's probably going on. For us, in the guards, it has been hard, because to mention magic means to acknowledge its existence, and the shepherd has made good work of preventing that from ever happening."

"What now?" Nellie said. She couldn't see how they as a small group of people would make any difference on a population that was likely to be controlled through magic they couldn't see.

"I'll go where you are going."

"We're going up the river, looking for a safe place to stay the winter and decide what to do next."

"And what to do next might include going back to Saardam and start a rebellion?"

"There won't be a point unless we can stop people being influenced by magic they can't see. No one in Saardam is ever going to agree with us, or see what is happening to the city, unless we can unmask what is happening."

Then another chilling thought. The kitchens were providers of food in the palace. By working there, had Nellie unknowingly contributed to the spread of the magic?

She had eaten the food herself—and only in the last few days when no longer relying on kitchen handouts had her plan come to fruition. Not only that, it had taken that long for the women to be prepared to support her.

Nellie's cheeks grew hot. It was likely no one in the kitchens had realised this.

Henrik was still talking. "Well then, if you are going to start a rebellion, you seem to be short of a few people who know how to handle a bow and arrow."

"But we have a dragon."

"True. I can't compete with that."

Nellie laughed, and he laughed, too, and then they both fell into an uneasy silence.

And then he said, "I'm sorry for the things I said to you. I could explain why I said them, but it would just sound like excuses to you. So I just offer my apologies."

"I accept them. I don't need to hear the entire story. I will have things to explain as well. I can imagine. I understand."

"Thank you."

And then neither of them said anything for a while.

Koby and Gisele were laughing, having a great time at the bow.

They should go inside because there was so much work to be done and people to be looked after. Jantien and her children, prisoners who were injured, and prisoners who were demanding—good grief, Madame Sabine was on the ship. Whatever were they going to do with her?

Nellie sighed and made to get up.

"Wait," Henrik said.

He put a hand over hers.

Nellie met his eyes. Grey, unwavering, honest. Her heart was thudding like crazy. She had just done all kinds of crazy stuff, but this little exchange made her feel like she was standing at the edge of a cliff ready to jump. It was ages since any man had shown any kind of interest in her.

"I'd like to make it up to you," he said, his voice soft. "I'd like to prove that I'm not a puppet who blindly obeys what my superior tells me."

"I know."

"No, you don't."

"Well then." She pulled her hand out from under his. "Let's prove it."

And she preceded him along the deck and into the cabin, swaying her hips. She hadn't done that for a long time either.

Thanks for Reading

THANK for you reading *The Wizard Priest*. The story concludes in *The Dragon King*, where Nellie embarks on a daring plan made necessary by Bruno's lust for revenge.

ABOUT THE AUTHOR

Patty Jansen lives in Sydney, Australia, where she spends most of her time writing Science Fiction and Fantasy.

Her story *This Peaceful State of War* placed first in the second quarter of the Writers of the Future contest and was published in their 27th anthology. She has also sold fiction to genre magazines such as Analog Science Fiction and Fact, Redstone SF and Aurealis.

Patty has written over twenty novels in both Science Fiction and Fantasy, including the *Icefire Trilogy* and the *Ambassador* series.

pattyjansen.com

BOOKS BY PATTY JANSEN

MORE INFORMATION:
PATTYJANSEN.COM